Your Love Was Breaking the Law

A Domestic Violence Anthology

Carmen Lashay, T. Nicole, Ty Leese Javeh, Eden
Mireya, Sparkle Lewis, Reign, & Armani

How Can You Hurt the One You Love?

Sparkle Lewis

This is dedicated to every female and male that has been a victim of domestic violence. And to my angel in heaven that died at the hands of her abuser, … may you forever rest in peace, Auntie!

I applaud myself for being able to escape a situation that could have resulted in death at the hands of my abuser … Not everyone is so lucky.

Carmen Lashay, T. Nicole, Ty Leese Javeh, Eden Mireya, Sparkle Lewis, Reign, & Armani

Prologue

WHAP!

"Didn't I tell you I better not even see you looking at no nigga? What the fuck! You thought I was playing?" Sayvion asked after having slapped me so hard I lost my footing and fell.

I couldn't understand why he even invited me to this party if he was going to show his behind the moment he got alcohol in his system. This was becoming so repetitive with him. He got drunk; I got my ass whipped. It didn't matter who was around. If he felt the need to exert his 'power,' he was going to do it.

"Sayvion, what are you talking about? I've been sitting in the corner all night. I had just come from the bathroom and got into it with this girl from Garvey. I wasn't even looking in Twin's direction. He's a little ass boy!" I whimpered, praying he wouldn't hit me again. *Prayer unanswered.*

Grabbing me up then dragging me by my dress to the front door, he pulled me down the steps, and once my foot reached the bottom step, he turned around, punching me as if he were hitting a dude in the streets. A crowd began to form outside, but no one stepped in. It was the nosey onlookers that achieved some sick level of satisfaction that had come outside to see what was going on.

As he maintained his grip on my dress, repeatedly smacking me, he yelled, "You ain't nothing but a fuckin' bucket! I don't know why the fuck I chose to wife a trick like you! You's a sneaky bitch!"

Which hurt worse? The physical pain he was inflicting or the emotional seeds he'd just implanted in me? I didn't ask for this. Or did I? I promised myself to never deal with a street dude, and I turned around and got involved with one of the biggest hustlers in Kings County. Nah, forget a street dude. I'd just graduated right on up to kingpin status. Regardless of whether or not he was that when I got with him, I stayed, knowing that was what he'd become once my brother gave him that authority. Now I was paying the price.

My unborn seed crossed my mind as he delivered one final punch, causing me to fall to the ground. I heard gasps, whimpering, and even some snickering around me. I wasn't surprised at all. Just about every dude at this

Carmen Lashay, T. Nicole, Ty Leese Javeh, Eden Mireya, Sparkle Lewis, Reign, & Armani

party feared him, and the majority of the females wanted him or just didn't like me because I wasn't from the same blocks. Either way, I didn't expect anyone to help me.

Right when I thought he was done with his performance, he looked down at me and spat in my face. "Your ungrateful ass don't deserve a nigga like me." He lifted his foot and repeatedly stomped down into my chest.

"Yo, nigga, what the fuck!" I heard Blockz scream once he came outside to see what was going on.

Damn, I wish Shalom were here, I thought before everything went black.

Talya

"Has the jury reached a verdict?"

"We have, Your Honor. We find the defendant, Shalom Barron, guilty of first-degree murder."

Those words changed my life forever. My brother, Shalom, was my rock, my everything. Having grown up in a household with a mother that put a drug habit before her children and never knowing who our fathers were, we were all that we had.

The day Shalom was sentenced to life was supposed to be one of the happiest days of my life. I had just graduated high school and was on my way to Michigan State to major in Kinesiology. Weird, right? I was a female that loved all sports, football being my favorite, and always wanted to study how the human body, muscles in particular, operated. I wanted to own a sports medicine clinic for athletes of all ages. My brother made sure he busted his ass on the blocks, from the time he was twelve up until he got locked up three years ago, to make sure that happened. Three years later, and I was a semester from graduating with my Bachelor's in Biotechnology here in NY. I refused to leave NY while my brother was locked up.

Carmen Lashay, T. Nicole, Ty Leese Javeh, Eden Mireya, Sparkle Lewis, Reign, & Armani

On top of that, I went and fell in love with his best friend. Now that shit was not intentional. Hell, it was damn near forbidden. But Sayvion swore up and down my brother wouldn't have wanted to see me with no other nigga but one in his camp. Even with that, we kept our relationship a secret for fear of what my brother would do if he found out.

Initially, we were going to go visit him to tell him face to face, knowing that was not a conversation you had with someone over the phone—not while they were locked. Over time, we just kept putting it off. Shalom knew I was dealing with someone; he just didn't know who. I was scared out of my fuckin' mind to tell him too.

"Tal, would you bring yo' ass on! I ain't got all day!" My smart-mouthed best friend, Shonday, just busted up in my crib like it was hers. I mean, what was mine was hers, but damn, she didn't ever knock.

"Shon-Shon, do you ever ring a bell? And why da fuck you standin' in front the door if you know my ass ain't ready? Have a seat, bitch. I shall be with you shortly," I told her impatient tail as I walked to the kitchen where she was standing, blocking the damn door.

"I don't understand why we make appointments if you never keeps 'em. Like, da fuck. Shit don't move 'round you, Tal. Ya slow ass. Bishhhhhhh, you heard about ya boy and 'nem shootin' up Garvey last night? Fuck dat was about?"

That was Shonday for you. Cursing you out one minute and ready to gossip the next. Never a dull moment with this chick. But she had definitely said something worth gossiping about because it was my first time hearing of it.

"Who shot up Garvey last night? What you talkin' 'bout?"

"I was in Key Food this morning and heard nice waist, no face Porsche, from Chester, talkin' 'bout Say and Blockz ran through Garvey and Van Dyke last night," she said like she was revealing some heavy-duty shit, all extra.

The reason this piqued my interest was not because of what she said happened but the fact I knew my brother had ceased beef with Garvey prior to him getting locked up. Things had been calm between Garvey and the 90's, so why would he go start the beef back up? Did

Shalom authorize him to do that or what? I was confused because SBD (Silent But Deadly) didn't do anything without my brother's permission.

"Shon-Shon, did they say it was all of SBD or just Say and Blockz?" I asked. Maybe that would give me a better insight as to what was going on.

"Nah, they ain't say if it was all dem niggas, but they did specifically say Blockz and Say. Ohhhh, and bitch, breezy that was wit' her is checkin' for Say. I meant to tell you dat shit first," she replied.

"Bitch, that should have been the first thing you told me. But truthfully, I don't give a fuck. If I gave one fuck for every bitch that wanted Say, I would really have too many fucks to give, and you know I gives no fucks!" We burst out laughing.

Hearing my phone blasting Fab's "You Make Me Better" made me jump up from the kitchen table. I knew it was Sayvion calling, so I decided to finish getting dressed while talking to him, taking the conversation in my room.

"Be back, Shon," I informed her before heading down the hallway. "What's good, bae?" I asked as I answered the phone.

"Fuck you at, ma?" Sayvion's deep voice penetrated my ears.

It wasn't hard at all for me to fall for Sayvion. He was dark skinned, stood at six two, and was buff as fuck. He kept a bald head with a nicely trimmed goatee. As Hershey as he was, he had the warmest set of brown eyes that changed colors when he got mad, with the deepest dimples, looking as if someone had drilled a hole in both his cheeks. His whole demeanor and everything about him screamed *that nigga*. Niggas hated and feared him, and females loved him.

"At da crib getting ready to go to the salon with Shonday. Why? What's up? You missin' me?"

"Always, ma, always. But look, I probably won't get in until late tonight, so don't wait up. And oh, Sha hit you up today?" he questioned.

Him questioning me about whether or not I heard from Shalom made me think back to what Shonday told me. I wasn't going to say anything now, but we were definitely going to have a discussion about it.

Carmen Lashay, T. Nicole, Ty Leese Javeh, Eden Mireya, Sparkle Lewis, Reign, & Armani

"Nah, not yet. And what you gotta do that's so important that it's going to be keeping you out all night?"

"Say what?" he asked, attitude completely changing.

Lately, he had been more irritable than ever. The smallest thing would make him flip out. I tried to keep my emotions in check because I knew I could go from zero to one thousand real quick, but our arguments had been becoming more heated lately, and I was trying to avoid taking it there with him.

"Da fuck you questioning me for, Tal? Matter fact, when the fuck did it start becoming a'ight for you to question me about what I do in these streets?"

See what I mean? He went from hot to cold in a matter of minutes. I didn't know what was on his mind, but he didn't have to take it out on me. Talk to me about it, but don't talk at me, and I felt like that was what he'd been doing as of recent. When I'd ask what was bothering him, he'd either shut down or tell me to mind my business—it was none of my concern. Today was too pretty of a day for me to allow Say to have me in my feelings, so it was whatever.

"You're right, babe. You need me to tell Sha anything if he calls?" I quickly diverted my attention from the conversation, not up for the drama. I focused on finding shoes to wear with my sky-blue BCBG maxi dress.

"Nah, I'm good. I'll hit you up later. One," he said and hung up. To hell with him. As much as I loved Sayvion, one thing I didn't do was stress niggas or the situations that occurred with them. I was focused on getting my degree and graduating December of 2016. Yes, in a couple more months.

I slid into my white with blue-trim Nine West sandal heels, grabbed my Chanel bag and my keys, and headed out the door. I started to leave my phone, but I didn't want to miss Sha's call if he so happened to call today.

Carmen Lashay, T. Nicole, Ty Leese Javeh, Eden Mireya, Sparkle Lewis, Reign, & Armani

Sayvion

"Bitch, if you bite my shit, I'm punching you in ya fuckin' kneecaps," I told this chick I had sucking my dick from Garvey. It was funny how I just shot the motherfucker up last night, and I had this chick feeding me info about who was saying what and what their plan of retaliation was going to be while I was feeding her the dick ... literally. And the bitch sucked a mean one.

"Ahhhh, damn, ma." I moaned loudly as I let my seeds shoot down her throat. She swallowed every drop like the bitch she was. That was why I couldn't wife none of these hoes. Talya may not have been my one and only, but baby girl had my heart.

I started fucking with Talya about a year after her brother got locked up. I was supposed to be looking out for shawty, but damn, how da fuck did he expect me to be 'hands off' when she had an ass that just kept screaming 'hands on!' Don't get me wrong. There was a multitude of bad bitches walking these streets, but shawty not only had it going on in the looks department; she was smart as hell, kept her head held high despite the odds of having a piece of shit ass mother and her only protector and financer being locked away, and she made that shit look so easy. Baby girl kept a smile on her face.

Talya was a whole foot shorter than me, and that was what made the shit so cute. Yeah, I said cute. That's what the fuck *they* said. We looked cute. Her dimples matched mine, her hair was real and stopped just right above her ass, and she kept that shit in funny looking colors. She had hazel eyes and was only a shade or two lighter than me. She wasn't what you called dark skinned, but she was for damn sure tapping on the door to it. Females hated her because she was ... special. She was too fucking perfect—a rider, smart as hell, took no shit, gorgeous as hell, and regardless of all the positive traits she possessed, she remained humble as hell.

"You coulda warned me you was getting ready to cum, nigga. How you know I wanted ya kids swirling around in my mouth?" this motherfucka had the nerve to ask.

"Shits ain't swirling in ya mouth; they down ya throat, ya dumb ass. Get da fuck up and get out." Her purpose had been served. I ain't even want the pussy. That shit was loose as hell. But as long as she had them vacuum cleaner jaws, she could suck me up anytime.

Carmen Lashay, T. Nicole, Ty Leese Javeh, Eden Mireya, Sparkle Lewis, Reign, & Armani

"You're rude as fuck, yo. I saw ya little girlfriend's homegirl this morning. Her nosey ass was standing there all up in my damn conversation, grilling me like she wanted me to put hands to her."

"Fuck you tellin' me for? As long as you wasn't sayin' shit you wasn't supposed to, you're good," I told her, waving her off.

"Please, nigga, wasn't nobody thinking 'bout ya stuck-up ass. Can you run me a few dollars, though? And don't act like that mouth wasn't worth it."

I had in-home pussy. I could fuck my girl in any hole, anywhere, any day, any time. Why in the entire hell this bucket thought I was getting ready to give her ass some money was beyond me. Before I could answer her, my phone began to ring. Looking at the caller ID, I saw it was my boy Blockz.

"Wa ah gwan, brethren?" I answered.

"Son, you spoke to Sha? These fuck niggas on some retaliation shit, and a nigga's ready to get it poppin'."

I was the only one that was connected with Shalom. When he ran these streets, *we* ran these streets. Everything from Flatbush to East New York was ours. I was his right-hand man, so of course, with him getting locked, that left me in charge. Still, shit never got handled without his approval. I was the only nigga he phoned in order to keep a low profile, and even our conversations were limited. When we talked, it was coded and brief.

"Nah, son, I ain't heard from him yet. That smut from Garvey put me up on game, son, so don't worry. I got shit handled. We gon' take care of that tonight. Do me one, though. Go holla at Tyrekka and dem boys from Union, and tell them to squad up. I don't want the rest of SBD on this shit. If we have any casualties, it'll be dem little foot soldiers and not squad, feel me?" I knew it was a war in these streets, and since Sha had been incarcerated, we hadn't lost one of our own. I didn't plan to any time soon.

"Say less. One," Blockz replied before ending the call. Forgetting just that fast that the human vacuum cleaner was still here, I turned around to see her mugging the fuck out of me. "Fuck you lookin' at?"

"And that shit, my nigga, is extra. Come on, Say. It ain't like you're hurting for it. You can break me off wit' a little bit ... or some dick. Either or." She smirked, and I wanted to whip my shit out, jack, and bust on her damn face, ol' stupid ass. But silence was golden, and I was willing to pay for hers as long as she kept feeding me the info I needed.

"Take this and get the hell on. Hit me up, though, if you hear some new shit," I told her, handing her two stacks. Yeah, she was a cheap one. Two stacks wouldn't have held wifey down for an hour.

After ... Tanjanekia, yeah, that was her name. After she left, I rolled up a blunt, sat back, and put a plan in action. Niggas had violated in the worst way, and it was now time for someone to feel my wrath. I was always the calm, laid back one between Shalom and me, but motherfuckas didn't realize that I was the damn enforcer. Every gun pulled, shot that was shot, and body that was dropped was all on me.

Once I had my plan in place, I scooped up my keys and headed up the steps from the basement at the house I had in the cut on 96th. It was crazy 'cause wifey literally stayed two blocks over on 94th, but I did all my dirt and shit here. I lived on Willmohr and 93rd, but I never took work or a bitch to my crib. Wifey was liable to pop up at any given moment, and them boys would never find shit at any place I actually laid my head. However, the 90's was where I felt most comfortable operating in every aspect of my life, so for that, I cheated a little too close to home.

I went in the backyard and, after feeding Rock, my pit, decided to walk up to Rutland and see who was on the block. I wasn't a corner nigga, but I kept my ears to the streets at all times. Hanging on the block gave me a feel of what the streets were saying, and at a time like this, I needed to know who knew what.

As soon as I hit the corner of Rutland, I saw Tal and Shonday going into the Dominican shop. I nicely turned my ass around and went back up the block. Fuck that! I jumped in my whip and pulled off, en route to Flatbush. I'd hear what the word on the block was another day. Wasn't getting ready to hem my ass up. I coulda sworn her ass got her shit done downtown, though.

Carmen Lashay, T. Nicole, Ty Leese Javeh, Eden Mireya,
Sparkle Lewis, Reign, & Armani

Shalom

198 .... 199 ... 200. These reps of sit-ups and push-ups were killing my ass, but I had to do something to take my mind off this bullshit ass bid. I was currently serving a life sentence for a murder I didn't commit. Don't get me wrong; I'd done my share of shit on the streets, but this one, I didn't do.

I had already appealed once and was turned down, but my lawyer contacted me a couple of weeks ago and said they had some evidence that would definitely get me out of here. He was supposed to be coming through this week to go over the details with me. I prayed like hell he wasn't on no bullshit because with all the incriminating evidence they presented at the trial, I didn't see how in the hell I was getting up out of here.

My bid started three years ago, and the only thing that kept me from spazzing out in here on the daily was one, I didn't have to worry about children or a girl on the outside world, and two, I knew that my niggas held my baby girl down. My sister was my life. She was all I had, and I was all she had. Our piece-of-shit mother didn't do a job of raising us at all. My sister superseded all other students in her class at an early age, and I knew she was destined for greatness. When I turned twelve, and baby girl was only seven, I made sure that I did whatever it took for her to not be a statistic and fall victim to these streets.

Talya had a weird liking for the human anatomy, so much so that by the sixth grade, she knew she wanted to major in Kinesiology. By that time, I was heavy as hell in the streets, and once I started SBD, I made sure she never had to want for anything. It didn't matter that it was only a five-year age difference between us. I was her mother, father, protector, and big brother all wrapped up in one.

"Barron, you got mail," I heard the C.O. say as he went around doing the daily mail delivery. Talya made sure she wrote me at least once a week and kept me updated on her grades along with this little punk ass nigga she was seeing. I wasn't feeling the situation at all, especially with me being behind these bars, but my nigga Sayvion said dude was on the up and up, so I took his word for it.

Sayvion knew Talya was my heart, and I would kill any nigga that disrespected her in any shape, form, or fashion. He adapted those same feelings toward her, so if he said dude was cool, I was gonna ride with it.

I opened the letter and smiled when the picture fell out. My shining star... Shorty had grown up so much, man. I couldn't believe the difference six months could make. That was the last time she'd sent a picture. This one was of her and her little thot ass friend, Shonday. I called her that, but shorty was a dollar and always had my sister's back. She was too young for me, but I knew she was crushing on me hard as hell. After staring at the picture a little longer, I began to read the letter.

My dearest Shalom,

I pray this letter finds you in the best of health and state of mind. As for myself, well, I don't have to say because the picture says it all. LOL. Just kidding. Anyway, I've been keeping my grades up and am actually expected to graduate two semesters earlier than planned. You know ya girl's smart as hell. I never thought I would actually make it through without you being here with me, but knowing that you'll be proud of me when I walk across that stage gave me the motivation to keep it pushing.

    Guess who I saw the other day? If you're thinking Mommy, you would be correct. Sha, she didn't even know who I was. Hell, I almost didn't know who she was. She looked horrible. I wanted so bad to take her in and clean her up, but I could hear you now saying that you can only help a person that wants to be helped, and it was obvious from her demeanor when I spoke to her that she was beyond help. I pray for her; that's all I can do. However, I will always be that little girl that yearns for the love of her mother. But I thank you for stepping in where she couldn't.

    Shalom, I have so much I want to tell you about this guy I'm dealing with. I know your face is balled up because you don't want to hear about him (LOL). I can guarantee you would approve wholeheartedly, though. I want him and I to come visit you, but you won't approve me for visitation. Why??? I miss you, and I want to see you. I'm almost forgetting what you look like (I'm lying but not lying).

    Anyway, I won't take up any more of your time. Again, I want to thank you for always being there for me. For every Mother's Day, Father's Day, birthday,

Carmen Lashay, T. Nicole, Ty Leese Javeh, Eden Mireya, Sparkle Lewis, Reign, & Armani

Christmas, and even my prom, my big brother held me down, being my mother, father, and brother. I love you always and forever. No one will ever amount to you. Until we see each other...

All My Love,

Talya

P.S. Shonday said you still her snack! (LMBOOOO!)

I had to crack a smile at the last part. That little girl was too much. Talya left me wanting to shed a tear after reading her letter. Yeah, thugs cried; let me be not the first nor the last to tell you that.

I lay back on my bed and soaked up everything that she wrote, glancing at all of her pictures every now and then. I heard my cell open, and one of my dudes from around the way walked in. He had a somber expression on his face, and off rip, I knew it was about to be some bullshit.

"T-Rock, what's poppin'? Walkin' up in here like you lost your best friend or some shit."

He sat down on my bunk and dropped his head in his hands. I ain't know what the fuck was going on, but I ain't do all this emotional shit for nobody but baby girl.

I knew T-Rock from around the way. Well, actually, he lived in the 90's and ended up moving to Garvey after junior high. When SBD had beef with Garvey, he never involved himself in the shit and stayed neutral. I respected the nigga for that.

"Sha, yo, when the last time you talked to dat nigga Say?"

The mentioning of Say's name caused me to perk up some.

"It's been a minute. Why? What's good?" I questioned, confused as fuck. If he was about to tell me something happened to my nigga, it was definitely gon' be some problems.

"I just got off the phone with Biggz from Garvey, son. Yo, ya boy in dem streets wildin'. Him and that other nigga Blockz shot up Garvey and either Tilden, Van Dyke or Seth Lo last night. Niggas fucked around and killed a five-year-old, son. Niggas is after his head."

What the fuck did this nigga just say to me?

Carmen Lashay, T. Nicole, Ty Leese Javeh, Eden Mireya,
Sparkle Lewis, Reign, & Armani

"Come again?" I had to make sure I heard him correctly because I knew damn well I ain't initiate no motherfuckin' war, so what was really good!

"Word is bond, son. Yo, I'm telling you this because niggas talkin' about killin' his bitch and all," he said.

I ain't give a fuck about that, because that shit didn't concern me. My only concern right now was getting ahold of this fuckin' livewire to find out what the fuck was going on. Say was the calm one. What the hell set this nigga off?

Talya

Talking about tired, Shonday and I shopped and pampered ourselves until we couldn't anymore. She was mad as hell at first because since we were late to our appointment, we had to backtrack and settle for a spot in the neighborhood. Her ass got over it, though. We even called up our homegirl Tricia. Tricia was the only Puerto Rican chick that I fucked with. Crazy as hell but cool as fuck. She dealt with Sha back in the day, but she didn't let their failed relationship interfere with our friendship. Both Shon-Shon and I looked up to her like a big sister even though Shonday was low-key crushing on my brother.

When I walked in the house, just as he'd informed me, Sayvion hadn't got home yet. I felt sticky as hell, and all I wanted to do was take a nice, hot bubble bath and read a book on my kindle. I was glad school was out for the summer, and although I'd elected to take two classes online, my workload wasn't that heavy. Even with studying, I always made time to read something from one of the ladies at Treasured Publications. Those girls could write their asses off!

I slipped out of my dress and went to the Keith Sweat station on Pandora. They were gettin' it in with all the old school jams. "He's Mine" by Mokenstef was playing, and my can't-hold-a-tune ass was singing right along with them.

After gathering everything I needed for my bath, I wrapped my hair, securely placing my scarf on it so no parts of it would get wet while I was in the tub. Before I could go in the bathroom, my phone chimed, alerting me I had a missed call. I looked at the number and saw I had missed Sha. Usually, he'd call right back, so I turned the water on to the desired temperature and let it fill up the tub.

As predicted, my phone rang not even a good minute later. After going through the spiel from the automated voice system, I was connected to my brother.

"Baby girl, what's good?"

Regardless of how old I was, when I spoke with my brother, you would think I was a child. My face would turn beet red, and I'd be blushing like hell.

"I'm good, Sha. Just got in from shopping with Shon-Shon and Tricia. How are you holding up? Have you spoke with your lawyer about another appeal?"

"Actually, ma, that's why I'm calling. My lawyer is supposed to be coming through with some news that should get me released. You know how long an appeal can take, though, so unless it's some off-the-wall, person-confessed type shit, I'll still be sitting for a while."

Although I didn't want to hear that, knowing that his lawyer had some new evidence did give me some level of hope. I decided to take this time and ask about something I'd mentioned in the most recent letter I wrote to him.

"Sha, will you please approve me for visitation? Please? Talking to you on the phone and writing letters is cool and all, but I haven't seen you in three years. I want to see you. We really need to talk."

I heard him grunt and knew that he was thinking. I missed my brother so much it hurt. When he was out on these streets, yeah, he was strict on me like a father would be on his child, and I felt like I couldn't breathe, but I'd rather have that back than him behind those bars any day. Even though he made sure that I was still good financially and didn't have to want for anything, it was nothing like having him here with me.

"Yeah, my star, I'll do it." He breathed out as if he were going against his better judgment.

Carmen Lashay, T. Nicole, Ty Leese Javeh, Eden Mireya, Sparkle Lewis, Reign, & Armani

I knew he didn't want me to see him in there like that, but I didn't care about all that. I just wanted to see my big bro.

"Thank you so much," I cried, glad he finally agreed.

"No crying, baby girl. Listen, I need to ask you a question, and keep it a buck wit' me. You seen that nigga Say in the last week?"

I froze. Did he know something? It had been two years, and we'd managed to keep our relationship a secret. If someone told my brother before I did, I would literally fucking kill them even though I couldn't fault anyone but myself.

"He came over the other day and dropped some money off from you. Why? Is everything okay?" I asked fearful.

"What's going on in the streets? I heard some fuck shit today, and I need to holla at him ASAP." Then it dawned on me what Shonday told me earlier. I wasn't going to speak with my brother about it. I now knew that he didn't authorize the hit. My question now was, what the hell was going on with Sayvion to start this beef shit back up?

"Nothing that I know of, bro." I hated lying to my brother, but I really wanted to find out what was going on first.

"A'ight, baby girl. Well I'm approving ya visits, so I better see ya big head. And tell ya homegirl I said calm her little hot ass down and stay outta trouble. That goes for both of you. I'm proud of you, Tal. I'm really proud of you, ma. Keep up the good work. Don't let ya little boyfriend take ya focus off them books, and keep doing ya thang. I'll call you back later this week, okay?"

"Okay, bro, and thank youuuu. I love you."

"I love you too, baby girl. One."

I hung up the phone happy that I was going to finally be able to visit my brother. Then the reality set in that I was going to have to tell him who I was dealing with. I would worry about that when the time came.

I ran some more hot water to heat my bath water back up and settled in.

I must have fallen asleep because some tumbling and shit knocking around woke me up.

"Tal, where you at, ma!" I heard Say yelling.

"In the tub, baby. I'm coming."

Before I could get out the tub good, this dude was already in the bathroom. I grabbed my towel and wrapped it around my body as he handled his business. After washing his hands, he joined me in the bedroom.

"Sha called me this evening," I said as I moisturized my body and slipped into my panties and nightie.

"Oh word? How's he holding up?" Say slurred.

"He's good. Finally approved me for visitation. Umm … he said he heard some shit that he wasn't too happy about. And Shonday told me that you and Blockz shot up Garvey and Van Dyke last night. What's going on?"

All of a sudden, it was like his drunken state was replaced by complete sobriety. Before my mind could began to register what was happening, he had grabbed me by my throat and pinned me against the wall.

"What the fuck I tell you about questioning me, huh? What the fuck I do in these streets ain't got shit to do wit' you. You gon' fuck around and I'ma hurt you, Tay, real talk. Shit's making me tight as fuck, yo." He released his grip on my neck as I gasped for air, looking at him like he had completely lost his mind.

One thing I didn't tolerate was a nigga puttin' hands on me. My brother never put his hands on me and always told me to never allow a nigga to do it to me. Trust, it was a rule I always lived by. As soon as I gathered my bearings, I slapped the fuckin' fire outta his ass. Umm, wrong answer. That nigga turned around and punched me with a closed fist. I thought that would be the end of it, but once he saw that I was getting ready to swing back, the brawl began.

Sayvion

Talya must have lost her everlasting fuckin' mind.
I wasn't for that shit tonight. I came home earlier than
expected, wanting some pussy, and she came questioning
me. I didn't mean to grab her up, and I definitely didn't
expect for her to swing back. When she did, I lost it.
Baby girl didn't deserve that, but her questioning me and
swinging back on me took me over the edge. Like damn,
you ain't even ask a motherfucka how his day went.

BAM!

I punched her one last time, making sure to get
my point across. Don't get me wrong; I didn't have a
habit of putting my hands on her, but lately, Tal had been
questioning everything I did, and honestly, I was fed up.

When Sha was out, she was a little hands on with
the business. Like I said, she was smart as hell, so she
handled financials, looked at investment properties, and
researched other legal avenues that we could use to wash
money. Her brains generated us an ass of money over the
last five to seven years, even at her young age. Since
when we started going legal with shit, all of us were

barely of legal age, she even went as far as securing businesses with investors. Once Sha got locked, he didn't want her to have anything to do with the business at all, so all the responsibility was handed over to me. Even though I still consulted with her on the legal aspect of shit, street shit had nothing to do with her, so she had no business questioning me about it.

I looked at her, and guilt consumed me immediately. I had fucked up. I was taking my anger out on her, and she was the last person in the world that deserved it. Yeah, I didn't like her questioning me, but shit was deeper than that. A nigga had a lot on his plate at the moment, and her questioning me added fuel to an already blazing fire.

"Ma, get up. I'm sorry."

"Don't you fucking touch me, Say. Get the fuck away from me! Da fuck you think I am!" she screamed.

Tears ran down her face, and I could hear the pain in her voice. *Damn, I fucked up.* I went in the bathroom and grabbed a washcloth then ran some cold water over it. When I walked back in the bedroom, baby girl just sat there crying.

"Why, Say? Da fuck I ever do to you to warrant you putting hands on me?"

Carmen Lashay, T. Nicole, Ty Leese Javeh, Eden Mireya, Sparkle Lewis, Reign, & Armani

I couldn't even answer her. Setting the washcloth on the dresser, I slowly grabbed her into my arms as I rocked her, allowing her to sob. When I pulled back and looked down into her face, one of her eyes was shut, and the discoloration was beginning to set in. Now I really felt like shit. I let her go, grabbed the washcloth, and went to the kitchen to get some ice.

Once I returned to the room, her tears had dried, and she gave me the deadliest look I had ever seen on anyone. I stopped in my tracks. See, what a lot of people didn't know about Talya was she was actually the true definition of silent but deadly. The way she moved about… She kept a smile on her face at all times, and though she didn't take shit, once she got to the point where you couldn't get a word out of her, you never knew what was going to happen. She became silent … but deadly.

"Say, if I was you, I'd practice the ten-feet rule. Stay the fuck away from me right now," she said with a snarl. Say no more. I turned the hell around. She ain't had to tell me twice. Bitch in my blood, never that, but I knew if I reacted, one of us would end up dead.

I went to the linen closet in the hallway, grabbed a blanket, and took my ass to the living room to sleep on the couch. As soon as I closed my eyes to try and sleep away this building headache, my phone vibrated. I looked down and saw it was a text from Tanjanekia.

Tan: *Change of plans. Them niggas hittin' ya spot in Flatbush tonight.*

Me: *Clarendon or Beverly?*

Tan: *Idk. They strapped up. Be careful.*

I know y'all probably wondering how a bitch I'm just bussin' know all my business, but it pays to get a person on the inside, and when you're feeding that person dick, it makes them a little more loyal even though you treat 'em like they ain't shit.

I texted Blocks and told him to send them Union niggas out to both spots in Flatbush and lay everything down. I ain't give a fuck who it was. The streets were dirty, but a nigga like me was grimy wit' no conscious for the game.

I went to check on baby girl, and as soon as I opened the door to the bedroom, she still lay in the same spot, icing me as soon as the door opened. *O-kay!* It

Carmen Lashay, T. Nicole, Ty Leese Javeh, Eden Mireya, Sparkle Lewis, Reign, & Armani

wasn't the time. I didn't even tell her I was leaving. I just grabbed my shit and bounced.

Talya

As soon as I heard the front door close, I counted backward from ten for the fiftieth time and got up to go to the bathroom to survey my face. I could not believe this nigga had the audacity to put his hands on me. And not only that, but he did the shit like I wasn't going to swing back. He had me so fucked up. This was the first time he had ever hit me.

Like I said, our arguments were becoming more heated, and I knew it was only a matter of time, but to be honest, I stayed because I knew my brother trusted Sayvion more out of anybody in his crew. He trusted Say with his life and my life. And even though Say put hands on me tonight, I trusted him with my life as well.

I went to the kitchen and saw the washcloth that he had grabbed earlier, I guess to tend to my face. I got it cold again and grabbed some more ice out of the freezer. My eye was shut closed, and I needed to get that shit to heal quick as hell. With Sha finally approving me for visits, I didn't know when the hell he would expect me to come up, but I for damn sure wasn't going up there with a black eye—oh, and a busted lip.

The more I thought about it, the more I was ready to kill Say. I didn't know what the hell was going on in

Carmen Lashay, T. Nicole, Ty Leese Javeh, Eden Mireya, Sparkle Lewis, Reign, & Armani

these streets, but your home was supposed to be your place of refuge, and granted we didn't live together, when he came here, he was supposed to have a peace of mind. Leave the hostility and street shit on the other side of the door.

Since I knew I was not going to be able to get any rest, I decided to knock out a week's worth of work in my Personality and Abnormal Psych class, which was one of my favorite classes thus far. For the next two hours, I crammed all the work that needed to be done. Needless to say, sleep came like a baby in no time following that.

I awoke the next day around 1:15 p.m. with a banging ass headache. I checked my phone and had ten messages from Shonday, four from Tricia, and a missed call from Blockz. *Blockz?* Fuck was he doing calling me.

As I viewed the text messages, my heart began to beat rapidly. Even with the bullshit that jumped off last night, what I was reading could not be right. I tried to call Say's phone, and it kept going to voicemail. I decided to call Blockz because I knew he would have the answers I was looking for.

Blockz

Man, what the fuck! Shit was getting crazy in these damn streets. And the craziest part of it all was I didn't know *why* this shit was jumping off. It was like I was doing everything that was asked of me when I should have been asking the question, *nigga, why?*

My phone rang, interrupting my thoughts. I looked down and saw it was Talya. I didn't know if mama knew what the hell was going on, but I knew that Sha left Say to look over her. Even though it was all of our responsibilities to look after baby girl if shit ever jumped off or if she was ever in need, Say was like her personal bodyguard. Plus, I knew the nigga was fucking her. I peeped that shit about a year back.

"What's good, ma?" I answered.

"Blockz, what's goin' on? I got hella messages on my phone saying Say got shot last night. Is he okay? Please tell me he's not dead. What the fuck is going on!"

"Whoa, slow down, ma. Nah, shorty, he ain't dead. That nigga's good. He just beat up at the moment. Some shit jumped off wit' some niggas from Garvey, and he got caught in the crossfire, but he's good, ma. He's at Kings. I got his phone and shit, but the shit's dead," I relayed to her, knowing she had probably blew his phone up when she got the messages. I ain't leave a fucking message when I called. Who da fuck relayed some shit like that through a damn text or voicemail?

"He ain't dead? They got phones at Kings County. Why da fuck he ain't call me? Oh, he gon' be dead. Da fuck!"

I couldn't do anything but laugh. Tay had some fire to her, and although we all knew a relationship was forbidden with her, having her was like having a diamond in the rough. That nigga Say was lucky as hell.

"I'm pretty sure he ain't want you to worry, ma. But what's good? What's up wit' my nigga Sha? How's he holding?"

"He's straight. He got some good news from the lawyer, so they're getting ready to appeal again. Hopefully, it's something that'll have him coming home. I forgot to tell Say about it since I barely saw him yesterday."

I made sure not to mention too much about the war going on, because for one, I didn't want her to worry, and for two, I knew Sha forbade her from being a part of that shit once he got locked up. Therefore, I wasn't getting ready to speak on it.

"That's what's up. Tell dat nigga we're missing him out here, and hold it down. You going to see Say?"

"Hell to the fuck no! Fuck I look like! He supposed to be guarding me; I ain't supposed to be chasing him. Fuck outta here!" Shorty was mad as fuck. It took everything in me not to burst out laughing in her ear.

"Yeah, yeah. A'ight, ma. Be easy and go holla at cha boy! One." I ended the call and thought about her saying Sha was getting ready to get a chance at becoming a free man again. I prayed the lawyer came through with something that could get him out because these streets were for damn sure getting crazy without him.

Talya
One Week Later

True to my word, I didn't go up to the damn hospital to see Say. I was glad he was okay and all, and I hated that he got shot, but after what happened the night before, I was not ready to be around him. I should have gone to the hospital if I knew I was going to endure the bullshit, though.

I had just finished taking an exam, and as always, I aced it. I decided to celebrate by having a nice, cold glass of Moscato. Walking into the kitchen to open the fridge, I turned on the light and was shocked like hell to see Say standing in the living room.

"Say, what the fuck! Why you just standing there in the dark like you 'bout to rob my ass or some shit?"

"Why the fuck you ain't come see me, Tal? I mean, I know you knew I got shot, so why the fuck you ain't come see me? Two fuckin' days in the hospital and not one visit from a bitch that claims she loves me. How dat look?" he questioned, wide-eyed, and I could tell from his voice and the way he was leaning that he was tipsy.

Carmen Lashay, T. Nicole, Ty Leese Javeh, Eden Mireya, Sparkle Lewis, Reign, & Armani

"You beat my ass, and a bitch is supposed to come run to your side? Not this bitch. I ain't beat for da bullshit."

I grabbed a wine glass and some ice, poured my Moscato, and was getting ready to head toward my room. Not quick enough. Before I could get to the entry of the hallway, my wine glass was flying out of my hand, and I was heading toward the floor, face first. Sayvion sat on my back, wrapped my hair around his hand, and commenced to banging my head on the floor.

"You. Is. The. Stupidest. Bitch. I've. Ever. Seen. Do you know how many fuckin' females wanna be with me?" BANG! "I can have any female I want, and I choose to stay in a damn secret relationship wit' yo' young ass!" BANG! "And ya ass can't even come see a nigga when he's down!" BANG, BANG, BANG!

I was defenseless. I couldn't even fight back if I wanted to. With his bodyweight holding me down, I couldn't even roll over. All I kept thinking was, what did I do to deserve this? Why now? Why me?

Never in my life had I been beaten to the point I had to be rushed to the hospital. I had a concussion, had to get twenty-two stitches in my head, my face was badly swollen, and my right eye matched the left eye that he had been blacked. I couldn't win for losing.

I was being released from the hospital today, and that night replayed over and over in my memory each day I sat in that hospital. Sadly, the fight in me was gone. The toughness I exuded and was always taught was gone right along with it. I was now doubting myself about everything, including school. But I knew I had to finish because I had to make Sha happy.

Speaking of Sha, he called while I was in the hospital, and I couldn't tell him where I was. He wanted to let me know that his lawyer definitely had a good reason to appeal, and he wanted to see me as soon as possible so he could tell me about it face to face. He also questioned whether or not I had spoken to Say because he couldn't reach him. Crazy ... I couldn't reach him either. He sent flowers, a big teddy bear, and a 'Get Well Soon' card up here like he wasn't the one that put me in this predicament, but as far as calling me himself or coming to see me, that was a no-no. I guess he was paying me back for not coming to see him.

Carmen Lashay, T. Nicole, Ty Leese Javeh, Eden Mireya, Sparkle Lewis, Reign, & Armani

Shonday was there with me every day. She took time off from her job to make sure that I was in good hands. Tricia came by twice as well, and even Blockz came through. When he questioned what the hell had happened to me—his exact words, not mine—I had to lie and tell him I got jumped up on the parkway. He found that shit un-fucking-believable, but he didn't question me anymore.

Shon-Shon and Tricia both were like raging animals when I told them what happened. It took everything in me to calm them down. Tricia swore up and down that she was going to find a way to get in touch with Sha to tell him what was going on. After hours of me begging, crying, and pleading for her not to do that, she finally gave in, but not until I promised that I would tell him on my own.

"Ms. Barron, make sure you get both prescriptions filled. One is for pain, and the other is an antibiotic to prevent infection once your swelling goes down. You will also need to follow up with your primary care physician in two weeks. Do you have any questions?" the nurse asked that was providing me with my discharge papers and care.

"No, ma'am. I thank y'all for everything."

"No problem, sweetie. Remember, love doesn't equate to pain. You didn't have to say anything to me... Your eyes told your story. Take care of yourself first, Ms. Barron," she said before leaving the room.

A lone tear fell from my eye as Shonday stood in front of me, shaking her head. She was hurting for me, but she was more mad than anything.

"Sis, I'm not going to tell you what to do, but you need to let Sha know what happened, and you need to leave Say the fuck alone, real talk. Is this the first time he put hands on you?"

I didn't tell her or Tricia about the first time it happened. I guess I was too embarrassed, and then with the shooting and everything, I just never got the time. Hell, the incidents happened so close together I barely had time to heal from the other. My silence must have answered the question for her.

"Well, considering *that* eye has some discoloration as well, I'll take that as a no. What the fuck! You are one of the strongest, no-nonsense females I know. Why are you even accepting this shit from this nigga?" she questioned.

I asked myself that as well. I mean, in less than two weeks, this nigga had put hands on me twice. But like I said, after this last time, I had no more fight left in me. Deserving of it, I was not, but no one would look out for me like Say did with my brother gone. Shit, he looked at me like a sister himself at one time. Disgusting, I know, but hey, he did. He may have put hands on me, but a muthafucka in the street had better not even make an attempt to look at me the wrong way. That went for male or female alike. In addition to him being my protector, he had my heart. He wasn't always like this.

When Say and I got together, even though we knew my brother would have a conniption, the attraction was undeniable. We built a bond that was unbreakable. He was like my best friend. I could talk to him about any and every thing, and we did any and every thing together. In the last month or so was when things switched up. What was going on? I didn't know, but I was losing my man and myself in the process. Scratch that. I had already lost myself...

Carmen Lashay, T. Nicole, Ty Leese Javeh, Eden Mireya, Sparkle Lewis, Reign, & Armani

Sayvion

I know y'all probably think I'm this fucked up ass nigga, especially since I said I didn't make it a habit to hit Tal, but when she didn't show up to see me, I blanked. I was dealing with enough shit in the streets, and who was supposed to have been my rock was nowhere to be found. She ain't even call up to the hospital to check on a nigga. What kind of shit was that?

The day I got out, I promised myself I was whipping her ass. I didn't know what the fuck time she was on, but the shit wasn't happening. So yeah, I fucked her up and sent her to the hospital. I didn't feel as bad this time as I felt the last time. Like I said, a nigga was stressed the fuck out with this street shit. But thankfully, all my problems had been solved. I hated that innocent lives were lost because of this war that was waged all because I was trying to get at one damn nigga, but that was how the game went sometimes.

I knew Tal was being released today, so I made it my business to be at her crib when she got there. I had tidied up and everything, considering the last time she was here, shit was all fucked up. I stretched out on the couch and waited for her to get home.

****

"Oh, hell no! Da fuck is this nigga doing here!" I heard Shonday's big mouth yell.

"Shonday, please stop yelling. Sayvion, why are you here?" Tal asked me like the shit was normal. I wanted to check her, but I understood her position.

"I came by to see how you were doing, baby girl. I know I didn't come up to the hospital and all, but it was a lot of shit going on that I can't go into details about right now. The shit is handled now, and I promise shit gon' get better from here on out," I told her, meaning what I said.

It was never my intentions for shit to go left with Talya like it did. I brought the streets into my home, and that was something that was not acceptable. I had been doing some fucked up shit, and it was catching up to me ... mentally and literally. They say you always hurt the ones closest to you, and I guess that rang true when it came to me. I took my frustrations out on the one person that held my heart. Although I *felt* she deserved that last ass whipping, deep down, I knew she didn't.

Carmen Lashay, T. Nicole, Ty Leese Javeh, Eden Mireya, Sparkle Lewis, Reign, & Armani

I heard her take a deep breath and sigh while Shonday stood there with her arms folded, looking back and forth between the both of us. I may not hit females on a regular, but I wanted to punch her in her shit, for real.

"Shonday, I'll give you a call later, sis. Let me talk to Say real quick," Talya said, and Shonday just looked at her and shook her head.

"I'll leave, no problem. But remember this hot shit, Mr. I Like Putting My Hands On Women. If Sha finds out, you're a dead nigga, bet that!" And with that, she walked out, slamming the door behind her.

"Baby, I'm sorry. I know I said it the first time, but I truly apologize. I know my words don't mean much of shit right now, but I can't keep saying it enough."

"Why, Say? Just please tell me what did I do that was so wrong for you to feel the need to put hands on me? I've asked myself that question every day for the past week, and I kept drawing a blank. I've been the perfect woman for you. Yes, bossy—I am. A smart mouth, definitely. But loyal, hardworking, and faithful, I've always been. I've even gone against my brother for you to some extent. So what the fuck did I do! How can you continuously hurt the one you love!" she yelled, making me feel like shit.

I could have told the truth and got everything off my chest, but I refused. Nah, she didn't need to be involved in this shit, point, blank, period. She already felt like she was going against her brother for me. If I told her what was going on, no doubt she would definitely feel like I'd betrayed her all this time. That wasn't the case. I legit loved Talya with all my heart. This street war ain't got shit to do with nobody but me, though.

Yet this street war was the reason I put hands on her. She did need to know that part at least.

"Look, ma. You're perfect. You know this. Do I fuck around on you? Yeah. Prior to this, have I ever put hands on you? No. Why now? I'm not using this as an excuse, but I was stressed the fuck out. I had too much coming at me from too many different angles, and I took the shit out on you. For that, I'm sorry because you didn't deserve it. You're my heart, Tal. You know that.

"Your brother entrusted me to protect you by any means necessary. Never in a million years was it my intentions to ever be the one to bring harm to you ... not physically, anyway. From the door, I told you I fuck other

Carmen Lashay, T. Nicole, Ty Leese Javeh, Eden Mireya, Sparkle Lewis, Reign, & Armani

bitches from time to time. That's just me. Never will them bitches ever run up on you or disrespect you because I'd end their lives. You know that, and they know that. And in all honesty, I never fucked the same broad twice to avoid catching feelings on either of our parts. Does that make it better? Nah, it doesn't, but I've always kept it real wit' you, and I won't stop now." Yeah, I was lying my ass off to some degree, but damn, I would say anything to get back on her good side at the moment.

"I understand you're going through shit in the streets, but that doesn't justify you putting hands on me. And then my brother is calling, asking me to come see him. How in the hell am I supposed to go see him like this?" she cried.

I couldn't answer that, because he would for damn sure know some shit wasn't right. Although he didn't know it was me she was fucking with, I was supposed to be the one protecting her. Blockz told me she told him she got jumped by some females, but hell, that shit didn't even sound right to him, so I knew it wouldn't fly with

Sha. First thing he would have asked was where the fuck was I, or what the fuck did I do about it?

Speaking of, I had been avoiding the nigga for a minute. I knew he was going to question me about the shootings since he wasn't the one to initiate them. I didn't want to deal with that at the time, so I just ignored his calls. Now that I was good, I needed to get at him.

I walked closer to where she stood, looked down at her, and wiped away her tears. The more I wiped, the more that fell. We had to find a way to get through this. We had to.

Carmen Lashay, T. Nicole, Ty Leese Javeh, Eden Mireya, Sparkle Lewis, Reign, & Armani

Shalom

Two months later

A nigga was stressing. My sister literally begged me to put her ass on my visitation list, and here it was a little over two months later, and her ass had yet to come see me. I had the best news for her, but I refused to tell her over the phone.

I didn't know how in the hell my lawyer found an actual eyewitness to the murder, but I wasn't questioning it. The witness went and spoke to the DA, and they were pushing for an immediate release. We were due to go to court next week.

I still hadn't been able to get up with Sayvion, and that shit was fucking with me—hard. I ain't know what was up with this nigga. My dude up in here told me the beef had simmered with Garvey and the 90's, but I still wanted to know what the fuck had started it back up from the door. I spoke to the nigga Biggz from Garvey and told him the shit wasn't on my command, and he explained to me everything that was going down. I was heated ...

heated as fuck, and Say was gon' have to answer to me when I hit them streets.

Since I couldn't get in touch with Say, something told me to call up my nigga Blockz. It wasn't sitting welling with me that Talya hadn't come to visit, and Say had gone ghost.

"What's poppin'? Who dis!" Blockz answered after the third ring.

"What's good, son? This Shalom."

"Oh shit, my mufuckin' nigga! What's up? You out? Don't an operator supposed to come through or some shit?" he laughed.

"I can't call it, my dude. And I'm callin' off a burner. What's good wit' you, boy? Holdin' shit down out there?" I asked.

"Man, the best I can, son, the best I can. Shit got real in these streets wit' that war for a minute, man. Too many bodies dropped on both sides." I could tell he thought I knew about the shit and was the one who'd actually called the hit, so I was going to play on that and use it to my advantage.

"My bad, son, and I hate I had to put y'all up in the middle of it. Just some old beef that popped up that needed to be put away, feel me? But then when niggas

Carmen Lashay, T. Nicole, Ty Leese Javeh, Eden Mireya, Sparkle Lewis, Reign, & Armani

was talking about kids got shot and running up in Say's girl crib, I had to dead that shit," I told him, using the little bit of information I'd obtained from T-Rock.

"Say word. I'm glad you deaded that shit before that happened, considering who the fuck Say's girl is," he said, almost mumbling the last part.

"Word? I know her or something? Shit, he's fuckin' one of my exes or something?" I laughed because I knew Say wouldn't do no fucked up shit like that. But hell, it ain't like I had too many exes I gave a fuck about.

The line got quiet as hell. You could hear a mouse pissing on cotton through that mothafucka. I had to look down and make sure the call was still connected.

"Nigga, da fuck. Who is the nigga's girl?"

"Man, I hate to be the bearer of bad news, but Say's been fucking with Talya, Sha. They been fuckin' around for a sec. Yo, don't shoot the messenger, son. You only fucked with Say, so you ain't leave room for nobody else to tell you shit," he said.

My heart literally stopped for a minute. I could not believe what the fuck my nigga was telling me. Say was like my brother, and he was dealing with my little sister? My heart? My star? Nah, this shit couldn't be right.

"So check it. Baby girl was supposed to come see me, and she ain't been up here. What's up with that?"

"Yo, she was in the hospital about two months ago. I went by there to check her, and she said some girls jumped her. You know that shit ain't even flying. After she got out, we barely see her. I'll call and check in with her, and she'll say she's studying or whatever, but she don't even kick it with Shonday like that anymore. Shon-Shon swears up and down that nigga Say beating on lil' mama," he informed me like he really didn't wanna do that shit.

And he probably didn't. Because any nigga that knew me knew that right now, a beast had awakened. Not only did this nigga violate me by dealing with my sister, but he had the audacity to put hands on her? Yeah, he had to see me.

"Say less, nigga. Yo, quiet as kept, you'll be seeing me real soon, son. And don't you open ya mothafuckin' mouth. I'll hit you when I hit dem streets. Stay up. One." I disconnected the call madder than a

Carmen Lashay, T. Nicole, Ty Leese Javeh, Eden Mireya, Sparkle Lewis, Reign, & Armani

mothafucka. This nigga Say ... he was a dead man walking.

Talya
A Week Later...

I listened to and believed every word Sayvion spit at me the night I came home from the hospital. So much so I allowed him to make love to me like he was a part of my soul. Needless to say, the beatings didn't stop. They actually got worse. I changed my locks and everything. That didn't do a thing. The nigga kicked my damn door in.

For the past two weeks, he'd made an attempt at changing. Two whole damn weeks. Since the last beating didn't leave severe bruising, nothing that makeup couldn't cover, he decided to invite me out to a party tonight. I only agreed because Shonday and Tricia invited me to the same party. I hadn't been seeing them, because they felt like I was a damn fool for staying, but unless a person went through what I was going through, they couldn't speak on it. I wasn't only a prisoner in my home but in my mind as well.

It had gotten to the point that I believed I deserved the beatings and couldn't do any better than Sayvion. He drilled that in me, and he also drilled in me that my brother wouldn't allow me to date anyone that wasn't SBD, because they would never be able to hold me down.

Carmen Lashay, T. Nicole, Ty Leese Javeh, Eden Mireya, Sparkle Lewis, Reign, & Armani

Yeah, I believed that too. But I knew that my brother would never approve of me allowing a man to beat my ass because the wind blew opposite of the way he was walking. Or because the sky was pretty and blue, and he wanted it to be gray and raining. He definitely wouldn't allow his niece or nephew to go through this. Yes, I was pregnant.

The last time I allowed him to enter me, which was the day I came from the hospital, another life was created. I'd just found out yesterday and was waiting to tell him tonight, knowing he'd be in a good mood. The party was for Kamar, Blockz's little brother. He'd gotten accepted into Harvard, and SBD was turning up for this one.

I was finally finished getting dressed and was putting the finishing touches on my makeup when I heard Tricia and Shonday ringing the bell like their minds were bad.

"Hold up, bitches! I'm coming!" I yelled.

Tonight, I was sporting an all-red Herve Leger bandage dress with some black suede Giuseppe Zanotti heels. As a matter of fact, my girls and I rocked the outfits in different colors. Shonday wore a hot-pink dress with white heels, and Tricia had on a lavender dress with purple heels. Head turners, yes, we were! All three of us were fierce.

I put the finishing touches on my makeup and headed out the door with my chicks, determined to have the best night I had in a long time. School was about to start back up next week, so this would be my last party for a while.

When we got to the address that Say gave me, I thought I was tripping. He said they were going all out. Why the fuck did we just pull up to a brownstone? Don't get me wrong. It was cute, but we were dressed to go to some exclusive shit. Who da fuck wore this shit to *this* shit?

"Girl, what the hell is this?" Tricia asked, and Shonday and I shook our heads in agreement with her.

"Hell if I know, but come on. I need a drink," Shonday's loud ass said.

"Umm, I may as well tell y'all now before we go in that I can't drink," I told them as I dropped my head.

"And bitch, may I ask why?" Of course, Shonday's ass would ask.

Carmen Lashay, T. Nicole, Ty Leese Javeh, Eden Mireya, Sparkle Lewis, Reign, & Armani

"I found out I was with child yesterday."

"Oh, mami, I'm so happy for you!" Tricia exclaimed as she grabbed me into a hug. Shonday, however, did not share in on the excitement. I knew how she felt because she knew I'd been getting my ass beat lately, but I did want her to at least be a little happy. Tricia only knew of the one time that landed me in the hospital, but I'd been in contact with Shonday. She was my best friend and would be the godmother of my child, so I needed her here for me.

"Shonday, you're not going to say anything?" I asked her.

She looked back at me before opening the door. With a hurt look on her face, she uttered, "Congratulations," and made her way out of the car.

"She'll come around. It's a hard pill to swallow, mami, but she will come around. Let's go, girl. I'm so happy for you." Tricia and I looped arms, got out the car, and walked up the steps of the brownstone.

Now once inside, hell yes, they went all out. The shit was like something from a fairytale. It was themed black and gold, and the décor was black crystal. Everything down to the forks and spoons were black crystal. It was gorgeous.

"What up, ma?" Say came up behind me and said as he kissed my neck. Yes, he was definitely in a good mood.

"Hey, baby. Don't you look handsome?" Handsome was an understatement. Seeing him like this made me remember one of the reasons I fell in love with him. The nigga was beyond fine. He wore a smoke gray shirt and slacks with some black Zanotti loafers, and the ice on his neck and wrist just popped. One single chain and one watch, both diamond encrusted all the way around. The one stud he wore in his ear was worth more than some people's salaries.

"I tries, I tries," he said with a laugh following. I wish I could have this Sayvion all the time. "Come get a drink, babe."

"Oh, about that, Say. We need—"

"Sis, what's good!" Blockz came over there screaming, obviously tipsy as hell already. He picked me up and swung me around. I knew SBD missed me because I had been cooped up in the house for a while, and that wasn't like me.

"I'm good, stupid, now put me down!" I couldn't
do nothing but laugh.

"I missed ya bighead ass. I need to holla at you
'bout something before the night's over. Make sure you
get up with me."

"I got you, bro." When I turned back around,
Sayvion had this look on his face, but he didn't say
anything.

"Yo, let me go holla at dis lil' nigga, Tyrekka, for
a minute, babe. I'll be back." And just like that, he was
gone.

I caught up with Tricia and Shonday, continuing
to admire the place. They had truly gone all out. We
found a seat in the corner since the place was getting
packed and just chilled.

***

The crowd was thinning out some, and I was
beyond ready to go home. Barely pregnant, but my ass
stayed very tired. All I wanted to do was crawl up in my
bed and get a good night's sleep.

"Girl, you 'bout ready?" Shonday asked. Tricia had already left since she got called in at the hospital. She was flaming mad too. Her one night off, and they called her ass in.

"Go ahead, ma. I'ma ride home with Say."

She looked like she wanted to object, but she kissed my cheek and told me to text her when I made it in. I sat there for a little while longer before I got up to head to the bathroom. I guess people thought this shit was a club 'cause they had fucked this bathroom up.

I squatted over the toilet seat, handled my business, and grabbed some tissue to not only wipe but to flush the toilet. That was how nasty the shit looked. Once I was finished, I heard the doorknob jiggling as if someone were trying to come in.

"One second!" I yelled as I washed my hands.

When I opened the door, I saw it was this bitch that I hated name Tanjanekia from Garvey. I was surprised her ass was even over here, considering the beef Garvey had with SBD earlier this summer. Choosing to ignore her, I walked right past her ass, bumping her on purpose.

"Excuse you, bitch!" she screamed.

Carmen Lashay, T. Nicole, Ty Leese Javeh, Eden Mireya, Sparkle Lewis, Reign, & Armani

Before I could turn around good, Twin, one of the street boys from Union, jumped up from nowhere.

"You don't want them problems, ma. Take ya thot ass on and keep it movin' before I let her fuck you up." Everybody knew how I gave it up, but she wanted to try me, of course.

She snickered and mumbled some shit under her breath, but I couldn't catch it.

The crowd had thinned, but there were still a lot of people here. SBD was nowhere to be found, though, except for the little block dudes. As I made my way to the kitchen to fix a to-go plate, I felt myself being snatched back.

"What the fuck you and Twin talking about? Why the fuck you keep looking at him?" Say asked me, gripping me by the back of my neck.

"Sayvion, I wasn't talking to Twin! Let me go! You are embarrassing me." I was not up for this shit tonight.

WHAP!

"Didn't I tell you I better not even see you looking at no nigga? What the fuck! You thought I was playing?" Sayvion asked after having slapped me so hard I lost my footing and fell.

I couldn't understand why he even invited me to this party if he was going to show his behind the moment he got alcohol in his system. This was becoming so repetitive with him. He got drunk; I got my ass whipped. It didn't matter who was around. If he felt the need to exert his 'power,' he was going to do it.

"Sayvion, what are you talking about? I've been sitting in the corner all night. I had just come from the bathroom and got into it with this girl from Garvey. I wasn't even looking in Twin's direction. He's a little ass boy!" I whimpered, praying he wouldn't hit me again. *Prayer unanswered.*

Grabbing me up then dragging me by my dress to the front door, he pulled me down the steps, and once my foot reached the bottom step, he turned around, punching me as if he were hitting a dude in the streets. A crowd began to form outside, but no one stepped in. It was the nosey onlookers that achieved some sick level of satisfaction that had come outside to see what was going on.

Carmen Lashay, T. Nicole, Ty Leese Javeh, Eden Mireya, Sparkle Lewis, Reign, & Armani

As he maintained his grip on my dress, repeatedly smacking me, he yelled, "You ain't nothing but a fuckin' bucket! I don't know why the fuck I chose to wife a trick like you! You's a sneaky bitch!"

Which hurt worse? The physical pain he was inflicting or the emotional seeds he'd just implanted in me? I didn't ask for this. Or did I? I promised myself to never deal with a street dude, and I turned around and got involved with one of the biggest hustlers in Kings County. Nah, forget a street dude. I'd just graduated right on up to kingpin status. Regardless of whether or not he was that when I got with him, I stayed, knowing that was what he'd become once my brother gave him that authority. Now I was paying the price.

My unborn seed crossed my mind as he delivered one final punch, causing me to fall to the ground. I heard gasps, whimpering, and even some snickering around me. I wasn't surprised at all. Just about every dude at this party feared him, and the majority of the females wanted him or just didn't like me because I wasn't from the same blocks. Either way, I didn't expect anyone to help me.

Right when I thought he was done with his performance, he looked down at me and spat in my face. "Your ungrateful ass don't deserve a nigga like me." He lifted his foot and repeatedly stomped down into my chest.

"Yo, nigga, what the fuck!" I heard Blockz scream once he came outside to see what was going on.

Damn, I wish Shalom were here, I thought before everything went black.

Carmen Lashay, T. Nicole, Ty Leese Javeh, Eden Mireya, Sparkle Lewis, Reign, & Armani

Shalom

A real nigga was fucking free. Some chick from Garvey witnessed the shooting but was too scared to speak up initially. As luck would have it, her man was running around telling people he saw the shooting, and it cost him his life. I was starting to put two and two together, and I wasn't liking what I was coming up with.

When I pulled up to the house I shared with my star, all I could do was smile. Shit looked exactly the same. I wanted to head inside, take a shower, and catch up with that nigga Blockz, but I needed to talk to baby girl first about this shit wit' her and Say.

I made my way to the door and rang the bell, but it went unanswered. I stood on the stoop for a good ten minutes, realizing Talya wasn't home. I forgot I had a damn key. I went to put the key in the lock, but the shit didn't work. What the hell made her change the locks?

I prayed nosey ass Ms. Dominguez still stayed next door and could let me use her phone.

Before I could step up on the stoop good, I heard someone saying from the window, "Shalom, is that you?"

"Yes, Ms. Dominguez. How are you? I was wondering if I could use your phone? I'm trying to reach Talya," I replied.

"Sure, baby. Give me a minute." I waited for what seemed like forever for her to come unlock the door.

"Thanks, Ms. Dominguez. I appreciate it. I'll only be a minute."

"Take your time, baby. It's good to see you out. You're staying out, right? No more trouble?" she asked.

"Yes, ma'am. No more trouble for me," I replied while I walked toward the old-timey rotary dial phone she still had hanging on the wall.

I tried to call Talya, but her phone just kept ringing out then going to voicemail. She probably wasn't answering because she didn't know the number. *Think, Sha, think. Blockz*. I quickly dialed up Blockz.

"Yo, who the fuck is this?" he answered.

"Yo, son, what's good? This Sha. I'm out, my nigga. I'm next door to the crib, but Tal not home. You seen her?"

"Nigga, you out? Fuck!" he yelled. I heard commotion in the background but couldn't make out what the hell was going on.

"Nigga, you at a party or some shit? Tal there?"

Carmen Lashay, T. Nicole, Ty Leese Javeh, Eden Mireya, Sparkle Lewis, Reign, & Armani

"Yo, son, shit is all bad. Meet me up at Brookdale. They don't think Tal gon' make it."

To be continued...

What will happen to Talya? What is Sayvion's fate? Who actually turned on Shalom? To get the answers to all of these questions and more, make sure to read *They Can't Stop Me: The Heart of a Savage.*

Carmen Lashay, T. Nicole, Ty Leese Javeh, Eden Mireya,
Sparkle Lewis, Reign, & Armani

Love Gone Bad
BY: CARMEN LASHAY

CHAPTER 1

LOVE IS BLIND...

"Yeah, he lives at 305 His Girlfriend Will Beat A Bitch Up Boulevard off of Bitch, Catch This Fade Lane. The gate code to get inside is 'one, two, three, bitch, come inside, and get your ass beat!'" I yelled, screaming into the phone at the hoe who had just called my boyfriend at 4:00 a.m. talking about coming over. I was sick of checking hoes left and right about my supposed nigga. All of my screaming must have woken him up because he jumped up out of his sleep, screaming at me.

"The fuck is yo' damn problem with all that damn yelling?" he asked, looking at me all crazy until realization set in that I had his phone. "I know you done lost your fucking mind. Give me my shit, El!" he yelled.

Feeling fed up with this same ole rodeo, I had had enough. I yelled back, "Naw, nigga fuck you and this damn phone! Who the fuck is April? And why this hoe feel like she can blow your damn phone up, talking about getting some more daddy dick? If that wasn't enough, then the hoe called, asking to come over, as if your woman and child don't live here!"

"Man, gone head with that dumb shit. A nigga don't even know no bitch named April. Now give me my shit," he said, reaching for his phone, but I quickly moved my hand out of reach and jumped out of the bed with it.

"Naw, since you don't know a fucking April, let me call this hoe back and see what she got to say," I said, typing his passcode in by heart. I had seen him putting it in a million times while he thought I wasn't looking. I didn't know what had come over me in this moment, but I was emotionally tired at this point and determined to get down to the bottom of this right now. I had put up with too much shit from Charles, and I refused to be a fool any longer.

Each time I found out about a different hoe, he would deny it to the end, fuck me silly, and that would be the end of the conversation until their asses would decide to make their presence known, which would end with me giving them the ass whooping they were clearly looking for. I hadn't had any issues in about five months, so I thought he had finally changed. Clearly, I was wrong; his ass just learned to cheat better.

"It's too early in the morning to be fucking doing this," he insisted.

"Nigga, who the fuck you telling? Shit, I'm the one been up all night waiting on your black ass to get home. Hell, considering you just got to this muthafucka at 2:00 a.m., you would know how early it is," I said as I got to the home screen, and his eyes bucked out at the fact I knew how to access his phone.

"Nigga stopped beating your ass, and you done started getting beside your fucking self. Apparently, you forgot who the fuck I was!" he screamed, advancing toward me. Before I could even dial the number, my arm was bent so far back that I didn't have any choice but to let the phone go.

"Arggg!" I yelled out in pain. The next few seconds of what happened became a blur as I slapped him across his face. That first lick he threw paused me, the next put me in a daze as I instinctively balled up, trying to protect my stomach.

"Stop it, Charles!" I yelled as I felt him kicking me over and over and striking me repeatedly.

"Naw, you're big and bad, bitch, so show me. I told your stupid ass to give me my shit, but you just had to fucking try a nigga. You wanted me to put my damn hands on you!" he yelled between every lick he threw, acting like a black mother when she was talking to her child as she whooped them. "All your fat ass do is sit around this bitch, eat, fucking complain, and constantly put a nigga down!" he yelled, seeming to get madder by the minute. I had no fucking idea what he was talking about because I always encouraged him daily to get a job and apply for a job. That wasn't putting him down. Finding strength to get up, I ran toward the bathroom and barely made it as I locked the door and collapsed onto the floor in a sobbing mess.

My whole body was on fire as realization set in that I was trapped with no phone and no windows to climb out of. My only option was to hope he left or did what he did best and turned to the bottle and drank himself to sleep. I couldn't believe he had put his hands on me again when he promised he would never hit me anymore.

BOOM! BOOM!

I jumped at the loud noise only to realize Charles was kicking the bathroom door.

"Stupid, ungrateful bitch. Yeah, I fucked that hoe because my own woman act like she can't give a nigga no pussy. We ain't fucked in months, so you damn right I'm running up inside everything I fucking see that got a pussy. It don't matter how the bitch look!" he yelled, crushing my soul as silent tears ran down my face listening to this.

Had I played a part in the failure of my relationship? Drove the love of my life to cheating? I didn't have time to ponder over that question, because before I could blink, the door flew back off its hinges, barely missing me. Looking into the bloodshot red eyes of Charles, I felt like I was looking at the devil himself. The ache in my side was beginning to be unbearable as I backed up until my back was touching the sink.

"Please, Charles. Your baby," I said, trying to reason with him.

"Fuck that kid. Where's all that mouth at that you just had and shit!" he yelled, grabbing me by my hair and forcing me out the bathroom into the bedroom, slinging me forcefully onto the bed. As soon as my body hit the soft California king, I wanted to give up the fight and rest, but thinking of my child made me push through the pain as I struggled to sit back up only to be met with a powerful push to my face.

"Lay the fuck down. Since you got all that fucking mouth, open them legs so I can fuck. Shit, a nigga came home without even getting a chance to get some pussy, and you're laying up here with this super soaker. You're about to give me some of this shit."

"No, Charles. The doctors already said I was high risk and should not engage in sexual activities!" I cried which was only partially true. I didn't want to catch another STD and risk my baby coming out retarded.

"Say another fucking word, and I'll break your fucking jaw," he said at the same time as he delivered a stinging slap to my face. At that point, I was exhausted and could no longer fight him, so I decided to just let him have his way with me. It was easier and safer than getting beat to death. Knowing him, it would be over in about two minutes. Not even bothering to make sure I was wet or not, he rammed his dick inside of me, and the shit was painful as hell. I wasn't aroused nor turned on in any way, so it was not only painful but very uncomfortable.

"Holding back this shit, and it's weak as fuck. Dry ass pussy," he snarled as he spat in his hands and rubbed it onto me for some lubrication as he began jamming his dick in and out of me, not bothering to be the usual gentle lover that he always was with me.

Placing my hands onto his lower stomach, I tried my best to push him back some.

"Move your fucking hands, bitch," he breathed out at me as he picked up the pace, seeming to be enjoying himself despite how I was feeling. Tears swelled into my eyes as he grabbed me neck and squeezed harder than he normally did when he choked me during sex.

"You're hurting me!" I yelled, unable to hold back my cries as I cried for him to stop.

"Shut the fuck up and take this dick, bitch!" he yelled, choking me harder until everything around me faded into black.

Beep, beep, beep!

When I opened my eyes again, I was hooked up to all kinds of machines. Looking around the room, my vision began to clear up, and I realized I was inside a hospital.

Knock! Knock!

Carmen Lashay, T. Nicole, Ty Leese Javeh, Eden Mireya, Sparkle Lewis, Reign, & Armani

Glancing up at the door, two officers walked inside my room, followed by my parents.

"She's awake!" my mom yelled, rushing toward my bed.

My father could barely look at me as he walked over as well.

"Ma'am, we want to ask you some questions about what happened to you. Are you up for answering them?"

Shaking my head no, I closed my eyes. I just wanted to be left alone. I heard my parents talking to the cops and heard my mom mention Charles's name and them saying they would put a warrant out. I blocked everyone and everything out, and I drifted off to sleep.

"What kind of love from a nigga would black your eye?

What kind of love from a nigga every night make you cry?

What kind of love from a nigga make you wish he would die?"

Lying in the dark room on the full-size bed back in the room that I grew up in at my parents' home, I listened to Eve's "Love is Blind" as the tears ran down my bruised face at a rapid pace. Each time I closed my eyes, I saw a fist coming toward my face, landing blows over and over again as if I were a punching bag at a gym. I also saw a hand choking me until I passed out. It was crazy because you would think I would be crying from the fractured bones in my body, my swollen, battered, and bruised face, or better yet, I should've been crying tears of joy that at almost eight months pregnant, my child survived the abuse my body had just been put through. However, sadly, none of these are the reason for my tears. My tears were for the love of my life: Charles. My tears weren't for the pain in my body but the ache in my heart at the thought of the life I would never have with him. It wasn't so much of what he did to me; it was the fact that he did it. My body became numb to the assault as I saw the man I love striking me.

That wasn't how it worked in fairytales and movies. The charming prince was not supposed to abuse the fair princess. He was supposed to love and care for her, and they were to live happily ever after. I knew after this, there was no way my parents would ever let me go back to him, so that happily-ever-after was more like happily-ever-disaster. Hell, there was no coming back after that night anyway—period. He almost killed me and his child, proving he didn't care about us. That revelation only caused the tears to fall harder because he was the only man I'd ever known and the father of my unborn child. I couldn't even imagine a life without him.

I just wished I could rewind time. I never would have been snooping through his phone like that. It was like he transformed into this demon that I'd never seen before. I knew that wasn't him but the alcohol that was threatening to take over him, yet and still the rage and pure hatred in his eyes as he woke up and caught me going through his phone was enough to make me have nightmares for the rest of my life.

Knock! Knock!

"El?" my mom said from the other side of the door.

Quickly wiping my face as best as I could, I had barely sat up good before she was opening the door of my room and turning on the light, walking in with a tray of food and the meds the doctors prescribed me. I sat up in bed, watching as she walked over to the dresser, setting the tray down.

"El, you didn't come to dinner, and you haven't been out of this room all day. You have to eat for the baby at least, and I brought your meds," she said, looking at me with concern and sympathy in her eyes.

"I'm not hungry," I said barely above a whisper as I stared straight ahead, dragging my eyes away from hers. I knew my parents were disappointed when they got the phone call in the middle of the night that their baby girl was laid up in the hospital, beaten barely conscious, only to get there and find out that I was also raped, and the culprit was somebody they loved and practically pushed me to be with. Not only that, but the doctor snitched on me, informing her of the past bruises on my body. They had high hopes for me, and I was disappointing them, and the sad part about it was I was just as disappointed in myself. I never in a million years at just nineteen pictured my life would turn out like this. But I fell for Charles hard, and I couldn't change that or stop loving him no matter how hard I tried. Since the first day I met him, he'd consumed my whole life.

Carmen Lashay, T. Nicole, Ty Leese Javeh, Eden Mireya, Sparkle Lewis, Reign, & Armani

"You can feel sorry for yourself and mope around if you want, Ellen Mildred Renaldos, but I will not allow you to starve my first grandchild and put more stress on the baby than it's already been through. I still can't believe…" she said as her voice trailed off and she put her hands over her mouth. Shaking her head vigorously as if she wouldn't accept the painful truth in front of her, she said, "As much as your father and I instilled in you, I can't believe you allowed this to happen without telling anybody, and the fact we missed this…" she said as her voice again trailed off, and tears began to flow down her face.

"Mom, don't cry," I said, reaching out to her. I didn't realize how much my problems affected everyone. Ever since the night we left the hospital, my dad hadn't said two words to me, and my brother was on his way home. I had been in a domestic violence relationship since my boyfriend, Charles, got laid off from his job almost a year ago, and the drinking started. It was always a slap here, slap there, pushed here, punch there, burned with a cigarette a time or two, etc. but nothing as drastic as last night. I had done a good job of hiding all of this until that fatal attack a few nights back. I was still unsure as to what triggered that amount of rage, but that just wasn't him. It had to be the alcohol.

"How can I not cry with my beautiful baby sitting in front of me looking like a punching bag? I'm going to kill his ass if the police don't find him first," she vowed, her tears drying up as sadness turned to rage. "I'm killing that son of a bitch!" she yelled. Being of mixed race, I had never heard my white mother speak like this, but as her entire face turned bright red, flushed with anger, I knew she was serious.

"That mufucka already got a bullet with his name on it," my daddy said from the doorway. "And I wish the hell you would sit up in my damn house and cry over that bitch-made ass nigga," he said, walking further into the room.

The tears I had held in when my mom came in suddenly betrayed me as my dad walked closer to my bed. I was truly a Daddy's girl, and I loved him so much. It broke my heart to see him this upset.

"I'm sorry, Daddy. I'm so sorry!" I cried as he held me in his arms, rocking me back and forth.

"You have nothing to apologize or be sorry for. I'm sorry for failing as a father, not realizing something wasn't right with my princess. I should have known something was up with Charles's ass. I missed all the signs," he said. "We gone get through this together as a family."

"I hope so," I said, not sounding too sure about it.

CHAPTER 2

ITS NOT EVERYDAY A MIRACLE COMES....

A few weeks later

"Okay, I need a big push on your next contraction," the doctor said to me.

"I can't do it!" I cried, shaking my head back and forth repeatedly.

"Come on, baby! Push," my mom said on one side of me.

"Yeah, push, push," my dad said as he held the camcorder to his face. I was beyond annoyed with his ass and that camera and was two seconds away from kicking him the hell out my room.

"Dang, you gotta squeeze a nigga hand that tightly?" my big brother, Karl, asked in agony. Ignoring him, I tried to remember the breathing exercises I had gone through, but it was hard to think when it felt like the lower half of my body was being ripped in half. As another contraction hit me like a two-hundred-pound football player rushing for a touchdown. I bit down on my tongue and pushed with all my might.

"Ahhhhhh, get this damn thing out of me!" I yelled in frustration and helpless pain. Crying hysterically at the point, I almost missed the tiny cries that filled the room. Looking down, I saw the doctor smiling hard as he turned to this left to hand the nurse something.

"Congratulations, Mommy. It's a girl," the doctor beamed. Calming my cries, I watched as the nurse walked off with a screaming baby in her arms.

"I want my baby," I said, lifting my head, watching them until I couldn't see anything anymore.

Carmen Lashay, T. Nicole, Ty Leese Javeh, Eden Mireya, Sparkle Lewis, Reign, & Armani

"What's going on, Mommy?" I asked as I lay with my legs still propped open on the table as my heart rate sped up, and I began to panic.

"Calm down, El. They went to clean her up. They're bringing her back," she said.

"That shit was beyond sick. Remind me to stock up on condoms when I leave from up here. I need them hoes like they're going out of style. Shit," Karl said.

"Watch your mouth" my mom said.

"Shit, hell yeah, yo' ass do. Hit every damn store until you get all them bitches," my dad chimed in. It was one thing when one of them was around, but it was tough dealing with two of their crazy asses. Together, they drove my mother up the wall.

"Don't get him started, baby," my mother fussed at my dad.

"So you want another grandbaby?" he asked her?

"Well, no. I'm too young for somebody to be calling me Grandma, no offense, El," she said.

"I'm glad y'all chose to have this conversation at this moment, but I just want to see my child," I said, beyond pissed at this point that they wanted to have a 'team no grandchildren' discussion when their first grandchild and niece was born.

"We didn't mean we don't want our baby princess," my daddy said.

"Yeah, Bug, I'm glad my niece is here," Karl said, calling me by the nickname he'd called me my entire life. Before I could answer him, the nurse came back inside the room with my baby, and my heart swelled with happiness and love. I never thought I would love someone as much as I loved Charles, but looking at his daughter, our daughter, I knew in that moment I loved my daughter more than life itself.

"Have we thought of a name for her?" the nurse asked me, placing her inside my arms wrapped in a pink blanket.

Thinking long and hard, I replied, "Miracle."

Carmen Lashay, T. Nicole, Ty Leese Javeh, Eden Mireya,
Sparkle Lewis, Reign, & Armani

CHAPTER 3

ITS TIME TO START LIVING FOR ME

"I'm angry, but I still love him,.

Pills and potions, we're overdosing."

"Bitch, if you don't put that phone down, turn that weak ass music off, and let's turn up," Kandice, my best friend, said to me.

Ignoring her, I sang my heart out along with Nicki Minaj.

"Ayo, they could never make me hate you

Even though what you was doin' wasn't tasteful

"Hell to the muthafucking naw, bitch. Not to-fucking-day you won't do that shit. It's my damn birthday, and your mom got the baby, so it's time to party, and you're playing this depressing ass shit, singing offkey, still stressing over that ain't-shit nigga," my best friend, Kandice, said as we headed to the cookout her parents had every year for her.

"I can't help it. Bitch, until you've ever been in love, you can't feel my pain," I said sadly as I looked at Facebook for the last time before I clicked off of it. Charles had posted pics of him and some chick on Facebook smiling and looking happy.

My parents had urged me to press charges on him, and while they thought I did, I simply got a restraining order. I was adamant that a stranger broke into our home and attacked me that night but couldn't lie my way out of the other hospital visits. The police seemed to know I was lying, but they remained quiet and allowed my lie to play out as they drew up the restraining order.

I never told my parents this, but Charles contacted me on Facebook shortly after I had Miracle, and we had been communicating ever since. He had apologized a thousand times and even promised that he'd stopped drinking and was getting himself together for the baby and me. Silly me for believing his lying ass and having a slither of hope that he would somehow come in like my knight in shining armor and fight to win me back. Shit, the trick was on me because here he was on Facebook, cheesing hard as hell, looking like he had the time of his life last night.

Meanwhile, I was at home with his hollering ass child, struggling to get her spoiled ass to sleep. My momma and my dad were always holding her ass all day every day then quick to give her chunky butt back to me, and she didn't want to sleep if I wasn't holding or rocking her like they did.

"Hell, if pain involves getting my ass beat all day every day, then I damn sure will skip on love and just take the dick," she said. She was the only one who I had confided in about the abuse I was going through. She also had a front row seat to all the pain and hurt I felt because of Charles blaming me for his misfortune of getting fired and not being able to get another job. I'd cried many of nights on the phone for hours, and she was always a listening ear. I didn't expect her to throw it in my face like that, though.

"Shit, you must not be getting the right dick then because if you were, you would definitely be in love because it makes you do and put up with a lot of shit. And I wasn't getting my ass beat like Tina Turner or some shit. I got slapped around a few times and pushed into shit; it's a difference," I said defensively.

"Naw, I'm getting dicked down properly, and like those 'for the dick challenges' on Facebook go, I'll do a lot of shit for the dick, none which involve getting slapped around, or in my case, in an all-out brawl, because I'd damn sure square up with a nigga quick. Seriously, El, I love you, and I don't want anything to happen to you. You have picked the pieces to your life up and started to move on. Don't go backward. You can't. You see what he did last time. He's progressed from slapping you to damn near killing you. That's not love. I'm glad you got out before that option was taken away from you," she said, looking at me with a concerned expression on her face.

Dismissing her, I said, "I hear you, best friend, and I'm not paying Charles or his busted ass rebound bitch any attention. I've been working out and done snapped this body back into shape, skin done cleared up, edges grew back, ass still fat. I just don't have time for a fuck nigga, but momma is looking for a new man," I said confidently even though I didn't feel it. I felt sad, heartbroken, and worthless. Seeing those pictures officially broke the last strand I had holding myself together. How could he be happy with someone else but hadn't smiled for me in forever? How could be get sober for another bitch but was drunk damn near my entire pregnancy? I was crushed, but I wouldn't dare show it. I was tired of people feeling pity and sympathy for me.

"Ayyy, that's what I'm talking about bitch. While you're at it, get you some new dick too 'cause, bitch, you had a bad batch last go around. Shit had you tweeking and shit," she said, laughing.

"Bitch, you have serious issues. I just had a damn baby two months ago. Dick's the furthest thing from my mind," I said as we pulled up to the crowded house. You could hear the music blasting without even getting out of the car.

"That's what the fuck I'm talking about!" she screamed as if this was all unfamiliar to her. This was the same rodeo year-round. The infamous birthday cookout had only gotten crazier the older Kandice got. She wasn't legally old enough to drink, but her parents let her get white-girl wasted for her eighteenth birthday, and last year, I would have sworn I was at a Bob Marley concert how smoked out the backyard was. I was almost nervous to see this year's event.

Walking through the gate into the backyard, everybody yelled, "Happy Birthday!"

"Let's turn the fuck up the Kandice way!" she yelled as she grabbed my hand and pulled me further into the backyard. I was resistant at first but said fuck it and decided to live a little.

A couple hours later and five cups of whatever kind of punch that was Mrs. Milton made, I was in the middle of the yard, dancing off beat to some song. I was barely focusing on the lyrics; I just heard the beat. Feeling arms sliding around my waist, I lay my head back on instinct into their chest, closing my eyes as I continued my horrible two step. It had been so long since I had been held that I basked in the moment and, for a second, allowed myself to believe that everything in the world was okay. The last few months was a bad dream, and I was back in my love's arms.

"You smell good, Ellen," the deep, masculine voice said, slicing through my fantasy like a knife destroying the dream I was having. Even though it was temporary, I felt so at peace for a split second like everything was going to be okay. I wasn't stressing myself out over the troubles of tomorrow, over being alone, jobless, broke, living in my parents' home, and most of all, a single parent. Upset at the intruder for stealing the feeling away, I pushed from his arms and turned around, preparing to curse him out only to lock eyes with Timothy Knight, my best guy friend as a child.

"Little Timmy?" I squealed, jumping into his arms. I hadn't seen him since I was fourteen when he moved away. We kept in touch all the way up 'til I was sixteen when he went off to the army. The last time I saw him, he was a scrawny nerd who used to follow me and Kandice around. Now, he had transformed into a grown ass man. Gone were the glasses and skinny frame. Instead, he had beefed up a lot and I guess was wearing contacts.

"Don't be sneaking up on me like that, fool. You almost caught these hands," I said, playfully hitting him with a two-piece combo.

"Girl, I'm hardly worried," he said, brushing me off like he didn't take me serious at all.

"What are you doing here?" I asked him.

"I'm home on leave, and I ran into Kandice's mom at the store, and she told me about the cookout. I couldn't pass up a chance to get the old gang back together," he said, flashing a panty-dropping smile. *Bitch, this is Timmy's Urkel ass. Calm your fast ass down*, I pep talked to myself as I felt myself becoming turned on with everything about him.

"You heard me?" he asked me.

"Huh? Shit, my bad. I've been drinking," I said, laughing.

"Yeah, I noticed your lightweight ass had a few. I been peeping you all night. Let me go fix you a plate so you can put some food on your stomach. I asked, how's your daughter? I saw the Facebook pics. She's adorable," he said, walking off.

"Bitch, I see you ran into Timmy. I tried signaling your ass, but you was zoned out," Kandice said, practically stumbling toward me.

"Yeah, bitch is it just me, or is that nigga fine as hell now?"

"Naw, it's not just you. The glow up was mad real for his ass, and he looks way better than grandpa woman-beater Charles. You better go work the fuck out of him,"

she slurred. "I'm 'bout to go find my man, bitch. Bye,"
she said just as Timmy was walking back up.

Laughing at her ass, I thanked him for the plate
and stumbled to the nearest table, preparing to bust this
plate work properly.

"So how's life been?" he asked me. My pride
wanted me to lie, put on a front like my life was grand,
and I couldn't be happier, but the damn shots of Patron I
consumed mixed with those five cups had me like a
person off *First 48* when they threatened to give them life
in jail. I was telling everything down to the rape that I had
endured. When I was done, he was squeezing the table so
hard that I was certain he was gon' break it. His eyes had
changed from hazel to a charcoal black. Reaching out and
touching his hand cautiously, he looked at me for a split
second before the anger faded, and he was back to the
person he was a few seconds ago. He had calmed down
that fast.

"That's a fuck nigga, and I promise on my life, I
bet not ever run into that boy, because I got something for

his ass," he said calmly, but I could tell he was still very much upset.

"I'm not thinking about him. I'm focused on moving on," I said, which was the partial truth. He looked at me long and hard as if he were looking through my soul.

"You deserve so much more than what you are allowing yourself to settle for. One day, you'll see that the road you want to travel down isn't the road you should be taking. You are beautiful, smart, and you have someone now who is looking up to you and watching everything you do. You honestly want her to think abuse is okay?"

Having just been read for filth, I didn't know what to immediately say to that.

"I-I, I'm seriously done with him," I said.

"I'm good at reading body language, one of the many skills the army taught me. So I know that just because your mouth is telling me something doesn't make it accurate. I hope for your sake I'm wrong, though, because I don't see this ending well," he said to me.

For the rest of the night, we just kicked it and caught up on old times. I truly enjoyed myself and his company as well. I must say it was the first time in a long

Carmen Lashay, T. Nicole, Ty Leese Javeh, Eden Mireya, Sparkle Lewis, Reign, & Armani

time that I found myself laughing and enjoying myself. Best of all, I was like, "Charles who?"

CHAPTER 4

A HARD HEAD MAKES A SOFT BEHIND…

"Bae, move," I said, laughing as Tim tickled me. Ever since the cookout, we had been spending practically every day together and had grown extremely close. He was funny to be around, cool as hell, a total gentleman, and best of all, he always wanted to include my daughter in stuff. When he asked me out, he would never ask if I wanted to go somewhere. He would always say stuff like, "Do you lovely ladies want to go to the movies with me?" or "Can I take you two ladies out to eat tonight?" It always involved me and Miracle, never me alone.

I told him my parents didn't mind watching my baby for me and were happy I was getting back out there and over Charles, but he insisted we were a packaged deal. and he wanted to win both of us over, not just me. Miracle's spoiled behind took to him instantly and would cry up a storm with me but would immediately stop crying if Timothy picked her up.

Moving my body under his, trying to get away from him tickling me, I felt something hard poking into me. We both froze, and laughter ceased as we gazed at one another. Breaking the silence, he reached his hand down between our bodies and readjusted himself.

"My bad. I apologize. I didn't mean to disrespect you. This damn perfume you're wearing and the way you're wiggling is fucking me up. He got a mind of his own. I already had a pep talk with him and told his ass to behave. Now he's in time out," he said, and I burst out laughing.

"Time out you say?"

"Yep, time out."

"So that means little Timmy can't come out and play?" I boldly asked. I didn't know what came over me, but I couldn't seem to stop whatever it was.

"Little Timmy, huh?" he smirked.

"Yeah, little Timmy," I challenged.

"Shit, ain't nothing little about Timmy, though. Don't make him come out of time out and show you something. It's only so long I can hold his ass at bay. He tends to not listen to me when he gets in his feelings."

Reaching my hand down between us, I moved my fingers around until I found what I was searching for.

Grabbing ahold of his dick, which was so thick that I could barely grip it in one hand, I pulled it out of the basketball shorts he was wearing. Looking up at him, he had closed his eyes as if he were fighting for control. Loving the way I was making him feel and how turned on I was, I began to stroke him up and down. The facial expressions he was making were giving me the confidence to go faster and apply more pressure.

"Shhhhh. You better stop that shit, El," he said to me as he opened his eyes and stared down at me. I could see the passion dripping from them as he struggled to resist what I was doing to him. Leaning up to kiss him, that was apparently the last straw for him as he growled at me and attacked my mouth at the same time that he slapped my hands away. Moving from my mouth, down to my neck, he was trailing passionate kisses all over me. At that point, I was leaking like a busted fire hydrant and wanted him in the worst way. I was so horny that I found myself taking control, something I never did, but it was something about him that made me feel sexy, beautiful, and most of all, safe and stress free Pulling his basketball shorts and boxers down a bit, I reached under myself and pulled my panties down, lifting up slightly so that I could get them over my ass and pull one leg out.

Carmen Lashay, T. Nicole, Ty Leese Javeh, Eden Mireya, Sparkle Lewis, Reign, & Armani

"You need to stop and think about this, El," he said as he allowed me to basically rape him. He didn't bother to stop me as I pulled his shirt off, revealing the sexiest, lickable abs I had ever seen. He didn't stop me when I leaned up and trailed a kiss from the top of his chest to damn near his stomach. He just shuddered and allowed me to do my own thing.

"You need to be absolutely certain this what you want because I'm telling you now," he said to me in a shaky voice as I ignored him and went back to stroking the beast he called a dick. When I grabbed one of his nipples into my mouth and sucked it, that must've been the straw that broke the camel's back because a ripple went through his body, followed by a growl and him taking his hands, planting them on each side of my thighs and yanking my whole body toward him so that I was straddling him from below and, in one swift motion, plunged deep inside of my dripping love tunnel.

"Fuck," we both said at the same time as he began fucking the shit out of me. I didn't know what exactly I was expecting, but it wasn't this as he began to give my body a serious workout. I didn't know half of the sexual positions he put me in even existed, but I had clearly bitten off more than I could chew.

"How long will it be before you come back?" I asked Timothy as I sadly watched him pack his things up.

"I have more vacation days saved up, so I can definitely come back soon. I hate to even leave you and baby girl alone, but it's nothing I can really do. I would suggest you guys move to the base, but I know that's moving too fast for you. For me, I've loved you since we were kids," he said, shocking me because I had no clue he even felt that way about me.

"It's a lot to take in. I would have to think about that. Let's just take it one day at a time," I said to him.

"My mom's having a going away dinner for me tomorrow before I leave, and I definitely want my two favorite girls to be there," he said to me as my phone started buzzing.

"We wouldn't miss it for the world. But listen, I'll see you later on. I have to pick Miracle up from my parents' because they going on a date," I told him, giving him a kiss and getting up to quickly leave. I didn't really have to pick up Miracle. Also, I was going to get her from my parents. It was just that Charles was blowing my phone up, and I didn't want to answer in front of Tim. I didn't want to ruin things by letting him know Charles and I were talking, and I was planning on taking Miracle to meet her daddy for the first time.

"Hello," I said with a little attitude as I finally answered my phone.

"Did I catch you at a bad time? I apologize if I did," he said to me. I had to pull the phone back to make sure that I was talking to the right person.

"Uhh, no, you didn't. I was in the store and didn't hear my phone ringing."

"Oh, okay. Well, I'm only calling to see if it was still okay for me to see Miracle today or not. If you are busy, then I understand, and I'll have to catch you guys at a later day," he said, sounding sad as if he had been really looking forward to this. It pulled at my heart strings how much he really had changed and wanted to see his child, so I agreed to meet up with him later on tonight at an address he would text to me.

"Where you guys going tonight? Back to Tim's place?" my mom asked as I packed myself and Miracle an overnight bag just in case it got late, and things were going well enough to spend a night.

"Yes," I quickly answered.

"That's good. I so love him for you, and he is so great with Miracle. I wish he was her biological father."

"Miracle has a father, Mom, whether you like it or not," I said with attitude.

"Just because she came from his sperm doesn't make that deadbeat a fucking father."

"How can he be a good dad if he isn't even allowed to be one? You can't call him a deadbeat, because you don't know if he is trying to do for his child or not," I said, coming to Charles's defense.

"He's a damn dead beat because he beat you when you were pregnant and almost made you lose the very child he supposedly loved. If that doesn't take the number one spot for deadbeats, then I don't know what does," she said with a frown on her face. "I know you're not in contact with him, are you?" she asked with her hands now on her hips.

"Of course not, Mom. Why would I talk to that bum? I was just saying. That's all," I said, hoping I sounded convincing.

"Okay, baby, have fun," she said, kissing me on my forehead and handing me my baby. "Bye, Granny's baby. I'll see you later," she said to Miracle. My baby was so lucky to be loved by so many people.

Ding!

Looking down, I saw an address come through from Charles.

"Okay, baby girl, time to go. Momma has a surprise for you," I said as I grabbed our bags and headed outside as my heart rate sped up. I was nervous about her meeting her father, how he would react, and most of all, us seeing one another again. I had not physically seen him in months, not since that fatal night.

The ringing of my phone jarred me out of my thoughts as I noticed Tim calling me. Ignoring the phone and allowing it to ring, I followed my GPS to the location Charles sent me, telling myself I was doing this for my child to see her father, and that was it. I mean, people could change, and I knew that it was the alcohol that night and not Charles. An hour and a half later, I pulled up to a beautiful brownstone home.

Before I could turn the car off good, Charles was coming out the front door and over to the car. Opening the back door first, he immediately grabbed Miracle up into his arms out of her car seat. I held my breath to gauge her reaction because she didn't take well to new people. She cried for a few seconds then stopped. She was taking to him, and I was glad.

Taking my keys out of my ignition and getting out the car, I watched the interaction between father and daughter as my heart melted. Walking closer to them, I glanced down at my baby clothed in her cute pink tutu dress her papa bought her.

"Momma's baby, meet your daddy," I said to her in my baby voice. Looking at Charles, he was tearing up just holding her, which was further melting the anger I felt for him away.

"Let's get you girls into the house," he said. Following behind him into the house, my mouth dropped in awe of what I was seeing. He had vases of red roses all over the entrance of the hallway leading into the living room.

"All this for me?"

"Of course, beautiful," he said as I smiled widely.

Carmen Lashay, T. Nicole, Ty Leese Javeh, Eden Mireya, Sparkle Lewis, Reign, & Armani

I know I shouldn't fall for him, and this visit was only for Miracle to see her father, but I was falling victim the more the night progressed, so much so that when he suggested we stay the night, I said yes fast as hell.

"El," Charles said to me, coming into the living room where I was.

"What's up?" I asked him.

"I ran you a hot bubble bath. Was wondering if you would like a glass of wine with it?" he asked me.

Who was this man that was becoming everything I dreamed him to be right before my eyes!

"Yes, please," I said, getting up to grab my pajamas. After I had them, I walked out the guest room that I was sleeping in and into the hallway bathroom. Entering, there were candles lit everywhere as well as soft music playing. Stripping, I stepped into the tub and sank into heaven as I slipped lower and lower into the tub. Soft music began to play as I closed my eyes, enjoying the feeling of the hot water against my skin. A few minutes later, I heard the door open, and my eyes popped open.

The tub was full of bubbles, so even when I sat up a bit, my body parts were still covered.

"I just came in to see if you wanted me to wash your back. That's all. I wasn't trying to disturb you," Charles said.

"Sure," I replied as I turned around, giving him room to wash my back as the fairytale I once had about us came rushing back tenfold.

"I'm better now, El. I've stopped drinking, and I have a job," he said. "I just want another chance to do right by my girls to prove to you guys. Will you let me have one more chance?" he pleaded as he washed my back and massaged it at the same time.

I was torn between the feelings I had developed for Tim and the way my heart ached for Charles. In the end, I couldn't deny my heart as I gave in and shook my head yes. No more words were exchanged as he lifted me from the tub and carried me to the room, laying me on the bed. After drying me off properly, he dove head first into my pussy, literally eating me into a coma before tucking me into bed. I went to sleep with my mind so at peace and a huge smile on my face, knowing I had made the right decision.

Whap! Whap!

Carmen Lashay, T. Nicole, Ty Leese Javeh, Eden Mireya, Sparkle Lewis, Reign, & Armani

I thought I was dreaming as I felt the burning sensation on my cheek. Opening my eyes, I saw a very angry Charles staring down at me with anger and rage as he held my phone in his hands.

"Who the fuck is this nigga Tim that's been blowing your phone up all night and asking about my muthafuckin' seed!" he yelled, and it felt like déjà vu all over again from when I woke him up after going through his phone.

"I-I," I said, finding myself stuttering. I was at a loss for words and didn't know what to say, but I knew my next words needed to be carefully thought out.

"Cat got your fucking tongue? Speak the fuck up, bitch. Got a nigga doing all this shit to get your stupid ass back, and you're out here popping pussy for the next nigga. You think I'm a joke, don't you?" he yelled at me.

"No, no, I don't," I said, shaking my head and saying a silent prayer that I made it out of here in one piece. The realization that nobody knew where I was hit me hard as hell as I tried staying calm.

Looking down at my phone, he seemed to get madder the more messages he read. Throwing my phone on the bed, he grabbed his belt buckle and begin taking it off. Thinking I was about to get raped again, I jumped up from the bed. I wasn't going through that shit again. Before I could get a word out, I was struck across my chest with his belt.

"What the fuck!" I screamed. "You haven't changed at all, and I'm taking my damn child and never coming back here," I yelled as the sting from the belt against my naked flesh began to burn. Smirking, he bent down and grabbed a bucket of water, throwing it on me swiftly as he then began hitting me over and over again with the belt.

"If you think you taking my fucking child anywhere, you got another thing coming, especially around another nigga. I'll kill both y'all first!" he yelled as he hit me harder and harder. Hearing him say he would kill both of us had me going into super mommy mode as I forced myself up, kneeing him in the balls and quickly running out the room and down the hall to the room Miracle was in. Grabbing her into my arms, I ran wildly until I made it to the front door. I had opened it and had one foot out the door when I was yanked back inside by my hair. Falling to the ground, I shielded my child as best as I could so she wouldn't be harmed during the fall. Hearing her screaming loudly broke my heart as I held her tightly.

"Don't do this, Charles. Just let us go. This is your child. She's an innocent baby," I said, pleading with him.

"I don't give a fuck about that baby or you, stupid bitch," he said, kicking me in my side. Doing my best to push Miracle safely away from me under a wooden table where she would be safe, I prepared myself for the fight of my life as I rose to my feet, refusing to just lie there and take what he was dishing out. Swinging on him widely, I screamed in fear and anger as I found myself back in the same situation I vowed to never be in again.

"Hell yeah, roll with the big dawgs. I like this shit, bitch," he spat as he delivered a powerful blow to me as if I were a nigga. The lick was so powerful I almost gave up the fight, but hearing the cries from my daughter seemed to rejuvenate me, but it also distracted me, allowing him the chance to hit me across my head with a trophy, knocking me to the ground. Lying sprawled out on the living room floor, I heard him laughing above me. Thinking this was it, I struggled to remain conscious as I tried to open my eyes to see what was happening when I felt water dripping onto my face. It only took me a few seconds to realize that it wasn't water, and that this bastard was peeing on me. I felt lower and lower and just wanted to die, but I somehow managed to get up when he turned around and ran into the kitchen, grabbing a knife.

"What the fuck you gon' do with that other than make me fucking mad?" he asked as I held the knife in front of me as blood dripped down my forehead into my eyes. I was losing a lot of blood at a rapid pace, but I was determined to get my baby to safety as I heard her cries grow louder and louder. *Why the heck haven't the neighbors called the cops after they heard me screaming?*

"I just want to take me and my baby and go," I said as my hands shook as I thrust the knife out further in front of me.

"The only way your ass is leaving me again is in a body bag!" he barked, advancing toward me. "I knew you would be back; that's why I waited a while to contact you then began feeding you bullshit, telling you exactly what you wanted to hear. I knew you would eventually fall for the shit and come back, and when you did, I had plans on making sure you never left again. You're my bitch, and I own you. It's 'til death do us part, hoe, so if you want to fucking leave, I'll gladly send you to meet Jesus!" he yelled, stopping directly in front on me. "You and that bastard ass baby," was the last thing I let him get out before I plunged the knife deep into his stomach over and over again. I felt myself loosing strength and consciousness as I continued to stab him as we both fell backward at the same time. If I were going to die, I was making sure I took him with me. There was no way I would leave him around my child.

"Whannnnnnnn!" I heard.

"Mommy's coming, baby," I said, struggling to roll onto my stomach and forcing myself to crawl into the living room. I could barely keep my eyes open as I slid on my own blood, using it as a slope to propel me forward until I reached the living room. When I got to the carpet, I lost the fight trying to get across the wool. Reaching out my hand, I wanted nothing more to do than grab her and hold her to me.

"I'm sorry, baby. I'm so sorry." I grabbed her as I rolled over onto my back.

"You deserve so much more than what you are allowing yourself to settle for. One day, you'll see that the road you want to travel down isn't the road you should be taking. You are beautiful, smart, and you have someone now who is looking up to you and watching everything you do. You honestly want her to think abuse is okay?"

As Timothy's word rang out in my head, I closed my eyes, thinking about how my stupid mistakes affected my child, and she would now be motherless. I should have listened to everyone and took heed to their warnings, but love clouded my judgement and allowed me to believe that it wasn't Charles; it was the alcohol, and he would never hurt me intentionally. Making excuses for any type of abuse was the ultimate mistake, and it had inevitably cost me my life. My last thought was that I hoped somebody found my daughter as I closed my eyes and allowed the darkness to take over me.

Carmen Lashay, T. Nicole, Ty Leese Javeh, Eden Mireya,
Sparkle Lewis, Reign, & Armani

EPILOGUE

I didn't die that night even though I thought I was
dead. When Charles had my phone, reading my messages
between Tim and me, he had somehow accidentally
called him, allowing Tim to hear everything that was
going on and realize that I was in trouble. After pulling
up *Where's My iPhone*, he was able to locate my phone
with the help of police and tracked me almost two hours
away at what turned out to be Charles's girlfriend's
house, who happened to be away for the weekend.

I flatlined twice on the way to the hospital from
the blow to the head and the vigorous beating I received. I
should have died on that living room floor, but it was
nothing but God that kept me alive. I learned my lesson
the hard way that it didn't matter if a man was abusing
alcohol or drugs; if abuse of any kind was involved, get
out and stay out. Also, just because you had kids or time
invested into the relationship meant absolutely nothing.
Be an example for your children and know when enough

was enough. Last, don't pass up a good man for a devil in disguise.

Timothy was a good man, and he was great with my child, and I almost let the fact that I had time invested with Charles and a kid cost me not only the best thing besides my child that ever happened to me but my life as well. Even if there weren't another man in the picture, just know when it was time to throw the towel in. Don't be like me and stay, thinking you could change a man, because the only thing you'll accomplish is a hospital bed or a casket.

Never lose yourself chasing a man; always remember that no matter what, you are beautiful. No matter what a man says or how low he tries to bring you, you are smart no matter how much he tries to belittle you. And you are so very strong no matter how much he tries to break you down. My name is Ellen, and I am a domestic violence survivor, and I hope that you are too.

THE END

Carmen Lashay, T. Nicole, Ty Leese Javeh, Eden Mireya,
Sparkle Lewis, Reign, & Armani

Love No

More

Reign

Copyright © 2017

Reign

Naomi

"Baby, that's my spot. Don't stop. Please go deeper." I hungrily moaned as Kango plunged his nine-inch dick in and out of my dripping, young, juicy center. My moans bounced off my girl Holly's spare bedroom walls as I spread my legs as wide as they would go, giving Kango all the access he needed to get me off.

"Shit, Naomi! This pussy tight as fuck and gripping the shit outta me, ma. You ready to take this shit to the next level? You know what I want right now. Come on, baby. Let's try it again. Mmm, let me pull out and put it in your mouth so you can make me feel good and finish this shit off," Kango whispered in my ear, and I didn't want to upset him by saying no again.

Kango loved getting his dick sucked, but I just wasn't the bitch to do it. I hated that shit and had only done it twice since we'd been having sex. I didn't think I was any good at it, and I didn't like it, so I avoided doing it and the conversation of head altogether.

Kango broke my virginity about three months ago, and he couldn't stop fucking with me even though his ass would end up in jail if someone found out we were fucking. I couldn't lie. Since he took my virginity, I'd been addicted to having sex with him but just wasn't a fan of oral sex.

"Uhhh uhhh, you know I don't like doing that, baby. Just don't stop. Let's just focus on making each other feel good in this moment. Is it good to you, baby?" I moaned, and I could tell that Kango was about to get angry.

His whole demeanor changed, and he started stroking me faster and harder, not caring that my moans of pleasure had quickly turned into cries of pain. As tears started to run from my eyes, I tried to close my legs and ease him out of me or at least give him a hint to slow down, and that was clearly the wrong move.

"Take this dick! This what you wanted, huh? It's all about you and you getting yo' fuckin' nut, right? Dumb, young bitch! Take this shit then!"

I hated when Kango was mad at me, especially over sex. I knew that this meant when I got out of school tomorrow, I would have to see him posted up at his car with other bitches randomly in his face. He would ignore the fuck out of me until I at least tried to suck his dick and then get mad and slap me when I didn't do it the way he liked. I was tired of going home with bruises and telling my parents that I was getting into fights with dumb girls at school.

As Kango exploded into the condom, he abruptly got up and started putting his clothes back on.

"Naomi, this shit is whack. Damn, that's what the fuck I get for fuckin' with yo' young ass. When you grow the fuck up, you know the number. Hopefully, it's not too late, and just maybe I haven't moved on to the next bitch who won't mind topping me off. Bitches swear they want this shit then act all shy and shit when it comes to sucking this dick. I eat yo' pussy, don't I?" he barked, not giving a fuck about my feelings as he disrespected me.

I was tired of him always threatening to be with the next bitch because of something I didn't want to do or didn't like. It was the same shit when we first started having sex. He told me that if I didn't give it up, that meant I wasn't ready to be with a nigga like him. Yeah, I wanted him—I wouldn't lie—but I wasn't ready to give up my jewel at the time. After all was said and done, I gave *it* up, and I didn't want to stop.

Kango always said that I had the best pussy he'd ever had. Why wasn't that enough? I didn't like his dick in my mouth. The few times I'd done it, I was constantly thinking about how many bitches he'd stuck his dick in before me, and let's be honest. He was more than likely still fucking other bitches while he was with me.

"Kango, I never asked you to eat me out. That's something you always did on yo' own. You're always talking about going to the next bitch and tired of my young ass, but you're always asking me if I can get away so that you can come fuck my young ass. If you want to go, fine. Go. I'll find someone else to fuck my young ass—somebody who doesn't pressure me to suck his dick. Maybe the next guy, I'll suck his dick just because he didn't make me do it and actually enjoy sucking it."

I was fuming. I hopped out of the bed and began looking for my clothes. I knew I was lying about finding someone else to fuck me, but I wanted Kango to feel just as bad as he was making me feel. I made up my mind that I would no longer cry over his ass anymore. I could always threaten him with the police, and he would leave me alone. I was only seventeen, and I had a few months before my eighteenth birthday. He was twenty-nine and in the streets, so I was sure he didn't want the police sniffing around him.

I bent down to find my shoes and was instantly pulled up by my neck.

"Who in the fuck do you think you're talking to like that? Bitch, I will fuckin' kill yo' ass. Play with me if you want to, and I guarantee yo' family will be bringing out the flowers and wearin' all black for yo' duck ass."

BOOM!

He slammed me into the wall, and I could have sworn I saw stars. I slid down the wall, instantly holding on to my head. I prayed he didn't start one of his attacks, but it seemed like my prayers were going to go unanswered again today.

"You wanna talk shit!" He began reigning blow after blow on my body and getting in a few face shots at the same time. Despite my cries for help, I could hear and feel at least two of my ribs crack from the force of his fists. I curled up in the fetal position, keeping my head tucked, trying to ignore the pain of my newly fractured ribs while I protected my core. I just knew that this was going to be the time that he landed a fatal blow that would kill me.

Time seemed to move in slow motion, and I was in so much pain that I was practically frozen. It was physically impossible for me to fight back at this point. I stayed down until he was out of breath and had finally finished beating my ass.

"Don't ever disrespect me again, and this is the last time I'm gon' tell yo' stupid ass."

Kango stormed out the room and slammed the door, and I cried in the corner, curled up in a ball. I groaned between sobs as I felt myself floating in and out of consciousness. Just as I was about to let the feeling take over me, my girl Holly rushed into the room.

***

"Naomi! What the fuck is going on? Fuck that nigga! You'd be a fool to continue to allow him to use you for a quick nut and a punching bag. This shit hurts for me to sit back, knowing this shit is going on and not being able to do anything about it. On the strength of our friendship, I'm trying to do what you asked and keep out of your relationship, but this shit is fuckin' deadly. I refuse to stand back and watch this mothafucka kill you, especially when the shit is taking place in my house."

Holly was in one of her preaching moods. Apparently, a neighbor had called her instead of calling the police to make sure she was alright. She came up with one of her many excuses and rushed home, knowing that Kango had delivered yet another beating. Every time Kango and I had a fight, she would come in, help me get myself together, and tell me how much I didn't need this shit. She constantly said that she wished I would allow her to help me out of this situation. I mean, come on now. No relationship was perfect. Everyone had good and bad days. Our bad days were just on the extreme end of the spectrum.

Holly was not a fool. She knew Kango would kick both of our asses if I allowed her to say something to him, so I chose to take the beatings and leave her out of it. I was just glad that we had a spot where we could meet, and it was sort of lowkey, so not many saw what I was going through.

Holly's parents were always working, and they pretty much trusted her with everything. Being a straight A student and having parents who were surgeons had its advantages. My parents weren't surgeons, but they were both supervisors at different buildings in a manufacturing company. They were a bit more on the strict side, which was why I did my dirt at Holly's house. She was the sister I'd never had and always wanted.

"Holly, sis, I love you for caring, but you and I both know that Kango won't kill me. He's a bit upset because I won't do ... you know," I spoke, sharing my sex details with my girl.

"Bitch, please. Donte don't trip on me about that shit, and if the nigga wanted his dick sucked so bad, why not have one of them bird bitches that's always in his face do it? Look, girl, you don't have to do shit you don't want to. You need to use that brain of yours and figure out a way to get out this shit. This shit ain't cool, and I won't promise you I'm going to keep my silence too much longer," Holly spoke, and I knew she was at her breaking point and wanted to tell someone. I had to make sure she didn't, because this could end badly for the both of us. I needed her to keep this part of my life a secret.

Attempting to change the subject, I quickly tried to act as if I had my shit together as I wiped my tears and smiled at Holly.

"Girl, fuck that shit. Let's talk about homecoming! So umm, you know it's senior year. We are both on the committee and both running. I would hate to have to do this to you, but I'm winning that crown," I said in a joking manner, but I knew that it was very possible for me to win.

I was popular. I always had the most amazing birthday parties, summer sendoffs, and 'welcome back to school' parties this school had ever seen. My parents may have been strict, but when it came down to showing off and spending cash that they worked hard to earn, they didn't hold back and weren't afraid to stunt.

"You wish you were getting that crown. What queen you know needs makeup to hide black eyes?" Holly asked, taking a dig below the belt at my situation.

"Holly, I get it. Damn. Trust me. I will handle this situation with Kango. Please don't worry about me, sis. It's going to be fine. Let's get through senior year and simply have a blast," I begged.

"Okay, Nae. I will back off, but I swear, I bet' not even think that he put hands on you again, or I can't promise what I will do," Holly said, and I knew she was serious. She was simply fed up with my situation with Kango, and being the loving person she was, she wanted to help me out of it.

"Nae, so ummm, who are you going to bring as a date to homecoming?"

That question kind of caught me off guard. I had never even thought of a date for homecoming. I was sure it would be nothing for me to be a third wheel with Donte and Holly, but I kind of wanted to be able to show my man off and show these bitches at Garfield High who really had Kango's heart. I held my head high and replied.

"Kango, of course."

Holly shook her head and walked out of the room. I gathered my things and went into the adjoining bathroom. I washed up quickly, sprayed on some body mist, and covered my bruises with Urban Decay makeup. Before I hooked up with Kango, I didn't even wear makeup. A little lip gloss and an eyebrow pencil was enough because my skin was flawless. As the beatings started, progressed, and got worse, I needed to start wearing it to cover the bruises and scars. At times, I looked in the mirror without makeup on and barely recognized myself. It almost looked like I had aged a few years from all the stress of being in my relationship.

I had to admit that I was much too smart and beautiful to be going through this shit, but Kango was my first, and at this point, I felt like I was in love with him. We were the cutest couple. I was five feet seven and 130 pounds. I had medium-length natural hair with a beautiful curl pattern. I had smooth, chocolate skin that most boys said reminded them of milk chocolate Hershey's kisses. Did I mention I had a voice out of this world? When I sang at the talent shows at school, many dropped out of the competition because they knew I would win hands down. I guess I could say I got my voice from my mom. Although she was a supervisor, she had once aspired to become a famous singer.

Now Kango? My man? Good lord, my man was fine. If you could say that I had a type, it would be Kango—caramel-colored, smooth, tatted skin, muscles that made my baby look like he was a professional athlete when he wore his wife beaters, juicy, thick, full lips, a strong jawline, and a nice low-cut, trimmed, wavy fade that easily connected to his mustache and goatee. He was like a sexier, more hood version of Omari Hardwick, and that was my baby. I knew when we got together, the hardest part about keeping Kango's attention on me would be keeping the random, thirsty bitches out his face.

I put my backpack on my shoulder and left out of Holly's spare room, limping and still dizzy. As I walked into the kitchen where she was entertaining Donte, I put my head down in shame.

"Thanks, Holly. I'll see you tomorrow. Hi, Donte," I spoke quickly in embarrassment as I prepared to leave.

"Nae, I love you, girl. Think about what I said. Oh, and your dad called a few minutes ago. He said to get home now. It sounded serious."

Letting out a deep breath, I pulled out my phone, noticing the twenty missed calls. I didn't feel like whatever drama that was coming my way with my parents, so I started up my 2016 Chrysler 300. It had been a sort of hand-me-down from my mother. I synced my phone to my car's Bluetooth and dialed my dad.

"Naomi, get your ass home now! You have fifteen minutes, or I'm coming to get you." He killed the line, and I shook my head, knowing that whatever it was he wanted, I was not going to like it. His tone said that he was not pleased. I just hoped my mom was home so that whatever I had done, she could help me out of it.

Carmen Lashay, T. Nicole, Ty Leese Javeh, Eden Mireya, Sparkle Lewis, Reign, & Armani

Kango

As I rode in silence, leaving that bitch Holly's crib, I couldn't get over how mad Naomi made me. Baby girl needed to stop with that slick ass mouth. All she needed to do was suck a nigga off when I told her to, and we wouldn't even have half of the fights we'd had. Bitch had the nerve to come at me as if I were a weak ass mothafucka. That bitch was talkin' 'bout going and fucking somebody else and even sucking another nigga's dick when she would barely suck mine. I wished she would let another nigga in my shit. I swear I'd kill both of 'em.

It never failed. Every time I left from being with Naomi's immature ass, I always needed to find a grown ass bitch to help me relieve my stress. I had a thing for chocolate, cute bitches too. It seemed like the darker the bitch, the juicier that pink pussy was, and I couldn't get enough. I headed to Greenville, leaving out of Anderson, knowing that this bitch Karina would let me beat the pussy up any way that I wanted to and suck me off real proper.

As soon as I jumped onto I-85, my iPhone 7 began to ring, and I allowed my hands-free system to answer.

"What's good?" I spoke as my voice bellowed throughout my whip.

"Nigga, where the fuck you at? We're out here waiting on yo' ass. You know damn well Bobby don't like it if we're late. We decided to wait on you so that we could all end up going together," my nigga Dooley spat, reminding me of a meeting that we had with our boss. I flipped around, heading back toward the spot in Anderson. Checking the time, I spoke up.

"Give me a good ten. You know how this traffic can be, but I'll be there shortly. I'll let Bobby know what's good when we get there."

I killed the line and got mad all over again. If I missed out on this money, I was going to beat the fuck out of Naomi again. She might even get it a little worse this time for interfering with me getting to the bag. I really needed to call this bitch Karina and tell her to keep that pussy hot and ready for me while I handled business.

Dialing her number, she picked up fast as hell on the first ring like she had been sitting by the phone and waiting for a nigga to call. That was that shit that I liked.

As soon as she started talking, I could tell by her tone that she was ready to be fucked. She was moaning with every other word that she spoke.

"Daddy, please tell me you're around the corner. I need you like right now. Mmm, I can't wait any longer. I've been bad, and I … shit … I need you to punish this pussy and my mouth."

Karina had a nigga bricked the fuck up just by the shit she was saying.

"Hey, ma. You gon' have to wait a little bit, but you better know that daddy's coming over to take care of that pussy. I'm putting this dick in the back of your throat. Can you handle that shit?" I asked, stroking my shit while I was driving. A nigga had just gotten out of some pussy, but I was ready to swim in some more. If a bitch could suck the shit outta my dick, I kept her ass on the team, and Karina was definitely in the starting lineup.

"Yes, daddy. You know I can handle whatever you give me. Hurry up and get here. I'll keep it hot and wet for you."

"I know you can. That pussy's trained to go. Go ahead and let daddy hear you cum. That'll hold you over until I can get over there and dig all in those guts."

Karina obeyed my command like she always did. I could hear her breathing get heavier as moans continued to ring through my car.

"Yeah, there it goes. Just like that. Rub that clit for me, and imagine how I'd be fuckin' the shit out yo' face if I was there."

I accidently hit the gas when Karina started moaning louder. I was full out beating the fuck off in traffic. I quickly grabbed one of my spare shirts from the back seat to catch my nut in as I felt that shit building. Just like always, we came at the same time. I immediately killed the line and focused on the road before I killed myself from fucking with that lil' chocolate freak. I couldn't wait to finish this meeting and get over to Karina to get my shit handled by a real bitch.

I made it to my boy Dooley's spot in record time. Killing the engine, I did the knock to alert them of my entrance so that I wouldn't get my ass lit the fuck up and riddled with bullets. I swear my niggas loved to shoot first and then think about questions and consequences later.

Carmen Lashay, T. Nicole, Ty Leese Javeh, Eden Mireya, Sparkle Lewis, Reign, & Armani

As I surveyed the room, my niggas looked as if they were suited up for war. We didn't know what the fuck Bobby needed with us, but whatever it was, we were prepared.

"Aye, fam, we need to get loose and roll out. We have about fifteen minutes before Bobby gets to blowing up our shit, and if we can make it on time, ain't shit to explain. Let's hit it," I spoke as we all filed out and switched up cars. We never took our own shit on missions. We always opted for old, beat-the-fuck-up bucket cars that blended into the neighborhoods we worked in so that we never stuck out like a sore thumb. Every now and then, I would borrow a chronic's car for almost nothing.

As we stepped on the scene in the hood, we were ready for whatever. Seeing our entire squad roll through and getting so much love from the block was a good ass feeling. We made our way to the spot where Bobby asked us to meet.

As we entered into the apartment, silence fell upon the room. Bobby's face was already turned up as his nose flared out. As we all took our positions, we remained silent, knowing not to speak in Bobby's meeting unless you were addressed. Even then, you better speak with caution. By the look on his face, this wasn't a meeting that any of us really wanted to be a part of.

Bobby walked around each of us as he held his steel bat in his hand. He slowly took the time to stop at each of us, giving us the same amount of eye contact and face-to-face action. *What the fuck is up with his ass today?* I thought as I found it hard to breathe or exhale. I was afraid to make any sudden movements or sounds. Bobby wasn't the boss to be fucked with.

Bobby hadn't spoken a word, and I was tired of the fucking silence. I wanted to know why we were here and what the fuck was up with all of the tension. Hell, we were supposed to be family. What the fuck was really going on?

"You niggas have no fucking clue why you're here, or are you niggas really as dumb as you fucking look?" Bobby posed that question to nobody in particular. We all remained silent as he continued to walk around.

"Kango! This is your team, right? You're handling these niggas, right?" he asked more so in a growl.

Clearing my throat, I replied, "Yeah, this is my team, and fo' sho'. I'm handling all these cats. We make and break bread together," I proudly spoke, looking Bobby dead in the face.

Without hesitation, Bobby walked behind me and hit my ass so fucking hard behind my knee with that steel fucking bat. I just knew that my shit was broken. None of my men moved as I fell to the ground in pain. No words left my mouth as I looked up at Bobby with fire in my eyes and only a pained grunt that I tried to stifle as hard as possible so as not to show weakness.

"So you allowed these cats in my camp? And what displeases me the most is how these bitches move, and your ass is proud about this shit. Stand the fuck up, nigga!" he bellowed as I rose to my feet with my leg slightly bent from the pain. I had no idea what the fuck Bobby was getting at, but I needed him to get to the point.

"Kango, for you all to make and break bread together, I guess the money you niggas pulling ain't shit. You got niggas on yo' team talking to other boss ass niggas, trying to cut deals and make a clean come up.

How the fuck you didn't know about this shit, and it got back to me? Are you apart of this shit too?" Bobby questioned as he raised his bat, wishing I said the wrong shit. I steadied myself, putting weight on my good leg and looked him dead in the eye.

"If you know of a snake in my camp, cut 'em off by the neck, and let's feed on his blood." I had death in my eyes. I couldn't believe one of my own niggas had me out here looking bad in front of Bobby. I hoped my words showed Bobby that I wasn't with that snake, undercutting shit. I didn't mind working for my shit and climbing my way to the top.

"Ha! Well, it's refreshing to see that your boss is not a bitch made nigga. I thought for a second that you 2017 niggas felt that disloyalty was the new coat of armor," Bobby spat as he looked at his second in command, Dru.

Dru held a smirk as if he knew some shit was about to go down. He walked up to Bobby and handed Bobby his pistol that had a silencer attached to the tip. I swallowed hard, not knowing if it was about to be my last day on earth. Thoughts of all the fucked up shit I had ever done started to run rapidly through my head as all I could think was, *karma is a bitch.*

Carmen Lashay, T. Nicole, Ty Leese Javeh, Eden Mireya, Sparkle Lewis, Reign, & Armani

Bobby smiled, kissed his pistol, and said, "May God have mercy on the souls of you disloyal ass niggas."

POP! POP! POP! POP!

Soft whistling sounds rang through the air, and I had my eyes closed until the whistles ceased. When I opened my eyes, Bobby was standing in front of me with a blank face and said, "Have your men to clean this shit up. You're my new right-hand man. We have a meeting at midnight. I'll send you the address."

Bobby walked out with his security and didn't utter another fucking word. I finally let out the breath I was holding as I looked around the room and noticed Dru and Dooley on the floor dead with their eyes wide open. Since Bobby just announced me as his right-hand man, I needed to get this shit in order and be prepared for my meeting. I had no time to dwell on or even mentally process what had just happened. A nigga was about to be a real boss ass nigga, fucking with Bobby.

All eyes were on me as I got up and paused to get myself together before speaking. Even though I was still in pain, I had just gotten bumped up the food chain in this game, and I couldn't show an ounce of weakness.

"Fam, I'm not sure what all of this shit was about, but as you know, Bobby works on a need-to-know basis. The information that came out will be the only information you niggas need. In the future, I'll always choose loyalty over anything. If you are loyal to me, I'll continue to be loyal to you. Just as I've told Bobby this evening, if we find snakes, we're chopping at the head and feeding off the blood. Let this be a lesson to you niggas. The next time I take a hit or bullet for some shit I didn't know about, just know that all of you niggas will need a burial plot. Get this shit clean and wait for further instructions before you proceed with our daily operation."

I left the men with their thoughts and the two dead bodies. Nobody spoke a word as I left. I limped back to my shit bucket of a car. I winced in pain and let out a low moan from the throbbing in my leg when I finally sat in the driver's seat, having had to suppress all of that in front of the other men.

I burnt out of the parking lot, headed to Dooley's crib to pick my real car back up. It was a damn shame his ass had been a snake ass nigga. His people wouldn't get shit from us, not even flowers, because he hadn't died honorably. He had betrayed the camp. I couldn't stand a fake ass, disloyal ass mothafucka. He had dug his own grave, and now it was time for me to build my empire.

I rode back to get my whip with a smile on my face. I had just been promoted, and glancing at my watch, I had plenty of time to get to Karina to celebrate. I was gon' dig her ass the fuck out and then call that young ass bitch Naomi and make sure her ass was in the fucking crib. It was going to be a lovely fuckin' night.

Nathan Warr

I couldn't believe Naomi had the audacity to stand in my face and tell a bold-faced lie. I understood that she was a young adult, and I got it that the kids were sexually active in high school, but my daughter, my princess, my love … she had so much potential that I refused to allow her to throw her life away over some clown who didn't mean her any good.

"I'm going to ask you again, and if you lie again, I'm taking the keys to your car, and you will have to figure out a way to get back and forth to school for the rest of the school year. Where in the hell were you from third through sixth period, and why in the hell am I getting a call from the school telling me that you were missing from those classes?"

Naomi stood in front of me with her beautiful, doe eyes. She had the saddest look that would make any father melt and give in. I hated when she tried to use that very look against me, knowing that I was a softie for her, to get her way or get out of trouble. She was truly a spoiled Daddy's girl, but I'd be damned if she thought she had my approval to skip class to go fuck up her life. That shit wouldn't happen on my watch.

"Daddy, I wasn't doing anything wrong. I have lunch third period, and Holly and I went to her house to eat. Her parents were home. Here, take my phone. Call them and see for yourself."

Naomi's eyes started to fill with tears. I was sure that she was lying, but I didn't want to look like the asshole father who didn't trust his seventeen-year-old daughter by calling one of her friend's parents. I did call the number she left for me, and Holly did answer. Shortly after, Naomi did come right home. Was I overreacting? Was I holding on too tightly as a dad?

Naomi had explained her third period disappearance logically enough, but somehow, I had a feeling she was up to no good or something was off. If I weren't mistaken, I'd just paid for her hair to be re-done. The fact that it was slicked back into a big, curly ponytail, and it was curled nice and cute when she left, had my mind going nuts.

Naomi's watery eyes turned into her all-out crying, and that shit tugged at my heartstrings. I hated for my child to cry, especially over something I had started. I pulled her in for a big hug.

"My love, stop crying. Daddy is just trying to make sure that you weren't out here fucking up. Naomi, you know I will give you the world, but if you come in here lying to me, I will take it all away, and you will live one very simple life. I do entirely too much for you to come in here and not appreciate the lifestyle that you have. All I ask is that you remain focused and keep your virginity until at least after college so that you can get your degree and be better than your mother and I were … until you decide to have a family of your own," I calmly spoke as I hugged my daughter to comfort her from her tears.

I had the perfect plan for my princess, and not a nigga on earth was going to stand in the way of the dreams that her mother and I had for her. Naomi dried her tears and looked me in my eyes as she spoke.

"Daddy, I promise I'm not going to mess up. I will follow the rules as always. You have to trust that you raised me right. I've had the talk with you and mom more than I care to even think about. Trust me, Daddy."

Her words made me feel like an ass. I had to believe that Patricia and I had raised her right. She was a straight A student and all. There was nothing in this world that I wouldn't do for her to keep her on the right track and make sure she succeeded the way that I knew she could.

Patricia Warr

There was nothing sweeter than watching this beautiful father/daughter moment between my husband and daughter. I loved their relationship, but like the old saying goes, mother knows best, and right now, I knew that Naomi was lying out the side of her damn neck. She could pull the wool over her daddy's eyes and push out those crocodile tears because he was a sucker for his baby girl, but Mommy wasn't going for the bullshit.

Carmen Lashay, T. Nicole, Ty Leese Javeh, Eden Mireya, Sparkle Lewis, Reign, & Armani

I walked up the winding staircase that led to my daughter's room. Her beautiful angelic voice was belting out the words of SZA's "The Weekend".

I stood there with the biggest smile plastered on my face, knowing that she got her love and gift of music from me. I watched her as she hugged her bear, singing to it as if she were singing to someone she loved. Only new love could make a young girl act like that. My baby had it bad for someone, and I was definitely going to get to the bottom of it.

Slightly tapping on her door to alert her of my presence, I pushed the door all the way open and walked in. Naomi quickly wiped away her tears, and somehow, I knew those tears had nothing to do with the conversation she'd just had with her dad.

"Sweetheart, what's wrong? This isn't like you. You know you can talk to me about anything. I've told you that before," I spoke in such a loving tone as I looked into my baby girl's eyes. She stared at me as if she were searching for answers to unasked questions.

"Mama, can we talk? I mean … like really talk? You have to promise me you won't tell Dad."

When Naomi spoke those words, I knew something serious was about to follow. I closed and locked her door, sat on her bed, and gave her my full, undivided attention. I was not going to make the mistakes my own mother had. I was going to listen to my child and try to understand her concerns. Naomi knew that her father and I were old-school parents. There were certain things that we weren't going to tolerate.

I did however believe that if your child really came to you with a true concern, you should be able to open up as a parent and hear your child out. You may not ever get the chance to have this opportunity again. Give the wrong reaction just once, and your child would probably never come to you again if they had problems with something.

"Sweetie, what's on your mind? You can tell me anything. Trust me. Unless you're telling me you're pregnant, we don't have to involve your dad," I told her, looking her right in her beautiful eyes and hoping that she felt comfortable enough telling me what was on her mind.

"Mom, don't get mad. I'm sick of pretending, and I know I talk to Holly, but I really feel like I need you and your guidance in this instead," she began, and she had my full attention.

"Go on, sweetie. What is it?" I questioned.

"Mom, I'm not a virgin, and I'm sorry that I didn't wait like you and Dad wanted me to. The truth is I felt as if I was ready, and even now, I still feel that way. I don't regret doing it. I just regret not being honest with you as you have asked me time and time again."

Naomi took a long pause as I tried my best to hold in the many emotions that ran through my body. I could see her studying my body language. I knew I appeared to be tense, but I wanted to know everything, and now wasn't the time to have a breakdown. I looked at her for a second longer before I replied.

"Is that all, sweetheart?" I asked in the most loving tone.

"No, Mom. There's more."

I don't think I was prepared for the news that she confessed to me. Part of me wanted to call the police, and another part wanted me to run down the stairs and have Nathan grab his gun to go hunting. Right now, my daughter needed me, and she had trusted me to come to me with this information. As a mom, I sometimes had some pretty hard decisions to make, but the simplest decision was always doing what was right for your child.

"Naomi, I won't sit here and say that I condone you having sex with a grown man, but I know that if I tell you to stop, then you will continue to sneak around and do it anyway. That's not what I want. Your father is five years my senior; however, we both were grown when we decided to get together. Sweetie, you have six months before your eighteenth birthday, and I'm begging you to please ask him to wait and not continue to have sex with you. Get to know each other. I mean, really get to know each other. You've already given him something so special that you will never be able to get back. Just take your time, and make sure that he's right for you. At the first sign of trouble, always remove yourself from that situation. Do you understand what I'm saying to you?" I asked.

As I leaned in and hugged her, the tears rolled from her eyes. I didn't know what it was that was causing her to be this emotional about this topic, but I assumed there was more to this story, and my motherly intuition was telling me that I was right in assuming so. The more that I inquired, the more that Naomi swore to me she was telling me everything.

Naomi and I talked about going to the doctor and getting her on birth control. Although I didn't condone what she was doing, now that I knew what was going on, I was going to help her take the necessary precautions to be sure that she didn't end up becoming another statistic… A struggling, single mom.

I smiled at my child, taking in her beauty. After a long silent pause, I spoke up.

"What does this guy do for a living, and what's his name?"

Holly

Two Days Later...

This bitch would get enough of using me in her lies to see this lame ass nigga who wasn't worth two dead flies... smashed. I swear I loved my girl, but ever since she got her cherry popped, her ass went dumb over this nigga. I'm not saying I was the sharpest pencil in the box when it came to my love life, but I damn sure wasn't about to allow a nigga to put hands on me and still be with his no-good, cheating ass, letting him get the pussy whenever he wanted to. No nigga was worth that shit. Nae was too cute and too damn smart to be going through that shit, not to mention too damn young.

I waited outside my car for Naomi to pull up and come grab my keys. I knew her ass was in the bathroom, trying to change clothes and fix her makeup before she saw this fool. I wasn't about to miss any classes, and I knew my parents weren't coming home anytime soon. I took the time to forward the house calls to my cell phone just in case. I never knew who might call and what lie I needed to tell to save both of our asses. I mean, my parents were cool, but part of them being cool was only because they thought I wasn't interested in boys or sex. I played that role well, but my ass had already been fucking for two years without them suspecting a thing. I simply keep my grades up, keep myself protected, and abided by my number one rule. Never get caught.

Nae was bouncing to the beat of whatever music she was playing in her car as she approached me. Rolling down her window, she damn near stuck half her body out.

"Why the sour ass look, sis?" she questioned. I rolled my eyes as I walked to the driver's side, handed her my keys, rattled off the code, and started back into the school.

"Sis, Holly, what the fuck is up? You can't talk to me now?" she questioned, and I stopped in my tracks, turning to give her my attention.

I sucked in air and blurted out without warning, "You are one stupid bitch, and I'm an even dumber bitch for allowing you access to keep this shit up!"

I knew my words hurt her deep. We were sisters, and we never spoke to each other like this. No matter what, we always said that we would discuss any and every thing. At this point, I was tired of discussing the same shit with her for her not to listen. It had been the same shit for the last three months, and I was tired of it. If Kango had been a good nigga, I wouldn't trip, but his ass was lower than the dirt on the bottom of my Nikes.

"Here we go with this shit again, Holly. You promised to stay out of it. Kango hasn't even so much as yelled at me since the other day. We have been cool. Can't you just be happy for me? If it's a problem with us using your crib, then just say that shit, and I'm sure we can figure something else out, but I don't appreciate the way you're coming at me."

Yeah, she was in her feelings, but fuck it. So was I. I walked back to her window, and we were damn near nose to nose.

"Nae, I love you like my blood sister, and I can't just sit around and watch this nigga make a fool out of you. We see him with hella bitches, and I watch you hold your head down and pretend that shit doesn't bother you. Nae, open your eyes. In a few months, we will be off to college, and his ass will still be here in Anderson, running these streets. You know there's no longevity there. Cut him loose, and just kick it these last few months of high school."

I tried not to cry, but the tears began flowing the more I thought about Nae being hurt. I wasn't trying to act as if I were better than her or anything. I just wanted her to know that she could do better—a whole lot better. I guess I wasn't prepared for what she said next.

"Holly, take your fucking keys. I don't need your judgement. Worry about what the fuck is going on with you and your man. Me and mine are fine. You want to stand here and judge what the hell I do and how I do it, but I challenge you to turn that same mirror around on your situation. I'm not asking Kango to marry me. Dammit, I just want to be happy. You act like you and Donte have the perfect fucking relationship, but the nigga always giving me the eye when yo' ass leaves the room. Keep your man happy before I show you how to do it. Bye, bitch!"

I didn't give a shit about anything she said with the exception of her mentioning that Donte was making passes at her or whatever. Fuck the dude. My sister was supposed to have my back and tell me if my nigga was fucking up. This right here showed me what type bitch I was dealing with. I was the one helping her. I was the one holding her secrets, and I was the one who made sure she was alright every time that nigga beat her ass.

"Cool, Nae. I'll play the same fucking game you're playing," I whispered to myself while walking off.

***

Nae had me fucked up if she thought she was just about to pop off at the mouth and talk to me any type of way because I was a good damn friend. I kept telling her that I only wanted the best for her, and in my eyes, Kango wasn't that.

My leg began to bounce up and down as I sat in the cafeteria, thinking about our fight. The nerve of her to call herself a friend and not speak on some shit about my man making passes or advances at her. Maybe Nae was talking shit, but I wasn't about to let anything slide. I knew my worth, and if the nigga didn't have eyes for only me, then he could keep it fucking moving. I was never pressed about a nigga or dick.

"Damn, ma. What got you all upset and shit? You're sitting over here with yo' cute ass frowned the fuck up. Where's Nae at?" Donte asked, and my blood began to boil. Why in the fuck was he worried about Nae? He may have asked about her a million other times before now, but all I knew was that Nae had been getting some type of signals. I was about to find out what the fuck was really good.

"So why the fuck you worried about Nae? You're trying to get with her or something? You want to fuck Nae?" I spat, and the entire section got quiet and began looking our way. Yes, I was loud as fuck and clapping my hands all up in Donte's face. I didn't give a shit how bad I looked doing it, but I wanted and needed answers. His ass was about to start talking.

"Whoa, Ma! What the fuck got you wired? I always ask you 'bout ya girl. You two are damn near connected at the hip. You're wildin' for nothing. You need to calm all that shit down," Donte spat, shaking his head. His boys started to clown him, and his nose began to flare. He started to walk away from the conversation, but I wasn't done with his ass.

"Oh, so you don't have shit to say, but you always ask about her? Be honest. Keep it one hundred like you promised, nigga. You're always looking at her and trying to make passes at her when I walk out the room or turn my fucking head!" I spat and didn't give a fuck who heard me or saw me.

"You really want to do this right here, Holly? You're straight playing yo'self, ma. All these bitches around here see how insecure yo' ass being, and that shit's not a good look. I don't want to disrespect you and shit, so I'm walking the fuck away. When you find my lady, then find me."

Donte walked away, leaving me standing in the middle of the cafeteria, looking dumb. He had never given me a reason to believe that he was doing me wrong, but I allowed Nae to get in my head and take me out of character.

I walked back to my seat at the table with my fist resting on the side of my head. As my friend Whitney walked up, I knew she was about to talk about my ass making a scene, and I wasn't in the mood. I killed that shit instantly.

"Whitney, not today. Right now is not the fucking time to be coming to me with the jokes. I'm not in the fucking mood," I spat before she even spoke a word.

"Holly, I can see that you're on bullshit right now, so I'm not about to go all the way in on you, because clearly you are in your feelings. What I will say is that you made yourself look extra dumb, asking that man about your bestie, who is like your fucking sister. Donte didn't deserve that shit. He curves bitches left and right and lets these hoes know what it is when it comes to you. You need to get yo' shit in order 'cause the moment you step off, all of these chicken heads are going for ya boy."

I listened to Whitney and felt like shit about how I had acted. After thinking about this shit, I realized how crazy I must have sounded and looked. The sound of the bell had students grabbing and emptying their trays. I saw Donte standing at the door, talking to his boys, and I shyly walked toward them. He glanced my way, and you could tell that he was still beyond pissed. Swallowing my pride, I walked toward him and instantly went in for his ear. His ear was one of his spots, and I wanted to start kissing on it to show that I was sorry for showing my ass.

"Go on with that, Holly. You're playing games," he said, turning his head away from me.

"A'ight, fellas. I'll see y'all in practice," he spoke to his guys as the warning bell went off, alerting us that we had three minutes to get to our fourth period class. I felt played, but I guess that was his way of paying me back for showing my ass in front of his boys and the entire school for that matter.

I looked at my phone and contemplated whether or not I should call Nae and apologize for our fight. I was only trying to be a good friend to her, and everything was all fucked up now. I had to find a way to fix it.

I walked out of the cafeteria with fourth period on my mind, but the buzzing of my phone got my attention. Looking down, I didn't know the number, so I hit ignore and kept walking. Moments later, the same number was calling back, so I picked up the phone.

"Hello!" I answered with an attitude because my mind was going a mile a minute with the bullshit I had going on.

"Hello, Mr. or Mrs. Lytle please," a very commanding yet familiar voice boomed through my ear.

"This is their daughter. Is everything alright?"

"Are you home?" the voice asked.

"No, I'm in school. Who is this?"

"This is Sheila, your next-door neighbor. We need to contact your parents. There is something seriously wrong at your home.

Carmen Lashay, T. Nicole, Ty Leese Javeh, Eden Mireya, Sparkle Lewis, Reign, & Armani

Kango

I was supposed to be knee deep in pussy, but this bitch had me out here in Greenville looking like a fuck ass nigga. I waited on her in that bitch Holly's driveway for twenty minutes and still didn't see her whip. I called her ass several times, and that shit was going right to voicemail. She really wanted me to fuck her ass up. I was sick of her young ass playing all these fucking games.

The longer I sat there, the more I began thinking. *This bitch is always here when she says she's going to be here. She probably wasn't expecting me to come on time, and she got another nigga in there.*

My thoughts had me in a fucked up head space. I started to imagine Naomi bouncing on another nigga's dick and got pissed the fuck off. I got out my whip, slammed the door, and began ringing the shit out of that doorbell. I didn't hear shit on the other side, but that didn't mean shit. For all I knew, they could be in there laughing at me and waiting on me to leave, so I began yelling.

"Naomi, if you don't get your apple head ass out here now, I'm breaking this fucking door down and dragging you out!" I barked, beating on the door, trying hard to knock that bitch off the hinges.

Minutes seemed like hours as I continued my rant. Having had enough of this bullshit, I went to my car, pulled out my pistol, and shot the fucking lock off. I walked all through that big mothafuckin' house looking for my bitch.

"Naomi, where the fuck you at, bitch?" I yelled as I went from room to room. These fuckers had a nice ass crib, and half of this shit, I hadn't noticed until now. I picked up my phone yet again and dialed Naomi, making sure to listen for a phone ringing or vibrating because I still had a feeling that she was hiding somewhere in this house. My anger was intense as I got the voicemail again.

"Naomi, I don't know what type of fuck games you're playing, but I'm beating the fuck outta you when I see you! You got me over here at your girl's house looking stupid, and you probably in here hiding and laughing at me and shit. Whenever I see you, I'm beating yo' ass! Don't get yo' shit pulled back!"

Naomi

I was fucked up in the head when I left Holly at the school. I tried to rent a few hotel rooms, but apparently, I wasn't old enough, and I wasn't trying to get caught up with Kango by asking him to get us one. The police would have probably arrested him on site. I wanted to take care of things on my own to show him I was a woman and could be the woman he needed. My phone had died, and I noticed I'd forgotten my charger at home. I figured I would call Kango later and explain what had happened.

***

I sat in the parking lot of the school, waiting for the fifth period to start. I'd missed lunch, and fourth period had already begun. I knew I was foul by eluding to the fact that Donte wanted me. That shit was so far from the truth. I guess in my own mind, I was a bit jealous because he was so attentive to Holly's needs, and that was all I wanted in a man. I thought I had it all by dating an older man, but it seemed like I should have taken my chances with a high school boy. At least I understood them better.

I was going over in my head the things I would say to Kango when I was finally able to talk to him. I was sure he was probably pissed off, waiting in the driveway at Holly's house. I knew I'd have to do something nice for him so that he would remain calm and understanding of what had happened today. I wanted to be with him so bad that I closed my eyes and went back to our last sex session before the abuse.

The things Kango did to my body, I didn't think anyone else could make my body do. I longed for his touch and scent. No matter what others thought, I knew he had a pure heart and was a teddy bear underneath the tough-guy act. I knew he had a lot of stress dealing with his street issues, and I was being understanding and trying to stay out of his way to keep him happy.

As my eyes remained closed, and I held a smile upon my face, I heard Holly's voice screaming, so I popped up to take a peek.

"Get your hands off me. I'm leaving and going to check on my house. You can call my parents if you want to. Fuck what y'all saying. This is school, not prison!"

Holly was going in on the school security guard. She mentioned that she needed to check on her house, and my heart dropped to my feet. Something must have happened, and thank God I never made it over there. I couldn't imagine something happening while I was there.

Holly stormed toward the student parking lot where I was parked. The security guard gave up and headed back toward the school's front entrance. Holly locked eyes with me, and it felt as if she wanted to say something, but I quickly turned away, hoping to talk to her another day. I kept my head down as I played with my nails, not paying attention to my surroundings.

I watched as her car pulled away, and sadness took over me. I scooted my body down into my driver seat as tears began to roll down my cheeks. I had fucked up bad with my bestie, and it didn't seem as if she wanted to try to make things right. I jumped and wiped the tears from my eyes as the banging on my window startled me.

As I looked up to see who it was, my heart began to pound as the look of terror and destruction was displayed all over his face. Knowing that this wasn't going to be good, I pressed the button for the window to go down to listen to what he had to say.

"So you sitting here crying, looking dumb as fuck because you fucking lied for attention behind a clown ass nigga?" Donte spat as I sat straight in my seat, wiping away my tears that began to rapidly fall. I sat quietly and allowed him to finish his rant. I knew I deserved that shit, so I didn't want to interrupt him.

"So now you don't have shit to say, but you were all in my girl's ear with some fucking bullshit that you and I both know wasn't true. I never tried shit with you. If you really want to keep it real, I'm too good for you. You're not into a man who doesn't beat yo' ass. That's right. You're into niggas who beat the fuck out of you and demand that you fuck and suck in order for him to keep his hands to himself while he's still out fucking bitches and not doing shit with his fucking life."

Donte was mad and spitting daggers at me with his words. As true as the statements were that he was spitting, I didn't appreciate him telling me about my business. More importantly, I needed to know why Holly felt the need to tell him what the fuck was going on in my life. Donte continued to go on for another minute or so until I stopped him.

"Donte, I get that you're mad, and you have every right to be, but I have never put out any of your business or put out anything that Holly told me about your sex life and relationship, so please don't bump off at the gums, spitting my business out like that. I'll admit I fucked up. I lied, but I was mad, and it had nothing to do with you. It was fucked up that I pulled you into my shit. For that, I'm sorry, but I'm not about to sit here and allow you to degrade me as if I don't fucking matter and if my feelings aren't fucked up by this. I'm sorry. I'll never bring you in shit again, and if you forgive me, fine. If you don't, oh the hell well. All I care about is getting my friend back. I fucked up! Dammit, I fucked up!"

I began crying like a baby, and Donte began to soften his stance as he opened my car door and pulled me out and into a friendly hug to console me.

"Nae, I'm sorry. I was out of line, but you know Holly and I want to see you with someone who treats you with respect. We are all friends, and we will have our moments to fight, but we can't go around lying on each other and fucking our own shit up when we have plenty of bitches and niggas waiting to do that shit for us."

I laughed at how true his statement was. Donte was a great guy. I was so glad that he and Holly were together. Donte wiped my tears, pulled me into his arms, and held me as he kissed the top of my head.

"Nae, you need to get yourself out of that situation. Holly would be torn to pieces if anything happened to you and she knew what was going on. Just think about the situation you have her in because she knows. Now that I know, think about how that makes us both feel if anything happened to you. You're my sis, with your lying ass."

He laughed as he hugged me tightly, and I took in a deep breath, knowing what I needed to do. I loved Kango, and I was almost certain that all he needed was to see me as a woman and things would be great between us. I had a plan.

***

After a few minutes of continuing to contemplate my broken friendship with Holly, I started my Chrysler and decided to head to her house to talk things out.

Holly

Carmen Lashay, T. Nicole, Ty Leese Javeh, Eden Mireya, Sparkle Lewis, Reign, & Armani

I pulled up to my house only to see my front door slightly open. I tried dialing my neighbor's phone number back before getting out and got sent to voicemail.

Against my better judgement, I nervously exited my car, approaching the door. I noticed the familiar car in the driveway and realized it belonged to Kango, but why the hell would he have kicked my door in? Naomi wasn't here, so he had no business being here.

I walked in and grabbed the bat that was always kept hidden behind the plant that was beside the door. When I got further into the house, I heard movement coming from the back room where Nae usually did her thing with Kango.

When I got closer to the door, Kango came charging out of the room with fire in his eyes.

"Nigga, what —"

No sooner than I opened my mouth to question this nigga about being in my shit, I noticed him reach for his waistband, pull out his piece, and fire. I felt all the air leave my lungs as I collapsed on the hallway floor. For the next few minutes, I heard muffled yelling and what sounded like a woman's voice before darkness completely surrounded me.

Naomi

I pulled up to Holly's house and immediately felt uneasy. If it weren't confusing enough that I saw Holly and Kango's cars both there, the feeling was elevated by the fact that the front door was wide open. I hurriedly got out the car, heading straight for the front door.

The moment I walked in, there was an eerie silence over the house that made goosebumps pop up on my arms.

"Holly!" I yelled, making my way through the living room and down the hall.

"Kango?" I said, barely above a whisper as my mind processed the scene in front of me. When I got to the hallway, all I saw was Kango standing frozen over my best friend's lifeless body with his hands on top of his head. Blood had pooled all around Holly, and it was enough to make me sick to my stomach.

"What the fuck did you do!" I yelled, breaking Kango from his trance. There were no words to describe the emotions that rose in me. I felt sadness mixed with confusion and rage as I took in what had happened.

"Fuck, man. I thought her ass was you!" Kango yelled, moving his eyes from Holly's body to me with rage all over his face. "I was gonna kill yo' hoe ass, but she showed up instead!"

I took a step back away from Kango at his mention of wanting to kill me, but my movement must have sparked something in him because he lunged for me.

"I'll kill you too, bitch! I'm not going to prison behind this shit!" Kango yelled out. I had tried to run, but his reach was too long, and he now had me pinned against the wall, choking the life out of me. I saw the crazed look in his eyes as I clawed at his hands and tried to gasp for breath.

Feeling myself slip in and out, tears began to fall because I knew this man was about to kill me. Why hadn't I seen that this was in him before now? Why had I stayed with Kango and subconsciously made excuses for why he treated me the way that he did? Now, my best friend was dead before I could make up with her, and I was about to die too.

I looked to the side, ready to close my eyes and succumb to the darkness of death that was coming closer with each second when something caught my attention. The subtlest glint out the corner of my eye caused my adrenaline to start pumping and my heart to race.

With every ounce of strength I had left, I kneed Kango in his groin and dove to the floor when he released me with grunt of pain, gasping for air. Grabbing the gun that he hadn't realized he had dropped, I pointed at Kango and emptied the clip into his body.

As I watched Kango's body hit the hall floor with a thud, I dropped the gun and broke down hysterically crying, interrupted by coughing, as I was still trying to catch my breath. After a few seconds, I stood up, slightly weak on my feet, and went to grab Holly's house phone. I picked it up, walked over to where her body was, and slid down the wall beside her.

"9-1-1, what's your emergency?" the dispatcher sang out into the phone as my heart sank into the pit of my stomach. The last few months of my life that were spent arguing, fussing, and fighting seemed to be pointless now. Everything was happening in slow motion as I scooted over to cradle Holly's head in my arms.

Carmen Lashay, T. Nicole, Ty Leese Javeh, Eden Mireya, Sparkle Lewis, Reign, & Armani

"I need help. He killed her, and I killed him. Please … somebody help me," I said almost in a whisper, in shock of what I had just done. Flashes of the past few months ran through my mind, and I couldn't help but think how this all began. This was all my fault. Hindsight was always 20/20, and now everything that Holly had been telling me was crystal clear.

Being free forever from the verbal and physical abuse felt like I had finally taken a deep breath of fresh air when I didn't even realize I'd been suffocating under Kango's so-called love the entire time we were together.

I clutched my best friend's limp body with her head in my lap until the police and paramedics arrived. Everything was so surreal to me from this point on. One minute, I was being lifted and pulled away from Holly's body while hearing a blood-curdling cry coming from the distance. It was only then I realized that the agonizing sound was coming from me when I was put in handcuffs and placed in the back of a police car. I had no idea what was going to happen to me and my life now, but ironically enough, riding off to the county jail, I felt freer than I ever had.

"I am beautiful with my scars. I am bigger than that pain. I am beyond those sleepless nights and months of walking on eggshells. I learned that jealousy is not a showcase of affection, choking does not make someone listen, a closed fist to the face is not an accident, and abuse is not love in any form. No matter what it takes, get out before it's too late." –Reign

Carmen Lashay, T. Nicole, Ty Leese Javeh, Eden Mireya,
Sparkle Lewis, Reign, & Armani

Shades of Love: Fighting for His Heart

Ty Leese Javeh

This is a work of fiction. Names, characters,
businesses, places, events, and incidents are either the
products of the author's imagination or used in a fictitious

Contains explicit language & adult situations

Contact Ty Leese Javeh:

Facebook: tyleesejaveh

Twitter: @tyleesejaveh

Instagram: @tyleesejaveh

http://tyleesejaveh.wixsite.com/tyleesejaveh

Shades of Love: Fighting For His Heart

A Domestic Violence Awareness Short Story

Carmen Lashay, T. Nicole, Ty Leese Javeh, Eden Mireya, Sparkle Lewis, Reign, & Armani

Synopsis

Khadafy and Zara have been together for thirteen years. Of the thirteen years, they have been married for eight. On the outside looking in, everything is perfect for the couple, but on their wedding day, things change, leaving Zara confused, wondering how her life has drastically changed within a blink of an eye.

As the years roll by, Zara finds herself alone, suffering in a marriage in which she feels trapped, abandoned, misused, and abused.

After losing his job, Khadafy starts drinking heavily, taking drugs, and taking out all his anger and frustrations on the woman he claims to love. Thinking that she can save Khadafy, Zara will stop at nothing to make her marriage work and hopefully change Khadafy into the man that she fell in love with.

Take a trip in Zara's mind as she seeks to understand life, peace, joy, happiness, and most importantly, freedom. Zara is on a journey to save her marriage, but in the end, she might just teach an invaluable lesson to her husband, Khadafy, even if it may cost one of them their life.

Carmen Lashay, T. Nicole, Ty Leese Javeh, Eden Mireya,
Sparkle Lewis, Reign, & Armani

Prologue-I Had Enough

After eight years of marriage, you would think that on my anniversary, I would be happy and excited. Usually, it was said that if you could make it past three years, everything else should be a breeze. What couple do you know that hasn't had their fair share of ups and downs? I wish people would stop lying on social media and making it seem as if life for them were simply crystal stairs and a bed of roses.

When it came to Khadafy, shit, I'd be lying if I said we were in marital bliss. Khadafy used to be the sweetest man in the world, paid attention to all of my needs, and only wanted to make me happy. The day I decided to cut off my family and only foster friends from hanging with his friends was the day that my life changed.

Affairs, drug abuse, arrest, baby momma scares, and of course, the ass beatings, yes, I'd been through it all, and when you were going through it, it was like you had on blinders of love that kept telling you that it would get better.

Tonight, after coming in from an Extended Stay at the hospital after sporting a black eye, broken jaw, and a pinched nerve, this nigga didn't even pick me up. He told me he was taking care of business.

I walked in the house and made my way upstairs, and when I reached our bedroom, who but Khadafy was lying back on the bed with his hands behind his head and feet crossed at the ankles, sleeping as if he didn't have a care in the world.

Thirteen years in total, and all he gave me was his ass to kiss, but this time, I was standing up for myself. Some people say if you had to go out, you went out with a bang.

Without making a sound, I walked into the room unnoticed, opened the top drawer, put my hand to the bottom, and smiled when I touched the chrome pistol. Today, the world would know you could never fuck over Zara Nicole Roberts.

"Khadafy!" I screamed to wake his ass up.

His cocky ass shot up in the bed, smirking at me.

"Oh, you're home. Good, now take off yo' clothes, and bring yo' ass over here and let daddy jump around inside you, pump you full of this dick." Licking his lips, he grabbed the bulge in his boxer briefs, squeezing it as if it were appealing to me.

I didn't respond, which made Khadafy angry. He sat all the way up in the bed, giving me an evil glare.

"Either bring yo' ass over here now, or get the fuck out so I can call the next bitch over here to take care of my needs," Khadafy stated as if he weren't in the wrong. He had to know that for every action, there was a reaction.

I revealed my hand, exposing the chrome pistol with a smile on my face. I had my mind made up, and he was going to pay for all of the hurt that he caused me, and what better day than today—our anniversary? The day I promised to love him 'til death do us part.

I boldly spoke. "I'm free, and so are you!"

POW!

Session 1

"Describe your relationship for me. Just kind of sum it up."

"That's not a simple question for me. If I'm going to tell you about it, I would want to tell you everything and not leave anything out."

"That's good, Zara. Talking about it will help us gain clarity for you to find out what you really want to do."

I sat in this office, going through the motions of trying to heal. No matter what I said, it still wouldn't change anything in my current situation. Nothing would.

"For the first four years of my and Khadafy's relationship, everything was perfect. Khadafy was the sweetest, most loving man that simply swept me off my feet. He was the perfect gentleman. He used to open doors, pull out chairs, and always made sure to hold my hand as we walked down the street. He was proud to have me as his woman, and I was damn proud to have him as my man."

"So what changed? Did something happen for this all to simply change?" I hated when this therapist would ask questions that he knew I didn't have the answers to. That was just like asking me why Khadafy beat me. I guess my answer would be because he woke up. I didn't have the answers to these questions. I could only take this doctor down the road as I saw things through my eyes.

"I wish I could answer that, but I don't know what changed. Maybe the signs were always there, and I simply ignored them."

"How so?"

"I'm not sure," I replied, being truthful.

"Well, Zara, you stated that the first five years were perfect, and you gave a few examples of what he used to do, but can you pinpoint when it stopped?"

If I told this man that every time Khadafy beat me, he would come home with flowers and candy and kiss my bumps and bruises and make sweet love to me, then he'd think I was a dumb bitch for staying and allowing this to happen, but it wasn't that simple. It had never been that cut and dry.

"I guess things weren't always so perfect; maybe that's how I envisioned it in my head. He's always been aggressive, demanding, and seemed to be a bit on the edge at times, but don't all men have a button that we women seem to touch, push, and jump up and down on?"

"No, Zara, and that's speaking as both a man and a professional. Zara, tell me about your wedding day. How was it?" he asked, and I started laughing.

"The wedding day. That's the day that my life became not so perfect." Laying my head back on the pillow, I began telling Doctor Li about my perfect wedding day.

"Like many women, you dream of your wedding as early as age five, and of course I wasn't any different. When Khadafy and I decided that we wanted our love to last forever, he got down on one knee in front of my family and my girls and asked me to be his forever and a lifetime."

"How did you feel when he proposed?"

"Special, loved, blissful, deserving even. This wonderful man has just chosen me to be with him forever. How could I not feel overjoyed? Of course, I knew exactly how I wanted my day. It was indeed one of the most important days of my life. I was emotional, full of joy, and at the time, had you asked if I'd go through the hassle of that day again, I would say yes without hesitation."

"Tell me about that day. It seems that your eyes were going a bit distant on me as you were talking. Talk to me about it."

"Well, it was the best and worst day of my life." I shrugged. As my mind took me back in time, I closed my eyes as I relived that very special day.

I was standing in the back of the church, and my bridesmaids marched to the wedding song of the old classic "Here and Now" by Luther Vandross.

"Are you ready to be mines forever and a lifetime?" Khadafy asked, and I was so in love because we made our own rules. We didn't do the traditional 'don't see the bride before the wedding.' We got dressed together and even walked down the aisle hand and hand.

I should have noted that as a warning sign, but I was blinded by love.

"Of course, baby, I'm ready. I'm already yours," I stated as we made our way down the aisle.

Tears flooded my eyes as we stood at the altar, and the pastor asked, "Who gives this woman to this man?"

Khadafy and I looked into each other's eyes and said simultaneously, "Our hearts."

There wasn't a dry eye in the church, and I was indeed the luckiest woman in the world; at least that was what I thought.

For a bride, you didn't really get to enjoy your wedding, but our wedding was different. I danced until my feet and my red bottoms had a major disagreement. When I sat down, Khadafy came over to me and stated, "They are playing our song," with his hand extended waiting on mine.

I wanted to dance with my husband, but my feet had different plans. "Baby, I just sat down. My feet are killing me," I stated and gave him my puppy dog eyes.

Khadafy walked away, and I couldn't tell by his face that he wasn't happy about me not wanting to dance. He simply made his way back out to the dance floor and found one of our friends and began dancing with her.

I smiled as I watched our friends enjoy our wedding.

After that dance, it was time to cut the cake. Khadafy made it clear that he didn't want cake smashed in his face, but that was a tradition I wasn't breaking.

Carmen Lashay, T. Nicole, Ty Leese Javeh, Eden Mireya, Sparkle Lewis, Reign, & Armani

After the toast and after the cake was cut, we took some amazing pictures, and then it happened.

I smashed the cake in Khadafy's face and was shocked by his actions.

"What the fuck is wrong with you, Zara?" he spat, and the few people within ear shot gasped at his reaction. He swiped the cake from his face, gave me a look that I would become accustomed to, and it seemed as if in that moment, many things changed in our relationship.

***

"Hurry up and get yo ass in the car," Khadafy said as we said our goodbyes to our guests.

I hurried as fast as my feet would take me, and when we got into the limo, that was when it started.

Slap! "Bitch, didn't I tell you not to smash cake in my face? Muthafucka, turn yo' ass around and drive this shit where the fuck you supposed to be driving us to." Raising the partition, Khadafy started slapping me and speaking to me with every hit.

"Didn't, I, tell, yo', dumb, ass, not, to, smash, cake, in, my, face?"

Tears spilled from my eyes as I shielded my face and watched the blood from my nose cover the front of my dress.

Khadafy sat back, out of breath, and then poured a drink.

"I'm sorry, Khadafy. I just wanted to have fun."

"Well, how fun was it to have yo' ass beat?" he countered, and I was shocked.

Thoughts of an annulment flooded my mind as we made our way to our hotel.

We walked in, went to the desk, and Khadafy immediately lied about me having nose bleeds and wanted to hurry to our room to rest before our honeymoon.

That night, we made love as if we would never see each other again, and magically, all of my thoughts about leaving went away.

Doctor Li's voice snapped me out of my memory.

"Here's a tissue," he said, passing me a box a Kleenex. I took a few tissues from the box, snickering. I didn't even know I was crying, and most importantly, I didn't even know why. I knew what I was dealing with but was too afraid to speak out against it. So I guess I was laughing to keep from crying.

"Zara, we are coming to the end of our session. We can pick this up again on your next visit?"

I shrugged my shoulders.

He placed his hand on top of mine and began to speak. "Zara, I can't tell you exactly what to do. I can tell you to be safe, and remove yourself from any situation that's not allowing you to be in a healthy environment."

"Thanks, Doc, but what is a healthy environment?" I questioned, really wanting him to tell me. I'd been stuck in my situation for so long that it seemed normal to me even though I knew deep down that it wasn't.

Doctor Li closed his notepad and turned off his recorder, signaling that our session was over.

"So Doctor Li, no assignment for me to do during the next few days?" I asked as the nurse entered the room.

Doctor Li was known to always have something for you to think about, and it was the first thing discussed on your next visit.

"Of course. I want you to really think about the terms happiness and perfect. What does happiness mean to you, and what would you consider to be a perfect life."

I allowed the doctor's words to seep into my system as I tried to understand the meat and potatoes of what he was really trying to get at.

"Okay, Doctor Li, I'll see you in a few days," I replied, nodding in agreement, and then the nurse escorted me out the office in a wheelchair.

With my head hung low to hide the bruises, the nurse wheeled me down the corridor of the hospital. On my way back to my room, I glanced around at the many people that were visiting their loved ones. Some looked worried or concerned, some looked as if they were nervous, and some looked heartbroken or sad, while life for everyone else goes on, I'm just here existing, as if nothing was wrong.

My eyes started to fill with tears. I had been in this hospital for almost two weeks now, and no one had even tried to visit me, not even Khadafy, my husband, the man who put me here.

"Is everything okay, Zara? Do you need anything?" the nurse asked, helping me out of the wheelchair and onto the bed.

Carmen Lashay, T. Nicole, Ty Leese Javeh, Eden Mireya,
Sparkle Lewis, Reign, & Armani

I shook my head no as I slid up on the bed, grimacing from the pain in my spine. She adjusted my pillow, fixed the tube to my IV bag so it wouldn't be in my way, and then jotted something down in my charts before exiting my room.

I wish I'd known then what I knew now because had I left when I first thought about it, I wouldn't be here suffering in this hell hole today.

Session 2

Most African Americans didn't talk about their issues with a counselor or shrink or whatever you wanted to call them. We were taught to keep our business in our house and pray for better days. Just like in *The Color Purple*, Celie's father told her she bet not tell nobody but God. But to me, I didn't even think God cared enough to listen to the hell that I was going through.

Things in my house had gotten so bad that I was now breaking an unspoken rule by sharing my thoughts and feelings. I wasn't sure what this would solve, but here I was, telling a perfect stranger my business.

"So Zara, last time, we talked a little about your relationship. I want to kind of go back to that. Tell me about Khadafy."

"What do you want to know? He beats me; that's about it."

"Did he take you places, like on dates?"

"Yeah, he loved having me on his arm. Sometimes, that's all I thought I was: a trophy wife. He loved to show me off but hated for men to look at me."

"How did it make you feel when he took you out and showed you off?"

"Like a piece of meat. But not all the dates made me feel like that. Some were good, some were not. And honestly, I don't know how they made me feel. I mean, what was I supposed to feel? Loved?"

"That's one way that dates should make you feel. Did you feel loved on your dates?"

"It's funny you should ask that. I guess people show love in different ways. I mean, dates aren't so cut and dry these days, right?" I stated as I looked at my counselor for confirmation in the question I just asked to him.

"Well, I want to know more about what you think and not so much about how society views dating."

"Well, when I was younger, I remember watching the movie *Miss Congeniality*. This movie always had me believing that even if the odds are against me, I could be whoever I wanted to be, and all I have to do is remain true to myself. My favorite part of that movie is when Miss Rhode Island gets a question about the perfect date. If life was only as romantic and perfect as she simply stated, April 25, because it's not too hot, not too cold. All you need is a light jacket!"

"So are you saying that you agree with her? This is the first time you actually smiled since we've been talking."

"No, I'm not really saying that I agree. I remembered that part of the movie, and it's funny because me and Khadafy met in April, and every year on that day, we went out on the night of our first date. At first, those dates meant something to me; they made me feel special and loved, I guess I could say. But a few years ago, Khadafy took those special feelings away from me. I remember getting dressed up for our date. I made sure everything was perfect from my hair being in a nice, neat tucked bun to my natural makeup and red popping lips. You couldn't tell me that I wasn't a show stopper that night. With my white, plunging V-neck with the cape pantsuit with my Ramour Suede Red Sole Pump, I knew I was looking good. I wanted to make sure my man knew that I did all of this for him. I arrived at the restaurant about twenty minutes before him. I ordered drinks and enjoyed the soft-playing music."

"So it was perfect—nice restaurant, soft music, and good wine," Dr. Li interrupted.

"No, not at all. It was, let's say, not so perfect. Khadafy arrived at the restaurant late, complained about the food, told me that I was dumb for picking the restaurant, and pulled me out as if he were a parent, disciplining his child. When we got home, he didn't acknowledge any of the things that I did for him around the house. He simply beat my ass for wasting his time. I was beyond hurt, and not just by the actions of him beating me but because I couldn't make him happy. I knew then that something needed to change."

"So what did you change?"

"Nothing. I created a pattern that was easy to follow. I allowed him to talk down to me and allowed him to beat me only to get in the room and perform any and every sexual task that he demanded. Now, Doc, you tell me. Was that a perfect date?"

"I'm only here to listen, record, and help you improve."

"That's cute, Doc. Well, help me to improve by removing myself from this situation."

"I can't. Only you can do that."

"Right… Only I can do that. Sessions over, right, Doc?"

"Zara, I will like to dig deeper into this next session. Think about happier times in your marriage. I will like to discuss those times."

"Happier times, huh? Did we ever really have those? See you next time, Doc."

Session 3

"I see you're walking better, Zara," Doctor Li mentioned when I entered into his office.

"Yeah, Dr. Bradshaw said that I'm healing well. I mean, at least I can walk with a cane now, right?"

"Small steps, Zara, small steps. So as I told you last session, I want to discuss happier times. Tell me about those."

"What's to tell? I mean, those times used to be my go-to place in my mind. Whenever he beat me or talked down on me, I would think about those times, hoping and praying that we could somehow get back to that place. At times, Khadafy can be so sweet, and I'll forget about the Devil that he has inside of him." I paused as I could feel a lump forming in my throat.

"Go on."

"Like this one time, I had just finished cleaning the house, and I was lying across the bed, trying to relax for a while before cooking dinner. I heard the door open and close, letting me know that Khadafy was home early. I'm not gonna lie, Doc. I was scared as hell. Khadafy was unpredictable, so I wasn't sure if he was gonna come in the room angry or not. I sat up on the bed, heart beating through my chest and holding my breath, waiting to see which Khadafy was coming through that door. I turned around, and Khadafy was in the doorway smiling at me. At this point in our relationship, I hadn't seen him smile in a while. It was a beautiful sight. I smiled back at him. He walked over toward me, scooped me off of the bed and into his arms, and twirled me around. He kissed me oh so passionately; it was like the first time he kissed me. I felt his heart and soul in that kiss."

"When you talked about that moment, you started beaming. How did that moment make you feel?"

"Special like Khadafy really loved me. After we kissed, he broke down and cried. He said that he loved me to death, then he promised that he wouldn't hurt me anymore. He started humming a slow tune, and it took me a few seconds, but I realized he was humming our wedding song. 'Here and Now.' He started rocking slowly from side to side as he held me tightly. He whispered in my ear, 'I'm so sorry for all the pain I caused you,' then he pulled away, and with tears in his eyes, he continued speaking. 'It's just that I love you so much that I don't know what to do. I never had a woman to have my heart, soul, mind, and my body. I'm all yours, baby, and you are mine. This is it for me. I will never love another woman the way that I love you.' He kissed me again then gently laid me down on the bed and slowly undressed me. His touch was so gentle, and his words were so kind, and I knew in that moment, he was genuinely speaking from his heart. And when he made love to me that night, he handled me as if I were a fragile piece of fine China. He paid extra attention to my body and made me feel wanted and loved. That's the Khadafy that I know and love. That's the Khadafy that I think about when I'm experiencing the wrath or the other one."

"You speak of him as if he's two people."

"Because he is. When Khadafy is drunk or high off drugs, he becomes a man that I don't recognize. But when he's completely sober, he turns back in to the loving man that I fell so hard for." Wiping tears off my face, I sat all the way up I my seat. "I think that's why it's been so hard to leave him. He went through a lot when he lost his job, and he became depressed, I think."

"What made you think he was depressed?"

"His increase in drinking and drug use. It became an everyday thing. I thought I could save him. Besides me, he only had his mother. But that bitch didn't give a fuck. In my eyes, I was all Khadafy had, and if I left, he had nobody. Sometimes, Doc, I think I love that man more than I love myself."

The dinging of the bell let me know that my session was over,

"Zara, I want you to think about happiness—what happiness looks like to you and what will make you happy."

"I can answer those questions right now." I chuckled as I grabbed my cane and stood up.

"Well, save that for the next session. I want you to think long and hard about those questions, and I want to see you again in two days."

"Okay, I'll clear my schedule. I guess I can pencil you in. Have a good one, Doc."

"You too, Zara."

Carmen Lashay, T. Nicole, Ty Leese Javeh, Eden Mireya,
Sparkle Lewis, Reign, & Armani

The Final Session

"Hello, Doctor Li. Did you hear? I'm getting out of here tomorrow."

"That's good news, Zara, but I want to continue therapy with you. I have an office outside of the hospital. I would like to see you there."

"I don't think so, Doc. Khadafy will never allow me to go to therapy."

"So you're going back?"

"Where else am I going to go, Doc? I have no one." I shrugged.

"You can reach out to your family."

"And say what? I'm sorry I haven't spoken to you all in years, but Khadafy beat the shit out of me. Can I come live with you?"

"That's a start."

I shook my head. "I don't think so, Doc."

"Zara, let's talk about your family. How was your childhood?"

"Really, Doc? My childhood? What you want me to tell you? I was abused, raped, or abandoned? I can't tell you that, because it would be a lie. My childhood was as close to perfect as you can get. I had two parents that loved me and showed me every day. I wasn't spoiled, but I got mostly everything that I wanted. My parents even spent a lot of time with me. If you want to hear about a fucked up childhood, you need to talk to Khadafy about that."

"So are you saying that Khadafy had a bad childhood?"

"No... Maybe... Well, I don't know. He never talked about his childhood. But for him to be the monster that he is, something had to happen. I mean, his mother is a piece of shit. You know the apple really don't fall far from the tree."

"You speak of his mother as if you have animosity toward her."

"Animosity? I fucking hate her," I chuckled.

"Why is that, Zara?"

"Why? Let me tell you why. See, my husband had a wondering eye, and soon, his whole body started wondering. So I was trying to keep my body right for my husband. So while he's out working and making money, I try to stay fit and hit the gym. I don't know why when we, as women, are faced with infidelity and things like that, we immediately attack ourselves and never realize that we might not be the problem. Nonetheless, I wanted my man to never have a wondering eye again. I wanted to be his everything and have a banging body in the process."

"So you blamed yourself for his infidelity?"

"Doc, I blamed myself for everything. Khadafy would tell me that if I didn't do this or if I didn't do that, then maybe he wouldn't do the things that he did. So naturally, I started believing it."

"So do you blame his behavior on his mother?"

"Hell yeah, I blame her because she never says anything. She knew what her son was doing, and she turned a blind eye to it. This last time, Doc, she was there. I was at the gym, working out, and I realized that I'd stayed ten minutes too long. I needed to rush to the grocery store and get dinner on the table before 5:00 P.M. I sped down the highway, getting off the expressway so I could stop at the seafood market to grab some shrimp, lobster, and crabs. I figured a seafood feast would be quick and easy. All I needed was to grab some asparagus and potatoes from the grocery store down the street and then be on my way to our beautiful home before Khadafy would get there."

"So you always had to be home before he did?"

"Yeah, I had to be home—period. He didn't like me to go out without him unless I was grocery shopping. When I arrived home, my heart dropped. Khadafy was already home, and there wasn't anything on the stove. As soon as I got in the kitchen, Khadafy started in on me. Doc, it's like if I close my eyes, I'm right back in that moment."

"Zara, tell me. Put yourself back into that moment. What happened that day?" I closed my eyes and began telling Dr. Li how it all went down.

"Where the hell have you been?" Khadafy questioned. I would've been a fool to tell him that I went to the gym and then finally to the store to get his dinner. He wouldn't be happy at being an afterthought, but he also wouldn't be too fond of my being at the gym around a bunch of men.

"I-I went to the store to get dinner," I stated in a shaky voice.

"Yo' ass don't fucking work, and you waited until it was time for me to get home to go get me something to eat? Da' fuck wrong with you?" he yelled.

I jumped, dropping the bags. I slowly leaned over to pick them up, nervous as hell because Khadafy was standing right in front of me. I had to brace myself because I knew it was coming. I knew he was about to punish me, but he shocked me. Khadafy didn't hit me. He lifted my chin and planted a kiss on my lips and told me that his mother would be there in an hour. Then he kissed my lips again. "Don't fuck this night up, do you understand?"

"What did he mean by don't mess up the night? Was it a special occasion?"

Not at all. Khadafy liked to keep up an image, and even though his mother knew what was going on, he still wanted us to appear as the loving, happy couple we pretended to be. He didn't want me to do anything to upset him. That's what he meant. I did what I was told. I nodded my head quickly and began taking out pots and pans and got my ass in gear to make the perfect meal.

With my mother-in-law on the way, I had a feeling it was going to be a great evening. So I thought. As I sit here and tell you this shit, Doc, I swear it plays in my head as if I'm watching a movie of my life. Khadafy went upstairs to get dressed, and when he came down, his mother was there, and I was still cooking.

"Bitch, I told you to have this shit on the table and ready! Didn't I?" Khadafy yelled and went upside my head."

I paused and took a deep breath, as I wiped the tears off of my face.

"I was so embarrassed that his mom was there, Doc, and she didn't say a fucking word. She just watched as her son beat me. For each blow that I took, I couldn't help but to be angry. This woman, a married woman, a supposedly God-fearing woman, watched her son beat the shit out of me and did nothing to help. Maybe she was getting her ass beat at home too. I don't know. I just don't understand how she could stand there and not try to intervene in no way. Honestly, Doc, if I was her husband, I'd beat her for having three chins, big, square coke-bottle glasses, a dry ass curly weave, and walking around with a baseball cap. Bitch is ugly as fuck and raised a pissed-poor piece of shit as a son."

Carmen Lashay, T. Nicole, Ty Leese Javeh, Eden Mireya, Sparkle Lewis, Reign, & Armani

"Zara, that isn't nice to say or to wish upon somebody."

"Well, Doc, haven't you noticed by now I'm not nice? Khadafy hit me so hard that I fell to the ground. He stood over of me, screaming in my face as he yanked me up by my shirt collar."

"Answer me dammit! Didn't I tell you to have this shit ready? Now my mom has to wait because yo' slow ass didn't want to do what the fuck I asked you to do. If you do the shit right the first time, we wouldn't have to go through this dumb shit," he stated, choking me as I begged him to stop.

"Khadafy, please stop. I can't breathe," I managed to get out as his massive hands squeezed my neck tighter. I was struggling to breathe as I tried to scratch at his hands.

I shook my head, chuckling.

"I swear, Doc, he seemed to enjoy my pain. He slung me across the room. That's when I managed to suck in as much air as my lungs could take in. I thought it was over but then slowly realized it had only just begun.

Punch after punch, kick after kick, Khadafy abused my body until he worked himself into exhaustion, then he threw me into the wall as hard as he could, making me hit my head. Then he started choking me again. I didn't fight this time. I was tired of the beating, and I happily welcomed the darkness. But right before I blacked out, I asked his mother why didn't she help. She said that's what men do, then she turned her head. It was in that moment that I knew for sure nothing would save me from this situation. Not even his ugly ass momma. When I opened my eyes, I had no idea how long I'd been sleeping. I moved, and a jolt of pain rushed through my body, and then I realized I hadn't been sleep. This was a result of Khadafy beating me. I tried my best to move. I was in so much discomfort that it was hard for me to find a comfortable position. I finally found one and started trying to focus so that I could see where I was. My vision was blurred, so I had to adjust my eyes so that I could focus. I glanced around room and realized that I was alone, here in the hospital."

I burst into tears.

"Zara, we can stop if you want so you can get yourself together."

"What's wrong with me that I can't find love? I mean really. I'm not sure what I'm doing to cause Khadafy or any man to turn his hands of love to the fist of fury."

"Zara, it's not you."

"It must be, Doc. When I think about each of my relationships, they either ended with a man cheating on me or a man beating on me. I was able to get out of those, and I know I can get out of this one, but there's only one thing holding me back... Khadafy is by far the craziest man I'd ever been with." Realizing that I had made the right decision, I cried my last cry, then I took a deep, cleansing breath and stood up.

"My session is over, Doc."

"Okay, Zara. I think you've had enough for the day. Will I see you in my office in a few days?"

"Will you?" I shrugged. "Goodbye, Doctor Li."

I left his office and headed back to my room. *Was there a way for me to get out? Could I make myself disappear? Could I just go back home and beg my parents and friends to accept me back into their lives? So many questions and not enough answers*, I thought as I started gathering my belongings so I could be completely prepared to be discharged first thing in the morning.

...

It was the morning of my release. I'd called Khadafy and asked him to come pick me up, but of course, he said he was busy. He sounded irritated and hung up the phone, so I called back. When Khadafy started yelling, I really had my mind made up that today would be the day that I became a free woman.

"Zara, here are your discharge papers. Your primary care physician will need to see you in a week, and Dr. Li is requesting that you come in for a visit within the next two days," my nurse stated, handing me my papers to sign.

I smiled, not because I was happy, but because I knew what had to be done, and today was going to be the day.

"Thank you so much. The staff here is amazing, and please tell Dr. Li he's helped me so much, and now I can see clearly, and I'm sure I will no longer need his services."

"Well, with patient confidentiality, I'm not able to discuss your personal needs with Dr. Li. I can only hope that you follow up as directed. Will you be needing a wheelchair?"

"No, I'm fine," I stated as I put the cane down and no longer wanted assistance.

I walked out of the hospital doors, and the Maryland breeze hit my face. Spring time. *All you need is a light jacket*, I thought as I opened my arms and stretched them wide, allowing all of my papers and documents to blow freely. They were blowing in the wind, flying like birds.

"Freedom." I smiled as I began walking with a limp as I made the journey home.

"I'm on my way home, Khadafy. I'm on my way home." I said as I walked, thinking about the good and bad times. The walk was about a good hour, so I stopped off, leisurely got some ice cream, and continued on my way.

"That's a nice purse," a woman said as I was leaving Baskin Robins.

I smiled, and I think I shocked her with my response. "Here. You like, you can have it." I hugged her, and she looked confused.

"Lady, your things are still in here!" she screamed and I ignored her because I had to get home to Khadafy.

"You can have it! Enjoy!" I called back as I knew freedom was just around the corner, as I was only about a few blocks away from home.

When I finally made it to my block, I took in the neighborhood and began looking at the grass. A piece of paper blew past me in the wind, and I used it as a sign.

"It's time to set him free," I said as I made the final few steps toward my house and finally opened the door.

Carmen Lashay, T. Nicole, Ty Leese Javeh, Eden Mireya, Sparkle Lewis, Reign, & Armani

Epilogue

Khadafy

I was kicking back on the bed when Zara came in looking all crazy with a goofy smile on her face. It seemed as if she'd lost a few pounds from her stay in the hospital. I was glad that she was back because Monique's ass stood me up, and I couldn't get my dick wet, so I was ready to pounce in that pussy.

I saw that chrome pistol in her hand, and my heart sank. All of the many beatings that I put this woman through were finally coming back to haunt me. I didn't have time to react. This was definitely the end.

I cocked my head to the side after Zara said, "I'm free, and so are you!"

POW!

"Shit! Zara what the fuck did you do! What did you do?"

Zara's body dropped to the floor as blood began to leak from her temple, and brain matter was now decorating our eggshell colored walls.

"Fuck! Fuck! Dammit, Zara, why did you do this?" I screamed as I immediately took to her side. As tears began to roll out of my eyes, I was again reminded by all the beatings I'd given her, the way I separated her from her family and treated her like shit, and I never appreciated her, and now she was gone.

"I'm so sorry, Zara. I'm so sorry! Why did you do this?" I cried as I held her body and rocked her as my tears began to mix with her blood. Blood, sweat, and tears was what she put into our marriage, and I treated her as if she were nothing.

My eyes darted to a white piece of folded paper, and my curiosity got the best of me.

Removing my wife from my lap, I picked up the paper, and it read, *Khadafy, you couldn't show me the love that I desired, so I'm going to set myself free. The only time you paid me any attention was when you wanted sex or wanted to put me into the hospital, so I'm setting myself free. If I try to leave, you will find me. If I stay, you will kill me. I'm doing this for the both of us. I'm setting me and you free. You are now free to do as you please, but I'm no longer here to allow you to beat me. I love you, but I'm choosing me, and now I'm free.*

Set me free

Carmen Lashay, T. Nicole, Ty Leese Javeh, Eden Mireya,
Sparkle Lewis, Reign, & Armani

Set me free so I can blow through the trees like a
nice, relaxing summer breeze
Set me free so I can fly high like the birds in the
sky
I feel like a prisoner, trapped in a cell. My
capture's pain is where I dwell
Set me free. I want to dance in the moonlight or
twinkle with the stars as they shine bright in the night
Set me free. I want to walk among the clouds
while I smile down on you, feeling oh so proud
I'm stuck in the darkness of your heart, behind a
closed, locked door
I don't see the person that I love anymore
It's like someone put out the light in you. Where's
the fight in you?
Set me free. You have a full life to live, and there
is so much more you have to give
Set me free because it's the only way that we both
can be happy. It's important so that our souls could
peacefully rest

Set me free. Life has ended for me, but for you, it's

not over. You can still live life to its fullest

But first, you must set me free

The End

From Author Ty Leese Jaweh

I give thanks to God for giving guidance when I needed it the most, for answering my prayers and blessing me with the gift of creativity, and most of all, I thank God for the readers who enjoy my books.

To my publisher, Treasure Malian, thank you for giving me this opportunity. I appreciate you even though there may have been times when you felt as if I didn't.

To my sisters, my daughter, granddaughter, family, and friends, I love you all so much. It's because of your encouragement as well as your support that makes me want to continue to strive for success.

T. Nicole: Words can't express the amount of gratitude I have for you. In this short period of time, we went from pen sisters, to friends, and now we are more

Carmen Lashay, T. Nicole, Ty Leese Javeh, Eden Mireya, Sparkle Lewis, Reign, & Armani

like sisters. You push me to my limits, and you give me a swift kick in the you know what when I need it the most. It's funny how we seem to always be in sync and thinking the same thing. I'm glad to have a beautiful person like you in my corner cheering me on.

Finally, to the readers, I can't thank you enough for supporting me, reading my work, and leaving reviews. It's your feedback that helps me to continue to grow as an author. I love and appreciate you all so much. I'm a firm believer in the quote "If it wasn't for you, then there would be no me." That stands true for me. Every book you purchase or post helps my dream become a reality. I promise that I will continue to grow and bring you entertaining storylines to keep you wanting more.

Words can't express how truly blessed I am. No matter how stressed out or discouraged that I've gotten, there was always someone in my corner who believed in me and wouldn't allow me to give up. I will continue to push myself and find my way in the literary world. With the continuing support from the readers, my pen sisters and brothers, and my family and friends, I'm sure that I can be successful.

Check out my other books available on Amazon and Barnes & Noble:

Survivor of Love 1 and 2

Adonis and Venus 1, 2, and 3

Lovin' You Ain't Good for Me

All I Want Is You

I Need Somebody Down for Me 1 and 2

Committed To Love 1 and 2

Giving My Heart to a Savage- Who Could Love You Like I Do?

Loving a Gangsta Isn't For The Faint Heart

Shades of Love: Fighting for His Heart

Carmen Lashay, T. Nicole, Ty Leese Javeh, Eden Mireya,
Sparkle Lewis, Reign, & Armani

"Broken Promises, Shattered Dreams: A Scary Thing Called Love"

Ms. T. Nicole

Copyright © 2017 Ms. T. Nicole

Thank you for taking the time to read my work.

Follow me on my social media to find out about upcoming projects and work

Twitter: Tomeika_Diva

Facebook:

https://www.facebook.com/MsTNicole/?fref=ts

Instagram: @creativediva12

YouTube: www.youtube.com/creativediva12

Carmen Lashay, T. Nicole, Ty Leese Javeh, Eden Mireya, Sparkle Lewis, Reign, & Armani

Acknowledgements

This book is intended to entertain and is recommended for ages sixteen and up. This is a book based on urban fiction, so please be advised that it will contain explicit language and adult content.

I truly want to thank God for giving me the gift to entertain through my words and twisted mind. When others thought and said that I was crazy, I used those words and picked up a pen. The day that happened was the day that changed my life. No matter what happens in my life, I want to truly take the time to say thank you to the family members and close friends who always stand by and support me. No matter what I pen, you all are always pushing me to do more and make me feel as if I could one day be great.

Mom, you are amazing; you never once allowed me to believe that failure was an option. Alexandria, you may not be able to read any of my books, but just know that Mommy loves you and will always do whatever I can to show you the same love and support just as your grandma has done with me. I love you, baby doll.

I want to thank my siblings for always being an ear and shoulder for me. No matter what I faced in life, and Lord knows the last six months have been trying, you all have been there for me, and I love you and can't thank you enough. When I wanted to give up and throw in the towel, you all wouldn't allow me to do that, so for that, I'm saying thank you.

My promise to you all is that I will continue to use this gift and allow my gift to make room for me. Let's get to the top. ☺ Love you all -MiMi

Carmen Lashay, T. Nicole, Ty Leese Javeh, Eden Mireya,
Sparkle Lewis, Reign, & Armani

**"Broken Promises, Shattered Dreams: A Scary
Type of Love"**

A domestic violence awareness short story

Synopsis

When it comes to domestic violence, many women suffer in silence, and it was no different for twenty-four-year-old Natasha. When Natasha first met Rome, she thought she had finally met the perfect man. He was tall, handsome, and a successful business owner. Natasha didn't think that a man like Rome would ever be interested in anything but sex, but she followed her heart and embarked on a journey of what she thought was love.

To Natasha, at first glance, Rome was different from the rest. He was a real gentleman; he was loving, caring, and attentive to all of Natasha's needs, and he was able to quickly capture her heart. Little did Natasha know, Rome's love came with a price.

Take a journey through the eyes of Natasha as she navigates through different aspects of her relationship, and find out how high of a price she paid for falling for the wrong man.

Please be aware that this is a short story concerning domestic violence.

Carmen Lashay, T. Nicole, Ty Leese Javeh, Eden Mireya, Sparkle Lewis, Reign, & Armani

Prologue

"Stop! Please, Rome, you said you would never… Ahhhhh, please… Ahh, pl-eee-aaa-se! I'm sorry, Rome, don't do this!"

"Shut up bitch!" *Boom!* "Natasha, I swear if the police come here, I'll kill you! Shut the fuck up with all of that screaming. You couldn't leave well enough alone, could you? You had to open your fucking mouth!"

Rome beat, kicked, and stomped me for what seemed like hours, but as I watched the digital clock while he dragged me around our three-bedroom home, I noticed that it had only been minutes.

This abuse seemed to have been getting worse and worse as the months continued to roll by. What did I do to deserve this? Well, the answer to that question was simple. I allowed a man to love me with his fists, and disregarded my own heart. I knew I had never been this weak of a woman to allow such things to happen. I needed to get out of this, and each day that I was alive, it was a struggle. Now, a better question was, *Will I be brave enough to make it out, or will he kill me?*

My name is Natasha, and this is my story.

Carmen Lashay, T. Nicole, Ty Leese Javeh, Eden Mireya, Sparkle Lewis, Reign, & Armani

How We Met

"Girl, this club is hella lit!" I screamed over the music into my girl Brittany's ear as we danced with each other, checking out the niggas who were popping bottles and hitting on these fake Instagram famous bitches.

"Girl, check out that nigga right there. He's been checking you out since we been working this fucking floor," Brittany said, and I slowly winded my hips in a full 360° turn so that I wasn't noticeably trying to check him out.

As I turned and continued dancing on Brittany, I noticed a tall, sexy, chocolate looking man wearing all white everything approaching us.

"Bitch, that nigga is coming this way!" Brittany squealed, acting like a thirsty school girl.

I played it cool and made it seem like I was only interested in having fun with my girl, so I danced and smiled, paying him little to no attention.

As he got closer to us on the dance floor, I really got a chance to take in all his features.

He was tall. He appeared to be about six two, and his smooth, ebony skin seemed to look as if it were glistening under the dim club lights. Although his clothes fit him a little loose, I could tell that this man's body was cut and chiseled to perfection. His face displayed a strong jawline, which made his goatee stand out on his face. His small, round eyes were set kind of deep, which made his cheek bones appear as if they were sculptured to fit his face perfectly. This man was a god, and I was too ready to be his goddess. He was standing directly in front of me, and I couldn't ignore the aroma that bounced off his body. God, this man smelled delightful, and his smile displayed a perfect set of white teeth.

"Hello, beautiful. Give your girl a break and dance with me," he said in this sexy, deep baritone voice that instantly had my panties moist, but I didn't want to appear too damn thirsty for this hot, sexy god of a man.

"I don't even know you!" I spoke over the music.

"Well, usually people meet when someone introduces themselves. I'm Rome, and you are?" he questioned, and I began to giggle.

"Her name is Natasha, and she don't have a man," Brittany blurted out, and I was too damn embarrassed. Brittany didn't know a thing about keeping shit cool, but

I was trying to play my part and not seem as desperate as she was making me look.

"I'm Rome, and I don't have a woman," he countered and held out his hand to shake my hand.

I took his hand, and the gaze that our eyes held had my stomach turning flips. I didn't know what had gotten into me, but I wanted to instantly bounce on this man's dick and ride him until the angels called my name to take me to the king.

"It's nice to meet you, Rome. Do you come here often?" I questioned, and he smiled and responded.

"Of course, I own it."

Yes, thank you, God, not another broke ass nigga trying to be something that he's not. I'm definitely fucking this man tonight, I thought as I smiled like a kid in the candy store, not realizing I still had his hand.

"May I have my hand back? But I'd love to get to know you so I can give you my heart."

"Um, you can definitely have your hand back, and you can keep your weak ass pickup line. I know your type. Try again, handsome. Not working over here," I stated, letting him know that I knew he was running that slick ass game on my ass.

He smirked, ignoring the fact that I called him out on his weak ass game, and then he took me by the hand. "You don't know my type. Don't ever compare me to another nigga, but I'm going to dance with you, we are going to exchange numbers, and you will be my woman," he stated with finality.

I was stunned, in shock, not really understanding how this perfect stranger had a hold on me. I didn't protest and followed his lead.

He led me to the middle of the dance floor, and I swear it seemed as if a spotlight came on, and we were the only ones in the club. I wasn't sure if he had the DJ to slow the music down, but when he grabbed me around my waist, K-Ci & JoJo began to blare through the speakers.

I will never find another lover sweeter than you
Sweeter than you
And I will never find another lover more precious than you
More precious than you
Girl, you are close to me, you're like my mother
Close to me, you're like my father

Carmen Lashay, T. Nicole, Ty Leese Javeh, Eden Mireya,
Sparkle Lewis, Reign, & Armani

Close to me, you're like my sister
Close to me, you're like my brother
You are the only one, you are my everything, and for you
this song I sing

The intense look that Rome was giving me as we danced had me ready to agree with whatever he was thinking. It was like we had this instant connection that I couldn't explain, and you couldn't tell me that I wasn't going to be happy with this cocky ass man forever.

The song went off, and Brittany was smiling like she'd won the lottery as we walked back over to her.

"Nigga, you better not be playing games with my girl!" Brittany yelled, and you could tell that the alcohol that she consumed was getting the best of her.

"Natasha, give me your number. I would like to call you and get to know you," Rome demanded, and I was lost in his eyes and couldn't say no.

I took his phone, saved my number, and handed it back to him. He stood with a cocky smirk, and I smiled while shaking my head.

"Well, you ladies have a wonderful rest of your evening, and Natasha, baby, I'll see you sooner than later."

Rome was sexy, and his swag was on a million. I didn't want to seem too damn eager, but when he walked off, Brittany and I both started screaming and cheering.

I was twenty-one years old when we met, young, naïve and full of life. I had no idea that this encounter would change my life tremendously.

Our First Date

3 Weeks Later

"Ma, no, I'm not driving up there. I'm about to run my errands and then relax for the rest of the day," I said, talking to my mom who was bugging me to drive home to see her and Dad. It was only an hour drive, but I just didn't feel like taking that drive. I was tired of always being the one to initiate seeing them. If they wanted to see me that bad, they would get in the car and make the drive to me.

After working these crazy swing shifts as a Walgreens manager, I enjoyed my down time to get things done for me, and that was exactly what I was planning on doing today.

"Well, Ma, I'm not coming. Just tell Dad maybe another time. I'm getting cold, and I have to finish getting dressed. I just got out the shower, Ma," I spoke, ending the call with my mom so I could get myself together.

I was fresh out of the shower, preparing for my day, and my phone started ringing again. I just knew it was my mom calling back to try to make me feel bad about not coming, so I ignored the call, and then the phone started ringing again, and although annoyed, I looked back at my phone.

Looking at the screen, Rome's name and picture displayed on the screen. I laughed because it was a picture that Brittany snapped the night I met him at his club.

I instantly got butterflies in my stomach. I didn't know what it was about this man, but every time I talked to him or thought about him, I got butterflies. I quickly snatched the phone up off the bed, and answered it.

"Hello, beautiful," he said as soon as I answered the phone, and I giggled.

"Hi, handsome," I replied.

"What are you doing?" he asked, and my smile grew wide.

"I just got out of the shower." I tried to sound as sexy as I could, but the never-ending giggles that I had made my little flirtation act seem a bit juvenile.

"Oh, yeah? I wish I was there, I could use a good cleaning myself," Rome replied, and I gasped.

"So you're just going to come straight out and say that, huh?" I stated, still smiling, knowing that I wasn't offended by him flirting but more so turned on. He'd been asking me out for the past three weeks, and I was playing hard to get, knowing that I was feeling this man.

"Stop playing yourself, girl. You know damn well that pussy's getting wet, thinking about a nigga," he continued, and I couldn't stop giggling.

"Why are you so straight forward?" I asked.

"Because there's no reason to beat around the bush. We're grown, right?"

"Yeah, I just haven't had a man to come straight out talking to me like you," I admitted.

"Well, that's too bad these niggas can't speak their mind. That's not me, and again, I don't like to be compared to other niggas; I'm my own man."

Cradling the phone on my shoulder, I continued getting dressed, and Rome continued speaking.

"So what's your plans for today?"

"I have a few errands to run, but other than that, nothing."

"Great, so that means I can finally get that date I been asking for." He sounded as if he were telling me instead of asking me.

I rolled my eyes at the phone in a playful way as if he could see me.

"I guess. I mean… are you asking me on a date?"

"Naw, I been asking for a few weeks, so now I'm telling you. You're spending the day with me, so after you run your errands, you need to call me, and I'll meet you at your house. Oh, grab a swimsuit." He ended the call without even waiting for my response. I shook my head and smiled at how direct he was, put my phone on the bed, finished getting dressed, grabbed my keys and purse, and headed out of the door to handle my business for the day.

***

Rushing through my door, I tossed my keys on the table and my purse on the sofa. I had to hurry and take a shower before Rome made it here for our date. He didn't tell me where we were going, but he did say to grab a swimsuit, so I decided to put on a pair of denim shorts and a white crop top with my brand-new two-piece underneath.

I hopped in the shower and lathered up with my Forever Red body wash from Bath & Body Works. As the scent filled the air, I started imagining Rome's massive hands rubbing the suds all over my body. I started to feel tingles down below. Shaking off the feelings, I quickly rinsed the body wash off, got out of the shower, and proceeded to get dressed.

As soon as I was putting the finishing touches on my makeup, Rome was knocking at the door. I gave myself the once over in the mirror then hurried to the door.

"Hello, gorgeous," Rome greeted, standing at the door, holding a bouquet of roses.

"Rome, they're beautiful." I put the bouquet up to my nose and took a whiff. "They smell wonderful. Thank you." As I was putting the roses in a vase, I noticed that it wasn't a dozen, only eleven. "Um… Rome, it's only eleven roses here. I think the florist made a mistake," I chuckled.

Rome grabbed my hands then turned me around to face him. Looking deep into my eyes, he responded by saying, "I asked for only eleven. The twelfth rose is you."

I was ready to fuck the shit outta this man. A mile-wide smile grew on my face as butterflies continued to grow in the pit of my stomach. *How romantic*, I thought.

"You ready?" he asked as he started leading me toward the door without waiting for my response.

Fifteen minutes later, we were pulling into East Green Lake Beach, Rome parked the car then turned toward me.

"I hope you like swimming," he stated and proceeded to get out of the car.

At first, I was a little disappointed. *Who has a first date at the beach?* I thought, but after spending the whole day swimming, playing, talking, walking hand-in-hand, having a picnic, and just being ourselves, it ended up being the perfect date.

This was only the beginning of what I thought was the start of something beautiful.

Since our first date at the beach, it seemed as if we were inseparable.

Our days started turning into months, and our months turned into years, and before you knew it, we were three years into our relationship, but subtle things in my life started slowly changing.

Carmen Lashay, T. Nicole, Ty Leese Javeh, Eden Mireya, Sparkle Lewis, Reign, & Armani

First Time He Hit Me

It had been three years, and Rome and I were stronger than ever. We'd moved in together, he asked me to quit my job so that he didn't have to wait to spend time with me, and I'd been enjoying being his trophy woman. Hopefully one day, I'd be his trophy wife.

"Rome, baby, you know I'm going out with Brittany tonight, right, baby?" I questioned as I got out of the shower and proceeded to get dressed.

"Yeah, where are you two going? You know I don't like you hanging with that bitch," Rome stated.

"Baby, she's not that bad. Be nice," I retorted as I came out of the bathroom and walked to my man and planted the most sensual kiss upon his lips.

"How long are you planning on being out, you know I need some of this right now," he stated, causing my love box to jump at his words. I loved this man so much, and there was nothing that was going to change the way I felt about him.

"Baby, you know we can't start, because I won't leave, and Brittany will be here soon."

"So! Fuck that bitch!"

I shook my head and removed myself out of Rome's embrace. Moisturizing my body, I made sure not to miss an inch as I massaged pure seduction into my skin. Spraying on perfume, I walked into our bathroom with my thong on and began to beat my face with the new Rhianna cosmetic line and made sure that my curls were cascading and swooped to the left as I put pins in my hair to give it an edgy side Mohawk looking style.

After putting on the perfect lip color, velvet teddy, I puckered my lips, blew myself a kiss, walked into the closet, and grabbed my white one-shoulder Doman-sleeve bodycon dress. I grabbed my nude pumps and nude clutch and called it good.

"Where the fuck you think you're going in that?" Rome asked, and I smiled.

"Now I know I look good." I chuckled, and he held a glare that was a cross of him being jealous and angry. Either way, I was loving it.

The doorbell rang, and I ran down the stairs with Rome fresh on my heels, and when I opened the door, there stood Brittany. She was dressed in a see-through dress that displayed her bra and panties. Not my style, but she had the body for it, but I would have liked for her to leave something to the imagination.

"Hoe," Rome stated while giving her an evil glance. I was sure Brittany heard him and just didn't want to argue.

After Rome and I moved in together after dating only for a short while, Brittany had a lot to say, and Rome started treating her like shit. My ass was stuck in the middle, but I tried my hardest to keep them both at bay.

"Where are you going, baby?" Rome asked me for the second time tonight, and I was nervous about telling him.

"We're going out, and that's all you need to know, nigga," Brittany stated, and I shook my head because I was sick of them going through this shit and constantly being at each other's throats.

"Bitch, shut the fuck up. Wit' yo' hoe ass," he stated and turned his attention back to me. Standing there with his hands on my waist and our noses touching, he said. "Baby, tell me where you are going." He planted a kiss on my lips, and I simply melted at his touch.

"We are going to Davion's all-white party," I said with my head damn near down and almost in a whisper. Davion was his boy, and he was known for having the wildest parties. I was young and still wanted to get out and experience things, but I also knew how Rome felt about niggas dancing with me and showing interest even if I weren't giving them any play.

"No the fuck you not! Davion, as in my boy? Shiddd … the world's coming to an end if you think you're going to that fuck fest. I'll be damned if you go and I'm not sliding through. My woman won't be caught at that shit. Fuck that."

"Baby, come on. Brittany is already here, we are dressed, and we are ready to get lit!"

"Fuck being lit. You better light yo' ass up those stairs and take that shit off. No, you not fucking going. Goodnight, Brittany!" Rome stated and pushed her ass out the door and slammed and locked it.

"What the fuck you tripping on, Rome? I'm about to go," I said, pissed off because he was acting like a real ass. I mean, I knew what Davion was on, but he never came at me like that, and I was really going just to keep an eye out for Brittany because she couldn't really control herself when she'd been drinking.

"You're not going, and that's final! End of fucking discussion."

"Rome, you're my man, not my fucking daddy. I'm fucking going. Now move!" I stated because I had enough of this shit.

Slap! ... "Bitch, act like you didn't fucking hear me the first time! I said you're not fucking going! Now take your slow ass up the fucking stairs and take that shit off."

"Fuck you, Rome!"

Slap! Slap! Slap!

He slapped me three more times as if he were trying to prove a point, and I was shocked, but I knew I wasn't taking this shit.

I held my jaw and looked at him as if he were crazy, I immediately ran up the stairs, and he was hot on my trail. I started snatching clothes out the closet and packing my shit to get the fuck away from him.

"What the fuck are you doing!" he yelled, and I ignored him and kept packing.

"Fuck you, Rome. I'm leaving. I will never stay with a muthafucka who thinks it's cool to put hands on me!" I spat and meant what the fuck I said.

"Wait, wait… Natasha, baby, wait, dammit! I fucked up, baby. I'm sorry. It's just that Davion be on some other shit at those parties, and I don't want you there. Hell, that's why I'm not going. Baby, I swear I didn't mean to do that shit to you. I was just angry. I'm sorry, baby. I'm so sorry. You have to believe me. I will never touch you like that again. I swear. I love you, girl. Please, baby, I'm sorry."

His words tugged at my heart as I felt the pain and hurt in his voice. He was sorry, and I was sure it was a freak accident. I calmed myself and softened my heart to allow myself to listen to his explanation.

Well, like most women, I believed him, and as for this day—this was the start of something evil in our relationship, and it was a pattern that I guess was never going to be broken. From here on out, I would only get broken promises and a broken heart.

Carmen Lashay, T. Nicole, Ty Leese Javeh, Eden Mireya, Sparkle Lewis, Reign, & Armani

A Broken Promise

4 Months Later

It had been four months since the night of Davion's party, and although I would like to say that things with Rome and I were going great, that was the furthest thing from the truth.

I didn't know why I allowed him to do things to me that I promised myself I wouldn't accept from any man. It had been four months of hell, and his beatings were getting worse and worse.

Ladies, if you are in a relationship, and you are seeing these signs, do what you can to get out before you find yourself in this revolving cycle of torture.

I was standing in my master bathroom, nursing the bruises that Rome etched into my body for what seemed like the thousandth time. I couldn't recognize the woman who was staring back at me. I was just a mere shell of the woman I used to be.

Standing at four feet nine and wearing a size eight, I was considered to be on the slim-thick side. My juicy thighs, slim waist, and perfectly shaped apple bottom ass seemed to always get me in trouble no matter how hard I tried to keep myself covered.

Who would have thought a simple thank you with a smile would have warranted my face to look as if I'd just left a boxing ring? After a few years together and many months of abuse, I knew what I needed to do, and I was going to try to get out of this predicament or at least die trying.

I closed the top on the peroxide and walked slowly out of the bathroom. Rome was sitting on the bed, breaking down a black and mild to prepare to roll up his blunt.

"Natasha, the next time I take yo' dumb ass somewhere, you better learn how to shut the fuck up. Do I make myself clear?"

"Yes, Rome. I'm sorry. I was only trying to be polite, and I never meant to disrespect you." I figured if I would explain my reasons as to why I said thank you and smiled, he would at least be nice enough to feel bad for a few days and not put his hands on me.

Two weeks ago, I was in the hospital at the hands of this man, and just when I thought he really meant that he would no longer touch me, he turned around and showed me that this was truly who he was. A woman beater.

I slowly moved closer to the bed so that I could rest my aching body. I felt as if he'd bruised or cracked a rib, and I dare not to say anything about it. I only wanted to get in bed and try to sleep this off. If I could forget the last few years of my life, I would be a much happier and stronger woman, but that wasn't my reality.

"Come here, baby. Sit on my lap." Rome grabbed me by my waist and pulled me over to him, causing me to whimper in pain.

I slowly sat on his lap. He swooped my hair to the side and started planting light kisses on my neck.

"You know that I don't really want to hurt you, right? It's just that I can't have another man trying to take what's mine. Shit, you're so damn friendly. A simple thank you can make niggas think you're trying to fuck. You think I want other niggas looking at my girl in that way?"

"No," I answered, hoping he couldn't tell that I wasn't interested in having this conversation.

It wasn't that I was being too friendly or anything like that. Rome was just a jealous man and thought that every man was trying to fuck me. I didn't know how he became so insecure; he used to be a very confident man. As of late, something changed in him.

"You love me?" he questioned, sliding his hand up my thigh.

"Yes," I replied, trying to fight back the tears. This was typical of him; he'd beat me and want to talk about love.

"Let me hear you say it," he demanded, kissing me on my cheek.

"I love you, Rome."

He kissed me softly on the lips. "Good girl," he stated as if I were a dog or something.

Rome began kissing and caressing me as he slid my shirt over my head and unclasped my bra. I closed my eyes to fight back the tears as he cupped and sucked on my nipples. His touch sent chills down my spine. Not the good 'I wanna fuck chills', but the 'I hate his touch' chills. Every time this man put his hands on me, he wanted to apologize and make love to me as if sex would make things better.

Carmen Lashay, T. Nicole, Ty Leese Javeh, Eden Mireya, Sparkle Lewis, Reign, & Armani

My body was in so much pain, but if I said anything, I knew how it would end. I would rather suffer in silence than to speak and tell him that I didn't think I could do this.

He pulled my panties down. "Get on the bed," he commanded.

I slowly crawled across the bed, trying my best to pretend as if my body weren't in pain. He put me in his favorite position: face down, ass up.

I took in a deep breath as I closed my eyes as I felt his strong hand grip me around the waist. I was trying to brace myself for the pain I knew I was about to feel upon his entry. But Rome did something entirely different from the norm. He spread my ass cheeks apart and licked around my hole, causing me to let out a loud moan.

"You like that, baby? You like for daddy to eat that ass?" He wiggled his tongue in and out my ass, making me damn near scream in pleasure. My pussy was throbbing and dripping wet.

"Mmmm…" I moaned biting down on my bottom lip while gripping the sheets. Although I was in pain from a horrible beating and what I was sure was a fractured rib or something, this was a different type of pleasure, so I allowed myself to enjoy it.

Rome started licking from my asshole to my pussy, and I was experiencing so many different sensations. I forgot about my pain and was trying to enjoy this experience. I arched my back, and a sharp pain in my side brought me back to reality.

I knew this was sad, but the throbbing pain in my side, reminding me of the ass beating he gave me, didn't matter. He was showing me that he was sorry, and I needed to accept his apology.

Rome was making me feel things that he'd never made me feel before, and I had a feeling that things were going to be different. My man was going to change.

"Come sit on my face," he said as he laid back. I moved closer to straddle his face as he parted my pussy lips with his fingers and went face first for my clit. He started bouncing me up and down on his tongue. I couldn't help but moan, scream, and beg for mercy as Rome's tongue fucked me into an explosive orgasm.

Using my hand, he guided his hard dick inside me. I immediately began to bounce and buck up and down, back and forth, taking in all ten inches of his thick rod.

"Fuck, baby!" he shouted as he rocked his hips under me. His dick filled my walls as I began tightening my pussy muscles with each thrust. He placed my nipple in his mouth, biting, licking, and sucking it as he paid close attention to both the right and the left.

"Aw fuck!" I yelled as I felt my body begin to shake and tremble.

"Right there, baby! Don't stop. Fuck me. That's my spot, baby! Hit that shit!!!" I coached as he kept his rhythm. My body began to tingle and shake as I exploded again all over his dick.

"Damn, baby, are you okay?" he asked, cradling my head against his chest.

I couldn't answer. I only held up a finger, signaling that I needed a moment to get myself together. Rome rubbed my back as I lay on my side, completely out of breath. With my body calming down from sexual euphoria, the pain returned, and I allowed sleep to find me. I went to bed wrapped in Rome's arms, feeling completely satisfied.

He was sorry for beating me, and this was going to be a fresh start to something new.

Carmen Lashay, T. Nicole, Ty Leese Javeh, Eden Mireya, Sparkle Lewis, Reign, & Armani

A Bad Trip to the Hospital

Sex with Rome was always so amazing. I guess that I may have been stressing him out and not really seeing things from his point of view. I got up with a new attitude and ready to do things his way so that we could get our love back on track. The man I met in that club a few years ago was still here. I just had to bring him to surface.

I got out of bed, legs still a bit sore from our sexual exploration last night, and I was fired up to make sure things changed for the better. I took an ace body wrap and wrapped my bruised side after taking care of my morning hygiene. I made my way down to the kitchen and began cooking breakfast. I turned on Pandora, and the soft sounds of Luther Vandross and Beyoncé's song "Closer I Get to You" was playing. I felt that it was a sign, telling me that things were going to be alright in my relationship.

I began smiling as they got to the bridge of the song,

Come a little closer so that we can see

Into the eyes of love

Just a little closer; let me speak to you. I want to
softly *tell you something*

Come a little closer; let me whisper in your ear.

'Cause I wanna tell you something

Move on in real close so we can celebrate the way
we feel about each other's loving

I had no idea I was in full concert until I turned around, and Rome was standing there, smiling at the sight.

"What are you making, baby? It smells so good down here."

"I'm making you an egg white omelet with mushrooms, spinach, feta cheese, and of course jalapeños. I also have the bacon going with pancakes. Give me a second, and I will use the juicer and get you some orange and apple juice mixed, just like you like it." I smiled and enjoyed the look of pleasure that rested on his face.

Rome stood behind me and began planting soft kisses on my neck and then began rocking to the soft melodies that played through Pandora. I swayed my hips from side to side and turned to face him. With my arms wrapped around his neck, we kissed, and I welcomed his tongue into my mouth as our tongues began to dance to the beat of their own tune. This was the Rome that I fell in love with.

I finished breakfast, set the table, and served him like the king that he was, and we enjoyed each other's company.

...

Breakfast was over, and I got dressed and was about to head to the mall with Brittany. I knew that Rome and Brittany didn't get along, so I didn't bother to tell him that I was going shopping with her. Rome's birthday was next week, and I thought it would be a great time to get him something special since we were on the road to repairing what we once had.

"What plans do you have for the day?" Rome asked as he was going through his books from the club.

"I'm just doing a little shopping for my man," I retorted, and a smile crept across his face.

"How are you shopping for me with my own money?" He chuckled, and I was a bit offended because he made it perfectly clear that he didn't want me working, and that was the only reason why I quit my job as a store manager for Walgreens.

"Don't give me that look. You know I'm just playing, but baby girl, I told you I didn't want you making a big fuss over my birthday," he stated, and I began to warm back up because maybe he really was just kidding.

I gave Rome a kiss and allowed him the space he needed to get through his paperwork. He was always so focused when it came to his business, and I didn't want to interrupt him.

"See you later, baby," I stated as I prepared to head out to pick up Brittany.

"Okay, baby. Call me if you need me. I'll be doing this shit," he said with his head down, and I planted a kiss on his cheek and left.

…

"Girl, I'm so glad you came out today. Usually, Rome be on bullshit, and last night, Davion said that he was starting that shit again," Brittany said as we made our way to the mall.

"What shit? And when did you and Davion get so close that you all are discussing me and Rome's business?" I questioned with an attitude.

"Don't even start that shit. You know I'm your girl. Davion and I actually been tight since the night of his all-white party. You remember. The one that you didn't go to, because that nigga of yours wouldn't let you."

"Whatever, Brittany. You don't understand," I said, trying to defend what Rome and I had.

"Look. Last night when we were out, Davion said the way that Rome was looking at you made him think about another girl he used to kick it heavy with. He said to watch you because he thinks Rome may try to put hands on you."

My heart dropped, and I began playing last night over and over in my head. Brittany did seem a bit cozy with Davion, but I was so focused on Rome that I hardly paid them any attention.

When one of Rome's investor's spoke to me, I remembered from the last time how he tripped out, so I made sure not to smile and simply said hello. Rome had an attitude until the investor left and then abruptly left with me, and then he beat my ass. He said that I embarrassed him and didn't nobody want to invest in black people with bad attitudes. I guess I cost him his deal.

"Natasha, did he trip out on you?" Brittany asked as if she'd asked me the question for a second time, and I quickly replied.

"Girl, naw. Davion needs to stop the lies and focus on whatever you and him got going on. My man was just in a rush to get me home to love on me," I added, and she gave me the side eye as she sat in the passenger seat.

"Natasha Deshay Longhorn, is he beating on you? Look, I'm not trying to be in your business. I only asked because that's Davion's dude, and you know these niggas talk. What's going on for real? I'm just concerned. Now, truth being told, you are wearing more makeup than usual, and you know I know; you have never been a bitch to cake that shit on."

"Hell naw, he's not beating me. You know me better than that. Drop the subject. Davion is way off with that, and I'm wearing more makeup because my man loves it and can't keep his hands off me." Yeah, he couldn't keep his hands off me, but not in the way I was saying to Brittany.

"Girl, I was about to say we can jump his ass. You know I don't give no fucks! I was two seconds from coming over there last night when Davion said that shit, but he said for me not to get involved, but you're my bitch, and I needed to get that shit straight. If he starts tripping, you let me know. I'll gut that muthafucka."

We both started laughing as I pulled up to the mall and found a parking spot. We were going in and out of stores, and before we knew it, time had completely gotten away from us, and it was a good four hours, and we had bags on top of bags.

I sat my bags down and searched for my phone. After finding it in a Neiman's bag, I realized the battery died.

"Shit!" I said aloud, and Brittany looked at me with confusion.

"What?" she questioned.

"Girl, my phone died, and I wanted to call Rome and tell him that I was on my way back," I continued.

"Girl, fuck him. We're out having fun. Let's go grab something to eat, then you can drop me off and get back to that nigga."

I laughed and agreed, and then we headed to Ruth's Chris.

We were seated and looking at the menu when I heard a laugh that I'd grown to love. I scanned the restaurant, and as sure as my name is Natasha Deshay Longhorn, there my man was, sitting at the table, laughing and being real chummy with a video vixen looking chick.

"Go cuss his ass out, girl! Fuck him!" Brittany said as my blood began to boil.

"No, it's cool," I said, and she was pissed and stormed over there.

"Nigga, why the fuck you over here with this fake, plastic ass looking bitch when you got a real one at home?" Brittany went off, and when Rome's eyes went up and landed on mines, the look of death that he held let me know that it wasn't the best time for Brittany to be showing her ass.

"Brittany, it's cool. You two enjoy your meal," I said as hot tears spilled from my eyes, and I pulled Brittany away yelling and screaming.

Carmen Lashay, T. Nicole, Ty Leese Javeh, Eden Mireya, Sparkle Lewis, Reign, & Armani

...

"So you're lying to me now? You're following a nigga? I was handling business, and you allowed that ghetto ass hoe to come show her ass when you know good and fucking well I told you not to hang with her. That's another reason why I was irritated yesterday; I hate that fucking bitch, and she's always trying to make it her business to be around and get in our shit! So you're spending my money on that bitch? Answer me!" Rome screamed as he choked me and began beating me as if I meant nothing to him.

"Rome, please. Baby, you said you wouldn't do this. Baby, please."

"Oh, so now you want to beg and plead with me. Fuck you. Talk that shit that you and that bitch was talking!" *Wham!*

I was taking blow after blow, punch after punch, and kick after kick. I knew my body wasn't completely healed from last night, and after the beating he put on me now, he had to rush me to the hospital.

I was in the hospital, hooked to an IV, and I had a broken arm with bruised ribs. Rome was sitting in the corner with a look that I couldn't make out. My room was filled with bears and flowers. The nurse told me that I was so lucky to have a man like Rome who came home at the right time to fight off my attacker. I knew to stick with that story, and I played the hell out of my part.

Everything in me was telling me to get away from this man, but deep down inside, I felt that our love would have pulled us out of this. Little did I know, there was only one way to leave this relationship, and I was going to find out a lot sooner than later.

Carmen Lashay, T. Nicole, Ty Leese Javeh, Eden Mireya, Sparkle Lewis, Reign, & Armani

The Never-ending Apology

As Rome was helping me up the steps, he told me to wait out front; he had a surprise for me. He opened the front door just enough for him to slip into the house. Honestly, I was sick of his damn surprises. They always came with an empty apology.

"Come on, baby. See what yo' man did for you," Rome beamed as he led me into the house.

"Welcome home," he added, pointing to the welcome home sign that he made, and the array of roses that were filling the room. Rome took my hand and got down on one knee, and all I could think was, *I hope this man isn't about to propose to me.*

"Look, baby. I'm sorry I did this to you. I don't know what came over me. I never meant to hurt you and put you in the hospital." He shook his head as tears rolled down his eyes. "I promise I will never hurt you like this again. I love you so much, and I couldn't imagine my life without you," he cried. He stood up and took me into his arms.

"Please, forgive me, please. I can't lose you. I swear, if anything happens to you, I wouldn't be able to forgive myself. You're the best thing that ever happened to me. Please, forgive me," he begged as he cried on my shoulder.

I slowly stroked the back of his head then replied, "I forgive you," as tears slowly rolled out of my eyes.

It wasn't that I forgave Rome for what he did to me; it was just that if I didn't, he would have gotten angry and beat me again. Plus, I hated to see a man cry, and it was just simply easier to tell him what he needed to hear so that he could feel better.

Rome cupped my face in his hands, looked me in my eyes, and said, "Baby, I don't know why you continue to do the things you do to piss me off. I try my hardest to be good to you, but it seems like you're not happy. Don't I make you happy, Natasha?"

Did he really just turn this around on me? Yep, he did, but I dare not answer incorrectly.

"Yes, Rome. You make me happy," I lied.

The truth was that I was miserable as hell, and all I wanted to do at that moment was go upstairs, crawl into bed, and go to sleep. Lately, that was all I wanted to do. Sleep. I guess it was safe to say that I was depressed.

Carmen Lashay, T. Nicole, Ty Leese Javeh, Eden Mireya, Sparkle Lewis, Reign, & Armani

I lost interest in so many things that made me happy, and it seemed like Rome had me just where he wanted me—stuck in this miserable ass relationship with no hope of ever getting away from him.

Last Trip to The Hospital
4 Months Later

"Uh … ahh … baby, that's it. That's my spot. Oh shit!" Rome was making love to me like it was the last time he was going to get my cookies. Yesterday, I had a woman calling me to tell me that she was pregnant by my man, and I didn't dare confront him about the allegations. I simply ignored it and pretended that none of it existed just like the past few times.

I guess you could say that I'd learned how to deal with this, and I simply continued my visits to the doctor to test myself for STD's and tried keeping myself as safe as possible.

"That's right, baby. Grip your man's dick. This pussy's so wet and tight for me, baby." He moaned as he dug into my honey pot of love.

I opened up to allow him full access as he took my body into a new place.

"I'm not ready to bust, baby. Oooh shit… This pussy's bout to turn me into a minuteman. Ahhh, I'm trying to hold this shit in, baby, but this pussy so good," he continued, and I moaned in pleasure, as Rome knew every inch of my body.

We continued making love until we both erupted on each other and remained in each other's arms.

"Baby, you know I've been stressed out lately with the opening up of my new club, right?" Rome questioned as he held me in his arms.

"I know, baby. I'm so proud of you, and I know you will make it just as successful as your first one," I replied.

"Thanks, baby girl. Your support means the world to me. I'm sorry we haven't been seeing eye to eye lately, but I swear to you that we will be good. You make me better, and shit is going to be right with us. You're my better half," he stated, and I only wished that I could believe his words, but with the girl Cynthia fresh on my mind, it was hard to believe anything he was saying.

Against my better judgment, we sat in the darkness, wrapped in our love juices, and I had to ask a question that led to one of the biggest ass beatings he'd ever laid on me.

"Baby, I got a call from a woman named Cynthia today, and I know you said I will have a lot of bitches coming my way with bullshit, but she knew about the birthmark on your dick and even said she was pregnant," I said in a low tone as I rested my head on his chest, stroking his chest, thinking we could have a calm conversation about this, but boy was I wrong.

"Bitch! Why do you insist on fucking up shit? Shit was sweet, been sweet with us, and you had to bring up some shit that another muthafucka is spitting!"

"Baby, please. I'm not trying to accuse you; I just wanted to talk about it."

"Talk? Fuck you! You think this is a fucking game? You're constantly hitting me up with shit about what you heard. Why haven't you heard about job applications? My ass is paying all bills. You're running up cards and shit but got the nerve to bring me some shit that another muthafucka's spitting." He sprang out of bed and grabbed a blanket to head out of the room, and I should have left well enough alone, but I decided to explain.

"Baby, I'm sorry. I just wanted to—" Before I could get the words out of my mouth, I was met with Rome's backhand.

Rome towered over me and began punching me in the face. With every hit, I was trying to stay conscious. He grabbed me by my ponytail and slung me over the banister. Landing on the floor, I heard something pop in my back, and I was in excruciating pain. With Rome running down the stairs, I thought he was about to stop, but he continued his abuse and beat me until I blacked out. I remembered him saying, "Hold on," as the sirens could be heard in the distance.

…

"Ms. Longhorn, I'm so sorry, but you lost the baby."

Baby? I internally questioned, as I didn't know I was pregnant. I looked around my room, and it was the same type of setup. *Typical Rome* was what I thought. He would beat me and then find a way to squirm back into my heart.

When the nurse left the room, Rome walked to the bed, and I was nervous. He bent down and spoke.

"You're always making me do shit to you. You better tell these fuckers that you have a crazy ex, and you think he's sending people to attack you."

I nodded my head.

"You stupid bitch. You can't even hold on to my fucking seed," he spat, and all I thought about was the fact that he was beating his seeds out of me, but I dare not say a word to him. The sad part about this was this wasn't the first kid I'd lost by his hands.

"I'm about to leave. Now remember, you better tell the fucking story I told you," he warned.

The nurse came in and said that she was about to end her shift in an hour, but a new nurse would be taking care of me, and I nodded my head.

After giving the statement that Rome fed to me, the nurse stated that she was going to get the police to make an official report because my visits were too frequent. She eyeballed Rome suspiciously, but she didn't dare challenge anything I told her.

The nurse left, and Rome gave me a knowing look. I knew that meant I had to stick with the story. I watched Rome leave the room and figured he was going out to cheat, but at this point, I didn't care. I was trying to plan my escape; I just didn't know where to begin.

My body was aching with pain, and I allowed sleep to take over.

…

Waking up from my dream, I found that it was just that. A dream. I thought that I was going to be surrounded by people who loved and cared for me, but I realized I wasn't worth anything. Not worthy of being loved and cared for. I was alone in a hospital bed with bandages covering my body.

Rome had so much control over me that I pushed my parents out of my life, and after this, I was sure I wouldn't be allowed to even see Brittany anymore, so it was simply Rome and me, and forever was sounding too damn long to be going through this.

I kept looking over, wondering if there were any tools that I could use to end it all. Nobody would care, and this was the perfect way to get out of the fucked up situation I was in.

With the way Rome was, he would probably beat my dead body and tell me that I was selfish for killing

myself before coming back to clean and cook first. *Ha!* I
had to laugh at the thought.

The door opened to my room, and a young nurse
who looked to be about my age stepped in and held a
beautiful smile.

"Hello, Natasha. You gave me quite the scare. I
usually get attached to my patients, and you were
determined to crash, but I was able to do everything in
my power to save you."

"Why did you do that? You should have let me
die," I stated as I stared at nothing in particular on the
wall. This new nurse had not a clue as to what I was
going through, and I wanted her to get the fuck out.

She looked at me with a puzzled expression, and
then she jotted something down, peered toward the door,
and then pulled up a chair and sat next to me.

"Natasha, I usually don't allow myself to get into
any of my patient's business."

"Then don't," I retorted before she could finish.

Taking in a deep breath, she said, "I refuse to
allow a woman who is the same age as me to go through

the same shit I went through without extending a hand of help to offer."

I looked at her and rolled my eyes. She didn't know shit about me, so how did she know my situation?

"Look, you may not want this advice, but I'm giving it to you. The coward that placed you here is a monster that you don't need in your life. It's by the grace of God that I was able to move from Tacoma and ended up here in Seattle and was able to get away from him. Not a long stretch, but back then, he was talking about starting his own thing with the club scene, and he kept blaming his temper on stress. I had to leave because his ass would have been stressed out so much that I would have ended up dead. The crazy part about it is that it's because of him that I'm a nurse. That man used to beat me so much that I couldn't get medical attention, so I had to learn how to care for myself. I started studying and studying, and then I realized I was good at it. He alienated me from my family, and last I heard, he was placed in jail for two years for doing the same shit to someone else. I can only pray that he's not putting his new woman through the hell that he put me through."

The nurse, who I now knew as Terri, continued. She talked to me, and I found that our stories were damn near alike; they were so similar that I had to ask what her ex-boyfriend name is.

"His name is Rome Healy."

When I heard my man's name, I could have pulled every plug from these machines and died. The shocked expression that I displayed on my face caused for her to become inquisitive and ask me about my man.

With tears already rolling out my eyes, I simply said, "Describe him."

I knew there was no way there could have been two Rome Healy's in this world, and the fact that she used to live an hour away from here told me that it was him before she went into every detail on his body and gave a full description.

As she finished her description, I added on to the conversation, completing some of her words. Yes, it was a small world we were living in, but how crazy was this that my nurse was beaten by the same man who beat me. My mind was made up. There was no escaping him. One of us had to go.

"Oh no, Natasha, we need to call the police!" she exclaimed.

"You know him. Calling the police and having him arrested for the night will only give me one night of peace, but when he returns home, I'll either end up back in here or in a box, having my eternal rest."

The reality of my words hit her, and she too began to cry. She promised me that she wouldn't say anything, but she slid me her card and told me to call her when I was released, and I was confused.

"Aren't you going to be here until I'm released?"

"No, I refuse to be your nurse knowing that Rome can come in and see you anytime, but just because I'm no longer your nurse doesn't mean I can't be a friend. We all need them. Please call me when you are released. You have a place to go."

She left the room as tears continued to spill from her eyes, and it saddened me that Rome had put other women through the same bullshit he was putting me through.

Call me crazy, but I wished he'd only done this to me. The fact that I knew he'd done this before was only telling me that this was a pattern that wouldn't stop, but I

Carmen Lashay, T. Nicole, Ty Leese Javeh, Eden Mireya, Sparkle Lewis, Reign, & Armani

had to do something. I had to find my strength and my voice to end this.

The Escape

It'd been two weeks since my return home from the worst hospital visit ever. My mind was made up that it would definitely be my last.

I was sick of hiding behind the bruises, listening to broken promises, shattered dreams, and this scary thing called love. Love wasn't supposed to hurt, but the type of love that Rome provided did.

My dreams were always to be a licensed pharmacist, but after I quit my job at Walgreens because Rome asked me to, I began to lose myself and became wrapped up in him and supporting his dreams.

I only wished that I'd been strong enough to leave long before now, but I knew today was going to be the day. I couldn't take anymore. I guess just knowing that another woman was able to get away and live out her dreams gave me hope to do the same.

When Terri gave me her card, I made sure to put it in my bra, and I planned to call her when I had my escape calculated and ready to implement.

Terri had Rome down to a science when it came to how he moved. I hated that she refused to treat me because she wanted to make sure she stayed as far away from him as she could, but I didn't blame her.

Carmen Lashay, T. Nicole, Ty Leese Javeh, Eden Mireya, Sparkle Lewis, Reign, & Armani

The only friend I had, I pushed her away just like I pushed my family away. There was no way I was going to allow Brittany to know what I was going through just so she could judge me, so it was easier to cut her off and save face.

It was time that I got out of this, and for the first time, I was choosing myself. Maybe when I got myself together, I would find the courage to mend the broken relationships that I caused due to this man.

Rome was in the shower, and I knew that meant he was going out soon. The fact that I'd recently gotten out the hospital meant that he would play it cool for a while. I just needed to play my part. It had already been two weeks, and things were relatively quiet, and I wanted to keep things just the way they were.

Stepping out of the shower, Rome spoke. "Tasha, I need for you to have this house clean, and plan a grand opening for my new spot. Do you think you can handle that?"

"Of course, I can, baby," I replied and put on the biggest smile as if I were happy to do it.

"Look. The way I see it, I want only my closest friends at the dinner party, here at the house, and then we will leave from here and go to the new club for a bigger celebration. Do you understand?" he questioned, and I nodded.

Rome began to approach me, and my heart rate started to speed up. I was so scared because I didn't know what he was about to do.

"Baby, I'm sorry. You know I never meant to hurt you like that. I've been stressed out lately with this new club. Thanks for always having my back and making sure to hold a nigga down. I'll never raise a hand to hurt you again, okay?" he promised as he kissed my lips, and what was funny was that I was saying the same speech in my head as he was saying it to me. I'd heard this shit so many times that I knew it was the biggest lie ever told.

Rome was so predictable at this point, and everything Terri said to me was slowly coming to the light. I guess you could say that I knew he wasn't shit and knew that he'd never change, but it was time for me to make that change.

"I know, Rome. I love you so much, and I promise I'll put on the best dinner party and grand opening celebration you've ever seen," I affirmed, knowing that I had no plans on being here any time after tonight.

Rome continued to get dressed and move around the room without a care in the world. I wanted to blow his fucking brains out, but I was so afraid of going to jail. Orange might be the new black, but my ass didn't look good in that color.

Rome left twenty minutes later, and I packed two bags and called Terri.

"Hello, Terri? I'm ready. Can you come get me?"

Without hesitation Terri was on her way. She instructed me to clear my phone log and reset my phone to factory settings without backing anything up. I did as she instructed once she told me that she was outside. She had me toss the phone in the nearest dumpster, and we were on our way.

I internally smiled, knowing that I'd escaped the big bad wolf and knew that he could never use me as a punching target again.

"You'll be alright, Natasha. I'm here for you. You need to call your parents…"

"No, I can't call them just yet. Please let me get myself together, and then I'll call them. I promise."

Terri didn't protest. We simply rode to Ballard to her beautiful beach home. I knew that I would be starting over, and I was ready to see what my life was going to be like without Rome.

Carmen Lashay, T. Nicole, Ty Leese Javeh, Eden Mireya, Sparkle Lewis, Reign, & Armani

Finding A New Love

It's been a year since I've managed to escape Rome and have a bit of relief. Terri kept her word and helped me out and was allowing me to stay with her until I found something permanent for myself.

This past year has been trying and I'm finally able to really get a grasp on life. Going to counseling and talking to Terri has been beneficial in helping me to see that I wasn't the issue in my relationship with Rome.

I've started volunteering at a violence against women association center and that turned out to be the best move for me. This allowed me to gain more support from other women and has afforded me the opportunity to work there part time, while I search for something permanently.

I'd just gotten out of bed and was ready for a new day. I'd been having nightmares, but Terri informed me that it was normal, as she too had some of those same nightmares.

"How did you sleep?" Terri asked as she sat at the end of the bed and held a smile as I sat up and stretched.

"This was one of the best night's rest I'd had in a while. Terri, I can't thank you enough for everything you have done for me, and as soon as I'm able to repay you, I will," I spoke with sincerity.

I didn't want to go from being dependent on Rome to depending on Terri, so I wanted to be clear that I wasn't able to do much now, but when I was able, I would do what I could to show how much I appreciated her for stepping in and inserting herself as a friend.

"Look, I told you I've been there, and the only thing I want you to do is focus on getting better and healing your heart. Don't allow what Rome did to shape and mold your thoughts about men and, most importantly, yourself. You are worth it, and you have to affirm those words daily."

I heard what Terri was saying, but I didn't believe the words she spoke, and that was why I still wasn't able to call my parents and tell them what was really going on after all this time. I knew this was all a process, and in due time, I should be able to heal and move on. *One day at a time.* I thought, reminding myself of the motto at the center.

...

Carmen Lashay, T. Nicole, Ty Leese Javeh, Eden Mireya, Sparkle Lewis, Reign, & Armani

I got out of bed when Terri left for work. I began to take care of my hygiene and prepare for the day.

After getting dressed and making myself something to eat, I turned on the television and started watching an episode of *Snapped*. I saw myself being able to relate to many of the stories that I'd watched. I shook my head and changed the channel until I landed on *The Haves and The Have Nots*. For the life of me, I didn't understand how Tyler Perry could create this black soap opera and people not see that this girl had been pregnant for the past four seasons and still hadn't began to show. Nowhere in sight did this girl have a belly bump. At any rate, I was drawn to Veronica. I loved her character on this show. I was hoping and wishing that I had the strength of Veronica one day. She was powerful and unapologetic, and I appreciated her role. While watching this episode, I nodded off and went to sleep and then woke up in fear. I felt a presence over me, and I thought it was Rome coming to get me.

"I got to get out of this house," I said as I got up from the sofa, went into the kitchen, and grabbed some juice. This neighborhood was quiet and beautiful, and some fresh air was all I needed.

After putting on some shoes, I grabbed the spare key and began to walk around and really tried to get to know the area. I had money that Terri made me pull out my account prior to my escape. She said once I was gone, it was important not to use that account or swipe the card. I guess this was to make sure Rome couldn't track me down. It was crazy how many things Terri told me to do just for my safety.

I knew that I only had enough money to get me through four maybe five months, so I needed to find a job or create a job for myself. Starting over might not be easy, but it was necessary for me and my sanity.

As I walked down the street, I noticed kids playing, and I started to smile. I could only dream of being a mother because the many times when I'd gotten pregnant, Rome beat my child out of me, and I was sure I wasn't able to have any kids now.

I continued my walk until I was in front of this cute little store that was filled with trinkets. I smiled as I walked in and started playing with one of the music boxes. After winding the box up several times, a man walked up behind me and spoke.

Carmen Lashay, T. Nicole, Ty Leese Javeh, Eden Mireya, Sparkle Lewis, Reign, & Armani

"If you love it so much, you should have it."

I turned around and was faced with the most handsome man I'd seen in a while. Physically, he was exactly the type of man that I was attracted to. He was tall. He stood about six feet five and had bulging muscles that I would love to feel wrapped around my body. He had a certain swagger about him that screamed confidence, and I was hearing him loud and clear. He was dark skinned, maybe a shade or two darker than brown. His dark hair was cut in a low, clean cut with more waves than an ocean, and his mustache was perfectly trimmed to match his neatly trimmed chin beard. He was casually dressed in a pair of black trousers and a gray Ralph Lauren button up. My heart began to skip several beats as I became flustered by his looks.

"Oh… ummm… I'm sorry I'm in your way," I managed to sputter out.

While quickly trying to get around him, I dropped the music box, and we both bent down to get it. Our hands touched, our eyes met, and it was as if we were speaking with our eyes.

"Allow me to get that for you," he stated in a voice that had my body ready to quiver with his touch.

As we stood in the store, staring in each other's eyes, he finally started a conversation that I wasn't sure I was ready to have. This was exactly the type of man who would treat me like Rome, and I knew I wasn't prepared to start that type of cycle again. I was barely out of the last one, but it was something about this man that had my full attention.

"My name is Ellis, and you are?"

After giving him my name, he was very direct in telling me what he wanted. This was oh so familiar, and everything in me was saying to proceed with caution, but Terri also told me not to allow what Rome did to shape my thoughts about another man.

"I want to take you out and get to know you because I see that you are new to this neighborhood."

"Who said I was new?"

"Trust me. I would have noticed a beautiful woman like you," he said, causing me to blush.

After talking for twenty minutes, he bought me the musical box, and I blushed all the way back to Terri's house. I couldn't wait for her to get home so that I could tell her what happened.

Carmen Lashay, T. Nicole, Ty Leese Javeh, Eden Mireya, Sparkle Lewis, Reign, & Armani

Not being able to give him a number had me thinking that it was time for me to get a phone. Terri told me not to get one in my name, but she wasn't here to get me one, so I walked over to T-Mobile and got a new phone and called the number that Ellis gave me. We sat on the phone and talked for hours. It was as if we were old friends.

He was a nice guy, or at least I thought he is. Only time would tell, but for now, I'd enjoy talking to him and feeling like a woman again. I loved hearing him smile through the phone, and he was making me feel special with his words.

This was a feeling that I would hope could last forever, but as we know, all good things have to come to an abrupt end.

This Crazy Thing Called Love

One year and three months I'd been free from Rome and enjoying this thing we call life. It had been a three months since I'd been talking to Ellis on the phone and really trying to get to know him. I made sure not to rush things and paid close attention to any possible signs. I'd just hung up from talking to Terri after I'd given Ellis the good news. Today, I received a call back from Walgreens after I put in another management application. I felt that it was truly my time to shine. It will be bittersweet leaving the center, but this management role will set me up for success.

After telling Ellis and Terri the good news, Ellis decided that it was a great time for him to take me out so that we could properly celebrate. After a bit of hesitation, I finally agreed.

"You can do this, you are strong, you are worth it, and love will find you." I affirmed, stating my daily affirmation, and ready to take the next step in my healing.

...

It was 7:00 P.M., and Ellis was right on time. He didn't do the typical candy and flowers, but he was looking good, held my hand, and showed me that he

Carmen Lashay, T. Nicole, Ty Leese Javeh, Eden Mireya, Sparkle Lewis, Reign, & Armani

didn't have any other motives other than getting to know me.

Ellis planned the cutest date. We'd gone to the Space Needle and had an amazing dinner and wonderful conversation. Things in my life couldn't have been going any better. After we finished our meal, we began walking around downtown Seattle and really just had a chill conversation.

"Thank you for coming out with me tonight. I'm having a good time. I thought I was ugly with a nice voice or something because you kept dodging me but always wanted to stay on the phone," he laughed.

"No, not at all. I was in a very bad relationship and didn't want to hop into anything else anytime soon. I didn't want to lead you on or anything, knowing that I wasn't mentally ready."

"I can dig that. I just wanted to take this opportunity to get to know you. You're a pretty cool woman, and I guess I'm looking pretty cool because tonight you're on my arm," he flirted, and I began to get those damn butterflies.

Ellis took my hand, and we were walking back to his car. He opened the door for me and allowed me to get in and buckled up before he closed the door and got in on the other side.

Taking my hand, he pulled out into traffic, and we were headed back to Terri's house. When he got on Aurora Avenue, I told him, "Let's go to your place."

A smile stretched across his face, and I knew I needed to clear that up with him.

"Um, I just don't want the night to end. You know I'm not ready for anything like that," I said with a smile.

"Can a man hope?" he asked and we both laughed.

"Hoping is fine, but seriously, I enjoy your company, and I'm enjoying this conversation."

"Good. I guess I'm not boring you to pieces," he continued.

Ellis pulled up to his place, and the view of the beach was simply breathtaking. "And I thought Terri had a nice home," I said with a smile.

"Well, I'm not sure how nice my home is, but I'm definitely loving it more now that you're in here with me," he stated, and those damn butterflies came back.

"Spend the night with me, Natasha."

Carmen Lashay, T. Nicole, Ty Leese Javeh, Eden Mireya, Sparkle Lewis, Reign, & Armani

"Ellis, I can't."

"Not like that. I simply want to hold you, and when the time is right, I promise to make love to you, but for now, I just want you in my arms. I won't try anything. I respect what you said. I promise you I won't force myself on you. As hard as it might be, no pun intended, but I will never force myself on you."

Chuckling nervously, I replied. "I don't have anything here, and I refuse to wake up with stinking breath."

We both shared a laugh, and Ellis promised to go to the store. He said that he needed some wine so that we could really get to know each other. He laid out a pair of shorts and a tee for me to shower and get comfortable in.

"I promise, I just want to hold you," he said, pulling me closer to him, and we finally shared our first passionate kiss.

No matter what my mouth was about to say, my body was saying something different.

"I won't be long. I'm going to get some wine and a few toiletries for you. Then we can continue whatever it is we were just doing," he said as he moved in for another kiss

"Hurry back," I said.

"I plan to," he retorted, and he grabbed his keys and left out the house.

I walked around his massive bedroom, admiring his décor. After being nosey, I decided that I would shower and freshen up.

I fell in love with his shower head that massaged my body better than any masseuse. After cleansing my body, I stepped out the shower and found some of his lotion. While moisturizing my body, I heard the door, and a smile quickly found its way to my face.

"Ellis, did you get everything?" I questioned, and he didn't say anything.

I walked down the hall and turned on the lights and jumped when a cat ran past me.

"Shit!" I said aloud, as I didn't know he even had a cat. I could have sworn I heard the door, but then again, it could have all been in my head.

I walked back into his room and sat on the bed. Ellis's bed hugged my body right as I sank deep into his pillowtop mattress.

Carmen Lashay, T. Nicole, Ty Leese Javeh, Eden Mireya, Sparkle Lewis, Reign, & Armani

I closed my eyes and figured I'd take a quick nap until he returned. Feeling a presence over me, I felt that my dreams were coming back. I opened my eyes and realized that my dream was a fucking nightmare.

"Ro-Rome?" I questioned, and he stood over me with a glare so strong that I could have sworn I saw Satan himself dancing in his eyes.

"Bitch, you think it's that easy to get away from me? You're out here giving my pussy away?" he questioned, and tears spilled from my eyes as I prayed Ellis would rapidly return.

"Rome, please."

"Please what? You love me, right? You was going to make me happy, right? Well, bitch, I'm not happy!" he yelled, and I jumped.

I tried running past him, and he hit me with a blunt object. Grabbing my head, I felt hot liquid in my hand, and I knew it was blood. I started blinking rapidly so I wouldn't pass out.

"Rome, please…" I begged, but my plea fell on death ears.

Rome beat me and continued to punch me, and I tried my hardest to fight him off. I stood as everything started to look blurry to me. I didn't want to black out, so I continued to coach myself to keep fighting.

"You've fucked with the wrong nigga!" he said as his foot connected with my stomach, sending me crashing into Ellis's closet.

I heard the front door and was relieved that Ellis was home.

I started screaming, "Ellis, help me! Please, help me!"

"Bitch, you have the nerve to call out another muthafucka's name in my presence?"

Boom!

He hit me again, and something cold fell at my feet. Realizing he had a gun, I reacted quickly and picked it up. My hands were shaking, and I now had the upper hand.

"Bitch, put that down before you really make me mad," he spoke as if he were a demon. I was scared, and then I heard Ellis.

"Natasha, put the gun down, baby. The police will be here soon," he said as he stood in the doorway, and Rome was standing with his hands in surrender.

Carmen Lashay, T. Nicole, Ty Leese Javeh, Eden Mireya, Sparkle Lewis, Reign, & Armani

"The police won't stop him. He will keep going and going with this. It was Terri and then me. I can't allow him to do this to anyone else. Broken promises, shattered dreams, and a scary thing called love."

I let off three shots and watched Rome's body hit the floor. With the sirens blaring in the distance, I thought about the question I used to ask myself after Rome would beat me. *Will I be brave enough to make it out, or will he kill me?* I guess I got my answer... I was brave enough to make it out, but I killed him.

I dropped the gun and walked over to Rome's body. "You can never hurt me again. No matter what, you can never hurt me again." I began to cry as Ellis wrapped me in his embrace.

I don't know what's going to happen to me, but now, I'm finally free. **The End**

From Author Ms. T. Nicole

This is my first short story, and although it was on a

subject that many of us are afraid to speak out about, I have to be transparent with my readers. I was in a toxic relationship while I was in high school. Although it has been over twenty years ago now, I'm thankful that I was able to walk away with my life and sanity. I may have a few scars that remind me of the pain, but those are the things that drive me to continue to press on.

I urge my readers to get out of toxic relationships that you know aren't good for you. It's okay to seek help. Your life is worth more than that man and that relationship. If you have kids, your children are worth more. I love you all for reading.

To my TP and Royalty family, thank you all so much for your love and support. Treasure Malian, I may be one of the craziest authors on your roster with a pen, but as long as you continue to be here for my foolery, you know I'm down for getting that treasured publication crown. TP authors, each and every last one of you ROCK! I mean, there is book release after book release, and it's some FIRE coming off each of you gems, and I'm happy to be able to pen with you all. Let's stay focused and continue to uplift each other in our journey.

Please check out my other titles listed on Amazon and Barnes & Noble:

Carmen Lashay, T. Nicole, Ty Leese Javeh, Eden Mireya, Sparkle Lewis, Reign, & Armani

I had to do it (1 and 2)

Love VS Trust (1 and 2)

Cold Case Love

Daddy Issues

No Loyalty in the Hood

True Undying Love-A Twisted Love Story

Fell In Love with a Bad Guy (1 and 2)

So Gone Over You (1, 2, 3)

It Hurts Me to Love You (1, 2, 3)

Giving My Heart to a Savage: Who Could Love You Like I Do

This Thug Turned My Heart Cold (1 and 2)

Broken Promises, Shattered Dreams: A Scary Thing Called Love

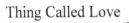

Unrequited Love

Eden Mireya

Carmen Lashay, T. Nicole, Ty Leese Javeh, Eden Mireya,
Sparkle Lewis, Reign, & Armani

Sighing, I fought hard to hold back the tears. I was emotionally and physically exhausted, and it seemed that the doctor was just as disappointed if not more, than my husband Shaqim and I were.

"I'm sorry, Mrs. Baker. We can try another round in three weeks—" he began to explain before I cut him off. I'd heard it all before and nothing Dr. Montgomery could say now could make me feel better.

"Nah. I'm good. I'm tired of this. It's always the same old stuff," I quickly shot back. After over three years of trying to conceive a child so that my husband would be happy and more fertility treatments than I cared to count, I was starting to feel like I'd never be able to give Shaqim the "honor" of being a father. Besides, I knew he still blamed us for the death of our unborn son. The moment that I glanced over at Shaqim and his heartbroken face, I fought my hardest not to burst into tears.

"Dr. Montgomery, can you give my wife and I a moment please?" he asked politely. I knew one of my baby's "talks" was on its way, and I was not here for it.

My husband didn't know the truth, but I did. Not being able to have a baby now was karma for me aborting my first pregnancy. Before I was the wife of Shaqim Baker, the celebrity fitness trainer, I was wife of Shaqim "Vice" Baker, the street lord of Los Angeles. He still dabbled in it here and there, but for the most part, you could consider my husband somewhat "retired" from the game.

Nodding his head, the doctor left the room as I sighed. Shaqim got out of his seat and walked toward me. "Miquel, what's up? I thought we had a plan... You can't just give up. You have to be strong. I thought you wanted this," Shaqim Barked as I gasped. I could not believe that nigga was acting like I hadn't put my all into giving him a baby.

"Nigga, you wanted this! It's always been you! But you're not going through any of this stuff! I'm tired of getting stuck and nothing happening! You don't even care about what this does to my body? You're all for it if you get your child even if you lose your wife!" I began to cry. Taking a deep breath, I tried my hardest to contain my composure. "My hair is falling out, Shaqim. I'm so stressed. I can't eat, can't sleep. I want a baby more than anything, but you want it more than me, and I know it. Shit, everyone knows it. Honestly, you're stressing me the fuck out," I added calmly as I stared at Shaqim's shocked face.

"So that's how you feel? I'm stressing you out?" he repeated as if I hadn't just said that. But remembering what happened last time I spoke my mind, I lost all my courage. I tried to swallow the golf ball that had suddenly lodged itself in my throat. But I nodded, and he instantly became defensive, so I tried my hardest to resolve this argument before it became a full-blown issue. There was no way I'd be able to hide a black eye. I didn't even have any of my makeup on me at the moment.

"I don't know what's wrong with me, Shaqim. I'm trying," I confessed, shaking my head. He didn't have to say anything, because his eyes told the entire message before his mouth had the opportunity to. *You're not trying hard enough.* "But you're not helping me either, Shaqim. I mean, ever since we lost our son—" I began to vent before Shaqim cut me off as usual.

"Why do you always have to bring it up? Let's not go there today, Miquel. Please," he snapped as I stared at him in disbelief. I couldn't believe we were having this conversation once again. It had only been seventeen months, two weeks, and three days since I delivered our stillborn son. Meanwhile, Shaqim was walking around like it never happened. He still called Immanuel an "it".

"Are you for real, Shaqim? Don't you dare call my son an "it" like he didn't exist! Maybe he didn't to you, but he did to me!" I yelled as Shaqim just stared at me. If you didn't know any better, you would never suspect Shaqim of being the reason that our son wasn't in my arms right now. His face was just blank, and that pissed me off even more. "Face it, Shaqim. Maybe we just weren't meant to be parents, or maybe it's not time yet. But either way, I need a break. My body and my mind just need a little break," I tried to explain even though I could tell by the look on Shaqim's face that he really wasn't trying to hear what I had to say.

"You know what? You're right, Miquel. Just like you always are. Maybe you just weren't meant to be a mother," Shaqim snapped, leaving the room before I could ask him what the fuck he meant by that. Taking my legs off of the stirrups and then pulling my pants on, I knew I couldn't catch up, so I quickly pulled my phone out and called his phone as I walked outside to the parking lot.

Carmen Lashay, T. Nicole, Ty Leese Javeh, Eden Mireya, Sparkle Lewis, Reign, & Armani

"What, Miquel?"

"Where are you, Shaqim? Why'd you just bounce out like that? Stop playing. I don't see you," I said, cursing in my head about how this dumb nigga had just left me to chill out in our car.

"You won't see me," he responded dryly as I looked around.

"I know, Shaqim. You parked in the front. Come—" I began to direct before he snapped, cutting me off.

"I left," he answered as I glanced at my screen just to make sure that I was still talking to my husband.

"I'm sorry. Wait. I think my phone is breaking up… I thought I heard you say you left me," I stammered as my heart began to race, and my eyes burned because I was trying so hard not to burst into tears. Shaqim was even madder than I thought he'd be when I told him I wanted to take a break from trying.

"That's what I said. I have somewhere else to be. I'll be back to the house later," Shaqim explained as if his last sentence was supposed to appease me. He didn't even ask me if it were okay. Don't get me wrong; I wasn't one of those types of women that needed her man to ask permission, but he hadn't even considered my feelings.

"How am I supposed to get home, Shaqim?"

"I'll call you an Uber," Shaqim offered. I became furious and held my tongue for only two seconds before I blew up.

"You know what? Fuck it, Shaqim. Fuck you. Don't even worry about me. I won't be at home when you get there," I announced, definitely not expecting his answer.

"That's on you, Miquel," he said before disconnecting our call. I didn't know what Shaqim's problem was, but if he wanted to show out, I could definitely show him how it was done. There was no way Shaqim was about to play me for someone's fool.

Calling my father wasn't an option. He already hated Shaqim, so this news would probably make him want to have Shaqim killed. My papí, Myron Rodrigo was extremely disappointed when he found out I was dating a dope boy… and when we announced that we were getting married, I had never seen my dad angrier. But now I was starting to think that my dad and my older brother, Miquon, had been right. Shaqim had never been any good for me. He just felt good to me. It was no secret that none of my family really liked Shaqim. But because they loved me, they simply tolerated him.

Dialing Miquon's number, the phone only rang twice before Quon quickly picked it up.

"What's good, baby girl?" he greeted, and I could instantly tell he was smiling. Before I could answer, Miquon had begun to ask question after question. "How did it go? What they say?" he asked, hoping to hear some good news. Too bad I couldn't give him any. My big brother was my best friend, so there were many nights he stayed up listening to me cry and whine about wanting to be a mother. At one point, I was so depressed about not being able to have a child that Miquon thought announcing that he and his girlfriend were expecting a baby would trigger me into some sort of mental breakdown. I didn't find out I was going to be an auntie until she was in labor.

"I-I don't want to talk about it. Can you come get me, please?" I asked, choking as the words came out of my mouth. Luckily, my brother knew when and when not to question me, and this was one of those times. My brother said the only three words I wanted him to ask me.

"Where you at?" Putting him on speaker, I quickly pulled up the address and sent it to him. "Alright, I got it. I'm on my way. The GPS says eleven minutes… so give me five," Quon explained before hanging up on me. It wasn't like Quon to be late, so like clockwork, in five minutes, Quon was pulling up with his music blasting. One of his homeboys was riding with him and when he saw me, he got in the backseat. The moment I sat, Miquon made sure to introduce me to his friend.

"Miquel, this is my boy Benz. Benz, this is my *little* sister, Miquel." The way Miquon introduced me always made me roll my eyes.

"Miguel, huh? That's unique… I never heard that name for a girl," Benz tried to joke even though I wasn't in the mood for all that. Not to mention, he'd called me "Miguel." Even Miquon heard his slip-up and chuckled under his breath.

"My name is Miquel, not Miguel," I snapped. When he laughed, I could've killed him right then and there.

"Where's that nigga Shaqim at?" Quon asked, making me roll my eyes.

"Let's not go there," I suggested as I fought hard not to say what I really wanted to say. *Your guess is as good as mine*, I thought to myself as I prayed for them to just drop the subject. I was not trying to get mad all over again. But when my brother pulled into the driveway of the four-bedroom house my husband and I shared, I just grew angrier.

Shaqim's car was parked in the driveway, which meant he had purposely abandoned me. "And he wanted me to bring a child into this bullshit..." I muttered to myself as I used my phone to open the garage door. If Shaqim thought I was just going to let this argument go like I did the others, he had another thing coming. My mom used to tell me that even the people closest to me could cross the most boundaries, and my husband had definitely crossed his. Now, I was about to show him exactly who the fuck he was messing with. Just as I was about to get out of the car, Quon grabbed me by my wrist.

"Don't do anything crazy, Miquel," he advised as I pulled away. If it were a show Shaqim wanted, I'd be more than happy to give him one. Climbing out of the car, I grabbed a bat that Shaqim had spent over a hundred dollars on just to use once. My brother must've not realized what the fuck was happening until that moment because he hadn't moved a muscle until he saw me advancing toward Shaqim's car.

"Wait, Miquel! Stop!" Miquon shouted as he hopped out of his car in an attempt to stop me. Shaqim must have heard my brother calling my name because before I knew it, he had run into the garage.

"What the fuck are you doing, Miquel?" he growled, running up on me like he wanted this problem. That was when Quon stepped in front of me.

"Step back, bruh. You know you don't want an issue," Miquon warned. Turning to me, he tried to pry the bat from my hands but my anger wouldn't let me let it go. "Sis, you don't wanna do this. Believe me," he tried to reason, but he could tell that I wasn't interested.

"No! Fuck that nigga! Do you know what he told me? He said I wasn't meant to be a mother! Me! After everything I've done for this nigga, and he wants to let some foul shit like that come out of his mouth?" I screamed to my brother. "Fuck you, muthafucka!" I screamed as I faced Shaqim. As I was yelling, Quon's friend stepped in and pulled me away by my waist. "Let

go of me! Get off me!" I screamed, swinging and kicking
in an attempt to get him off me. Benz seemed unfazed.
"Seriously. Let me down!" I snapped, growing tired of
getting manhandled.

"Not until you calm down, little mama," he
refused. I took a deep breath and counted to ten, relaxing
until Benz's strong-armed ass relaxed his grip and let me
go. The moment that he did though, I took full advantage
of the head start and rushed right past Shaqim, swinging
as hard as I could until the bat connected with his
headlights.

"What the fuck! You're crazy, Miquel!" he yelled,
only adding fuel to an already uncontrollable fire.

"I might be, but if I am, it's because you made me
this way! You're blaming me, and I already do that
enough! What if we can't have a baby because your dick
is fucking weak?" I yelled, and Benz, who once again had
tried to contain me, couldn't even control himself any
more. He burst into laughter, and Quon followed in suit.
Both of them laughed until tears ran down their cheeks.
Shaqim, who had been standing there, looking stupid as

hell, stormed back into the house, and my initial thought was that he was going to get his gun. Quon must have thought so too because he turned toward Benz and me.

"B, take Miquel to the car," Miquon ordered, but I shook my head and stood my ground. He was somebody's dad, but he wasn't mine.

"First off, Miquon, you're not my father. Last time I checked, my father's name is Myron Rodrigo. Is your name Myron Rodrigo?" I snapped back, giving him no time to respond. "I didn't think so. Therefore, I'm staying right here," I argued as Miquon stepped closer to me, clearly not playing around.

"Get your ass in the car, Miquel Lataysia Baker. I'm not arguing with you right now," Miquon barked back. The tone in his voice scared me, so I dropped it and walked to the car, Benz following behind me to make sure that I followed through. The moment my ass touched my brother's custom interior, I could hear him yelling. "You are one pussy ass nigga!" he shouted, making both Benz and I turn our heads to see what was going on. Getting back out the car, I followed behind Benz closely as he went to investigate. I could only gasp when I saw Shaqim throwing all my clothes onto the front lawn. By now, our chaotic fight had drawn the attention of the neighbors, and people were starting to come out of their houses to see what was going on.

"What are you doing?" I screamed as Shaqim stared at me with fire in his eyes before walking into the garage as all three of us watched his every step. Instead of answering, Shaqim just threw daggers my way with his eyes as he searched relentlessly for something. Then before I knew what was happening, he rushed toward me and sprayed me with some sort of liquid. My mind only raced with confusion for a few seconds before my brain registered the smell. This nigga had just doused me in gasoline. Realizing what was happening, Quon's eyes grew wide, but as he stepped closer to me, Shaqim grabbed me by my hair and put a lighter only mere inches from me.

"Come any closer to me, and your sister will go up in flames. I swear," Shaqim threatened as tears rolled down my face. Miquon raised his hands in surrender as he backed away, doing anything to appease Shaqim until he could get his sister out of harm's way. Meanwhile, Benz was trying to get close enough to Shaqim to subdue him without putting me in danger. I could see him creeping our way out of the corner of my eye, but Shaqim was so focused on Miquon that he didn't even realize there was another threat coming right his way. With his hands still gripping my hair, I felt him fumbling in his waistband and then he pulled out a gun. Considering I was drenched in gasoline, and I knew a bullet was just as capable of sparking a fire as an actual flame was. Every move that Shaqim made, I flinched, terrified. Shaqim had hit me before, but it only had been a small smack here or there and nothing of this caliber. Once I got out of this situation, I'd never look back. Shaqim could kiss my ass.

"You have two options, Miquel. You can come back inside, and I'll wash you off and clean you off … and we can work on our family and our marriage. Or, you can do you. But, if you do that, I won't allow you to parade around with the clothes or the jewelry I bought," Shaqim snapped as I stared at him in horror. Yes, Shaqim had been a little jealous before we got married. Sometimes, he could get a little loud and rowdy. He'd grown up watching his stepfather beat his mother down on the daily, and he reassured me that I'd never have to worry about him raising a hand to me. But recently, he was starting to turn into the exact thing he despised.

By this time, Miquon had become anxious and started to talk his shit.

"The fuck would she need your clothes and jewelry for? She had all that shit and more living with her family, nigga." Miquon growled, clearly not seeing Shaqim's finger quivering on the trigger. I didn't see it either, but by the way the barrel was rattling against my temple, I didn't need to see it. Having enough of Shaqim's antics, Quon spun around in an attempt to get the help of one of the people just standing around, watching what was unfolding. Some people even had their phones out recording as if my life weren't in danger.

"Aye! Is y'all niggas serious? You're not even gon' try to help, huh? Someone call the police!" As a real street nigga, calling 5-0 was the last thing for Quon to do. If he were suggesting it, that meant we were out of any other options, and that scared me to death. However, with Miquon's back turned, he couldn't see that Shaqim's gun was now pointed right at the center of his back.

But Benz did. The moment it seemed that Shaqim was about to flip his lid because he was, Benz tackled him to the ground and tried to wriggle the gun out of Shaqim's flexed hands. Even though Benz probably beat Shaqim in height by about a foot, easily outweighed him by quite a few pounds, and Benz was way more muscular than Shaqim, the fight for the gun wasn't an easy win-lose situation like I thought it would be. I suddenly rushed over to where they were fighting, but just as I was about to attempt to break it up, four gunshots rang out, causing me to duck out of the way, to run and hide. My heart was pounding, and I could've sworn that Benz was behind me, but as I ducked on the side of my home near my rose garden, I only heard him shouting for help. Without looking, I thought that maybe Shaqim had been shot when the gun went off, but as I peeked back around the corner to see what was happening, my heart sank, and I could only mutter three words.

"Oh. My. God," I whispered as my heart broke. Without any other care in the world about what was happening, I ran as fast as my feet would take me to where Quon was lying face down in the grass. Everyone who had been standing around watching just minutes earlier were now scattered and screaming for their lives. The moment I got to him, I could see two red holes staining his fresh white t-shirt.

Carmen Lashay, T. Nicole, Ty Leese Javeh, Eden Mireya,
Sparkle Lewis, Reign, & Armani

Only repeating what I had practiced so many times in nursing school, I ripped off my sweater and pressed it to his back then turned him on his side so he wouldn't suffocate with his face in the grass. My big brother had just been trying to protect me, and now he was dying on my front porch.

"Quon, get up. Please. Let's go home... please." I began to cry, shaking him in desperation when blood began to spill out of his mouth like a waterfall. He coughed and stuttered, struggling to get words out. He must've been wearing his energy out because he soon threw his head back in exhaustion, and I watched my brother, Miquon, slip away. I did my best to keep him alert by talking to him.

"You gotta stay with me, big bro. For me, for Marisol," I began to count, giving him all of the reasons I could think of as to why he should fight to stay with us. "Amiris will be so heartbroken without you, Quon. You and her have that special bond since the moment she was born... I don't think her eyes will ever even light up the same without you here," I tried to explain not even realizing Shaqim was still in my presence until he spoke up.

"I always told you, you were going to let your loud-ass family speak up for you and get your little rebellious ass fucked up. Look what you made me do." Shaqim snickered as he came closer to me. Benz had run to his car for his phone in order to call 9-1-1, but when he saw me racing toward Shaqim, not caring that he had a gun, he sprinted toward me. I didn't even see a gun honestly. I barely even saw Benz. All I saw was Shaqim's blood that I was about to spill.

"What I did? You shot my brother!" I yelled, paying no attention to the sirens that seemed to be getting closer to us. Benz reached me the moment that I swung on Shaqim, but it was too late for either of us. The moment that Benz snaked his arms around my waist, Shaqim reached into his pocket and pulled out his lighter. With one quick motion of his thumb, Shaqim flicked the lighter, firing me up instantly like a charcoal grill.

"I don't really remember much of what happened after that, doctor," I explained. Nearly two months after 70% of my body had been burned when my husband set me on fire, the bandages that had engulfed my face were finally coming off. I had expected to look bad just by the look on the nurses' faces, but I hadn't expected to look like *this*. I was unrecognizable, and even worse than that, I was ugly.

When he came up behind me, I did my best to turn my head when Benz walked up to me. They were still searching for my soon-to-be-ex-husband, and all the while, Benz had never left my side. Luckily, the paramedics had made it in time to save Miquon, but unfortunately, the bullet was too close to his spinal cord to move, and it left him in a paralytic state. He said he didn't blame me, but I knew he did. Hell, I blamed myself too. I deserved what happened to me, but my brother should've never been placed in the middle of it.

"You don't look any different to me," Benz whispered as I wiped the tears from my eyes almost immediately. Causing them to stay on my face too long meant that my skin would start to burn, and I didn't have time for that. I could tell that he was lying because when I looked up, his eyes told me the truth. I didn't want to even imagine what kind of monster I looked like to him.

"Yeah, right," I snickered. Shaqim had always told me that I wasn't meant for anybody but him, and now he'd made sure that anybody else that ever looked at me could see how scarred my last love left me, literally.

But Benz wouldn't leave it at that. Instead, he pulled me by my hand and sat me down on the bed, waiting until the nurse left the room to begin talking to me. Then he pulled up a chair and sat at the same eye level as me.

"Listen to me, Miquel. What that no-good son of a bitch *"husband"* of yours did. That was some sucka shit. Ma, when I tell you as long as I'm here ... none of that will ever happen to you again—" Benz began to explain, but I cut him off.

"Why do you care so much? You don't even know me." I genuinely wondered.

"Your brother asked me to make sure you were good." He shrugged as if I hadn't heard anything he said while I was sedated.

"But I've *been* good. For a while now, and you still stayed. Why?" I retorted, staring at him while I waited for him to lie to me again. He chuckled under his breath before rubbing his hand over his face and scooting his chair as close to me as it would go.

Carmen Lashay, T. Nicole, Ty Leese Javeh, Eden Mireya, Sparkle Lewis, Reign, & Armani

"Fine, you caught me. I stayed because well…" he said, before taking a deep breath in. All I could hear was the alarm on the clock ticking while I waited for Benz to talk. "Well, when I was eight, my mom's husband pushed her through a glass door… and I remember just thinking that if I was bigger, I would've been able to help her in some way, got him off her. But, I honestly probably would've killed the dude. So I told myself and I promised my mom that when I got old enough, I would never just stand around and watch a woman get beat on by a man," Benz explained.

That was when I grabbed his hand. Neither of us were sure why, but the moment that we touched, electricity practically went up my arms, and I got instant goosebumps. But being that I was still technically married and far too concerned with what other people might think about me, I shrugged his affection off even though affection was exactly what I needed. It was what I craved.

"Well, I'm sure your mother is very proud of you," I changed the subject, but I watched as he took a deep breath in and then began to talk again.

"I honestly wish she could be, ma. My stepdad killed her when I was fifteen. Stabbed her right through her heart and took mine in the process," he said, causing tears to water up in my eyes again. His voice sounded vulnerable, and every word he spoke sounded so sincere. I had no interest in my brother's friend before that moment, but I just wanted to make him feel better. So I grabbed his hand, and when it was firm in my hand, I outstretched all of his fingers and kissed his palm.

"I know she is proud of you, Benz. Because I'm proud of you… and I thank you with all my heart. I owe you my life," I admitted honestly. Even though I could tell that he wasn't expecting it, he rewarded me with a small smile.

"You can repay me by letting me take you out when they let you out of here." Benz thought he was slick by sneaking that part in there, and the goofy look on his face made me burst into laughter. My first instinct was to say no, and I almost did, but something stopped me. Laughing, I blew Benz an invisible kiss before shrugging as if I didn't care.

"Yeah, we'll see." I chuckled before my mood turned somber. "What is it that you want from me? If it's a relationship, I'm not sure that I can give you that—" I tried to explain before he cut me off.

"I'm not looking for a relationship either, ma. I'm just looking for a dope-ass friendship with a dope-ass chick," Benz argued softly.

"I hardly consider myself dope right now." I mumbled as my attention went back to the mirror. But then Benz grabbed my hands and focused my attention right back to him.

"That's because you don't see what I see." He smiled, and for once, I could actually feel the validity of the words he was speaking. I felt myself getting choked up, but after clearing my throat, I heard my voice no longer cracking.

"And what is it that you see?" I asked purely out of curiosity. That was when Benz took the opportunity to sit next to me, now being the one to take my hand in his.

"I see a beautiful woman who got into the hands of the wrong man. Now, she's hurt. She's bruised. She's angry, and she's a little bent out of shape, but she's not broken. Not by any means. And with the right person, she can flourish into the woman she's meant to be. The queen, the deity, that she is meant to be," Benz exclaimed.

My jaw dropped until I realized he was probably used to saying that same speech to a lot of women. I remembered noticing him before, but with us being so close to one another, I had no choice but to really see him now. With skin like melted chocolate and neatly shaped up hair, I couldn't help but wonder what motives he had for sticking around for me. I wasn't pretty, he wasn't getting any ass, and I couldn't pay him, so there was nothing he could get out of it.

"Even with this stuff all over me?" I began to cry. Benz leaned in and gently kissed my lips, barely touching me so that I couldn't feel any pain.

"*Especially,* with this stuff all over you."

"How is it that you're so enamored with me, and I know nothing about you?" I asked, seriously starting to believe this man was too good to be true. Benz chuckled under his breath and then stared me dead in my eyes.

"What is it that you want to know?"

Carmen Lashay, T. Nicole, Ty Leese Javeh, Eden Mireya, Sparkle Lewis, Reign, & Armani

"Anything that you want to tell me. Tell me everything. As you can tell, I have nothing but time," I responded quickly.

"Well, my real name actually is Benz, believe it or not. But it's not my first name. My full government name is Omeer Benz Morgan. I'm twenty-five years old, and my birthday is on Christmas. My favorite food is chicken enchiladas, and my favorite color is green," he rambled, counting on his fingers as he talked. "I'm the youngest of five and the only boy." That was when my eyes went big. Growing up with Miquon, we were afforded luxuries that a small family allowed us to do, but that didn't stop me from wanting a sister and Miquon wanting a little brother.

"It's just me and Miquon," I responded. That was when Benz burst out into laughter.

"Oh, trust me. I know. Me and Miquon been boys for years now, and pretty much all he does is brag about you and fantasize about beating up your husband. I think if he had another sister that was as fine as you, he would've been told me. If you guys had a brother, I would've met him already," Benz explained before diverting his attention to his ringing phone.

"Hello?" he asked before standing up. Whatever news he was getting, it wasn't good because his brows began to furrow, and he immediately made a beeline for the door. Turning back around, he kissed me lightly on the forehead and then exited the room. Shortly afterward, the nurse rebandaged my head and gave me some pain medicine. I was out like a light.

A few hours later, I woke up to a shadowy figure in the corner. At first glance, I thought it was Benz, being a creep like he obviously was doing while I was sedated.

"Dang, that was fast. How long was I asleep for?" I asked as I wiped my eyes and waited for my vision to refocus. But my heart started racing because when my vision finally focused, this man was clearly not built like Benz, and being with him for so long, I could recognize Shaqim from the back, the front, and the side. I made a quick attempt to scream, especially when he rushed toward me, but before I could, Shaqim had clasped his hand over my mouth.

"Don't… do that. I'm serious, Miquel. I have nothing else to lose," he whispered, brandishing a gun as tears now escaped my eyes, and because my head was

Carmen Lashay, T. Nicole, Ty Leese Javeh, Eden Mireya, Sparkle Lewis, Reign, & Armani

wrapped up in bandages, all of my tears were now sticking to my face, causing my skin to burn. "I can't lie, though. I almost didn't recognize you. You... look like a mummy." Shaqim laughed as I stared at him in horror.

There was nothing funny about what happened to me—about what he had done to me—but now he was sitting in my face, laughing like my life was some kind of joke. Doing the only thing I could think of, I quickly and quietly hit my nurse's station button, hoping that someone would just come in like they had been doing and check on me. If they could just see Shaqim, I knew that someone would call the police, and I'd be saved.

Except when the nurse popped in, her eyes grew big, and instead of going to call for some help, she froze there like some big dummy while this nigga who was obviously on some type of drugs, held a gun to my chest. Before I knew it, he'd dragged the nurse into the room and locked the door. The nurse was so scared that her knees and legs were now shaking, and I couldn't blame her. Shaqim looked mad and deranged like he hadn't slept in days and was coming straight off of a cocaine binge.

"Do not test me! Do not!" he yelled as the nurse tried to subtly reach for her phone. I wasn't sure what the bitch was thinking about doing now that she had already missed her chance.

"I-I-I-I'm sorry," she stammered, raising her hands up in surrender.

"Yeah, you gon' be real sorry when I blow your fucking head off too, bitch," he spat, pressing the gun so far into the back of her head that it left a dent. But something must have clicked in his head because his attention left straight from the nurse back to me. "You're lucky that this one is the one I'm here for." He smiled, pointing to me. Grabbing my arm, he seemed to grip harder when I yelped out loud. "Shut the hell up," he said, pulling me out of the bed. He gave no fucks about my health or my current condition and yanked the IV out of my arm.

"You can't do that! She'll bleed out!" the nurse yelled, almost stepping in between Shaqim and me before he pointed the gun back at her.

"I said you weren't the one I came for. Don't be the one that gets shot the fuck up, trying to play the hero," he warned, and she nodded her head. "Get on your knees," he demanded, waving the gun erratically as she cringed and covered her head with her hands doing what Shaqim told her to do. Quickly, he tied her up, making sure that the four knots wrapped around her wrists were tight enough to where she couldn't move, before coming back over to me. He barely spared me a second glance as he pulled me by the arm and out of the exit. Blood was leaking down my arm, and my head was starting to pound, but it didn't matter. A security guard at the front entrance saw what was happening and stepped in front of us, which was a horrible mistake. Shaqim pulled out his gun and fired one shot into his chest, sending the whole hospital into a frenzy. Lucky for him but not so lucky for me. We made it out before the doors shut and they went into a lockdown.

The entire time Shaqim was driving, tears were escaping down my face. I just knew I was about to die. My "husband" had turned from a star among celebrities to a fugitive in the streets. It wasn't my fault, but he was still blaming me. I knew that because the entire drive was filled with him talking to himself about how it was my fault that his life had been ruined.

"All of this because you didn't want to give me a child! That's all I wanted, Miquel! A fucking baby, but you made it so hard! Why?" he screamed, slapping the steering wheel with every word that he spoke. I remained silent, but when he grabbed me by a fistful of my hair, I had no choice but to respond. "Just tell me why!" he repeated, screaming loudly as he drove.

Needless to say, his attention was not on the road any more, and it was all on me and making me suffer. "You don't think I saw you with him? Tell me why you don't deserve to die! You broke our vows, bitch. Now it's death do us part! Don't you remember?" he screamed, finally focusing back on the road. Sending me one quick glance, Shaqim puckered his lips before swerving into the lane next to us and right in front of a semi-truck speeding our way.

"What the fuck are you doing!" I screamed.

BOOM!

THE END!

Carmen Lashay, T. Nicole, Ty Leese Javeh, Eden Mireya,
Sparkle Lewis, Reign, & Armani

"Definition of Love"

A domestic violence awareness

short story

Armani

Carmen Lashay, T. Nicole, Ty Leese Javeh, Eden Mireya, Sparkle Lewis, Reign, & Armani

Definition of Love

Prologue

"Where the fuck have you been, LaDonna!" my dad yelled as I jolted from my slumber. I inched my way to the door of my bedroom and listened to what I thought would be one of their many fights.

"I went to see Nadine! Why the fuck are you tripping? Damn! I fed Leticia before I left! What are you screaming for, nigga?" my mom responded, and I heard a loud slap.

Slap!

"Bitch, don't get smart with me! Learn yo' fucking place! You are a fucking mother, and running around the streets with yo' hoe ass ain't a good look. You weren't with no damn Nadine! The bitch came over here looking for yo' dumb ass," he spat in anger, and my heart dropped when I heard the sound of breaking glass.

"You just gon' hit me like that, Craig? Fuck you! I'm getting Leticia, and we're out this bitch!" my mom continued, and I scurried to my bed, placing the covers over my head.

"LaDonna, if you wake my daughter up, I'm fucking you up. Play with me if you want."

They were standing in my room as I heard them arguing over my trembling body as I tried to remain as still as possible with the covers over my head and my eyes closed tight.

Trying not to make a sound, my mother shook me. "Leticia, wake up! Yo' daddy's on bullshit, and we're leaving!"

I didn't know whether to open my eyes or remain still. My mom shook me harder, and I remained like a possum and played sleep.

The arguing continued as I felt my mom moving away from my body. My dad had her full attention as they continued to go back and forth with the argument.

"I told you not to bring yo' dumb ass in here fucking with her, didn't I?" he asked as if he were chastising his child rather than speaking to his wife.

"Craig, get your fucking hands off me. You wanna talk that shit, talking 'bout I'm a hoe! Well, my hoe ass is getting the fuck outta here, and I'm taking my daughter with me."

"LaDonna, touch her again, and I'm fucking you up!" he warned.

Carmen Lashay, T. Nicole, Ty Leese Javeh, Eden Mireya, Sparkle Lewis, Reign, & Armani

My mom shook me and called out my name. I remained as quiet as a church mouse, trembling underneath my covers with my eyes shut tightly.

"Bitch!" my dad yelled and knocked my mom backward into the door.

Boom! Was all could be heard as they began exchanging punches and kicks. I knew something had gone wrong when I heard a loud thud, but I was too afraid to look.

"Oh shit! LaDonna! Get up, baby. LaDonna!" my dad screamed with panic laced within his tone.

Still afraid to move, I silently prayed that my mom was okay, but judging by the eerie feeling that came over me, I knew that this was bad.

"LaDonna, baby, I love you. Come on, baby. Get up! I'm so sorry!" my dad continued, and I finally peeked out and witnessed a horrific scene.

My dad had my mom cradled in his arms, sitting next to my dresser. Tears were rolling down his face as he rocked her like she was a newborn baby.

"I love you. I swear to God. I love you." He cried as blood began to soak my bedroom floors, and the life slowly moved out of her body. I saw her chest rise and fall and had a bit of hope until my dad started screaming, *"Noooooo!"*

I jumped from my bed and slipped on my mom's blood. The look of sorrow that displayed in my dad's eyes would be a look that would forever be embedded in my mind.

My father immediately began to apologize to me as he took his phone out of his pocket and called the police.

"9-1-1, what's your emergency?" the dispatcher answered as tears were now falling from my eyes as well as my dad's.

"My wife. There was an accident. I need help," he managed to get out as he continued holding my mom, planting kisses on her lifeless body.

At twelve years of age, that was a bit much for any preteen to encounter. I stood there, gawking at the scene, not knowing what I should do.

Sirens filled the air, and when the officers came, my dad confessed to what happened. I was questioned

Carmen Lashay, T. Nicole, Ty Leese Javeh, Eden Mireya, Sparkle Lewis, Reign, & Armani

about what I heard and saw, and then my dad was taken away.

After the officer helped me put on clothes, I saw my mom being taken out in a black bag. I didn't see my mom anymore after that. She was buried by the state, and I was sent to a group home.

If I didn't learn anything else about that night, I knew that my father loved my mom. He said it repeatedly, and that was when I started to ask, what is the definition of love? ...

Reflection:

I was twelve when my mom was taken away from me. I guess you can say that I lost my mom and dad on the same day.

Now at twenty-four-years-old, I was questioning, *what is love?* I guess that was a question with many answers. I'm sure most would want to be politically correct in saying that love is a variety of different emotional and mental states. Well, typically it's supposed to be viewed as a force of nature. For me, Leticia Daniels, I found out what love was the night my father loved my mother to death.

Today, June 25, was the twelfth anniversary of the day that I lost both of my parents. Although my father was yet living, I had yet to go see him locked away in the cage that they sentenced him to. I loved my father. He was the first man who really taught me what love was. I was sitting here with this single cupcake, reflecting on my life. It wasn't all perfect, but at least with my high-school sweetheart, Montrell, he showed me love.

Carmen Lashay, T. Nicole, Ty Leese Javeh, Eden Mireya,
Sparkle Lewis, Reign, & Armani

What is Love?

"Hey, baby. I'm so glad you're home. Are you ready to go to the cemetery so that I can eat my cupcake?" I asked Montrell as he walked into our two-bedroom apartment, carrying his backpack full of work.

Montrell wasn't a kingpin, the man in the streets, or a big-time drug dealer, but he knew how to slang on the corner, bang in the hood, and lay that pipe in the bed. We'd been together since high school, and although we had our ups and downs, I knew this man loved me.

"Ey, I'm not going to that shit. I need to get out here and make some money. You cook?" he asked, and I held my head down, not wanting him to know that he hurt my feelings. I didn't ask for much, but if I asked for something, that meant that it meant a lot to me, and my mother meant everything to me.

"Montrell, you know what today is, right?" I questioned as I tried to make him understand that this was really important to me.

"Leticia, on some real nigga shit, I told you I'm not fucking going. I need to make this money. Now did you fucking cook?" he asked, elevating his voice.

"No, baby, I didn't cook," I retorted in a defeated tone.

"So you want me to take my ass to a cemetery so you can cry and eat a fucking cupcake, but you can't make a nigga a meal? Fuck part of the game is this?" he interrogated, making me feel like shit.

I had quite a few memories of my parent's arguments, and many times, I would wonder why my mom would look down and try to remain quiet. For the most part, it kept your man at peace, and allowed him to be in control. Sometimes I'd forget and lash out just like now, but I knew he was going to love me afterward, and that was all we ever needed: love.

"Montrell, out of all 365 days of the year, I don't ask for shit but for one day. One fucking day. This might not mean anything to you, but it means the world to me," I stated as tears started to form in my eyes.

"Bitch, fuck all that shit. Every year, you want a muthafucka to feel sorry for you. Shit, muthafuckas die daily, and people do what the fuck I'm telling yo' slow ass to do. Get the fuck over it. Now get yo' ass in that fucking kitchen and get me something to eat on the table!" he demanded.

"No, I'm going to the cemetery!" I screamed, grabbed my cupcake, and proceeded to the door.

Wham!

Montrell kicked me in the back, and my purse and keys flew out my hand. Trying to hold onto my cupcake, I began screaming.

"Montrell, stop! What the fuck is wrong with you? Stop!" I screamed, trying to gain my composure.

"Bitch, you want a fucking cupcake? Here! Take this shit! Here!" Montrell smashed the cupcake all in my face and hair, then he began to kick and stomp me into the floor.

Crying in the fetal position, Montrell towered over me. I looked up into his light-brown eyes as blood discharged from my mouth and coughed out, "I love you, Montrell. I'll get up and cook."

Out of breath, Montrell took a water bottle that I had on the table, opened it up, and slung it at me.

"Clean this shit up, and hurry up with my food," he demanded, and I began to internally coach myself.

This is love.

Carmen Lashay, T. Nicole, Ty Leese Javeh, Eden Mireya, Sparkle Lewis, Reign, & Armani

Love is Patient

My junior year of high school, I found the answer to my question *what is love?* when a star basketball player took notice of me.

Montrell Jones, the most popular boy in school. I remember the first time he spoke to me. I had gone to a party with my girl Chantay. I really wasn't feeling the crowd, because unlike Chantay, I wasn't one of the popular girls. I was sitting in the chair in the corner by myself. Chantay had found some boy to dance with and was up in his face most of the night. The song "Make It Rain" by Travis Porter came on, and everybody went wild. Bitches started hiking up their skirts so they could bend over, and shake their asses while the boys danced behind them, holding them by the waist, smacking them on the ass. I was shaking my head, staring at the whole scene in disgust.

"Wanna dance?" asked a deep voice that came from the side of me.

I turned my head, and there stood Montrell with his hand stuck out. He was tall, already standing at six three, with skin the color of toffee. His light-brown eyes were big and bright, and they appeared to be sparkling under the dim lighting. I was speechless as my eyes scanned his athletic frame from his curly, faded hair, then his thin mustache and chin beard that made his thick, full, kissable lips stand out, and finally landing on his size thirteen shoes. My heart started pounding through my chest.

I started glancing to the side of myself then looking behind me, trying to see who Montrell was talking to. There was no way that this fine ass nigga standing over me was actually talking to me, especially when he could've had any other girl in school that he wanted.

"I'm talking to you, shorty." He chuckled as if he knew what I was thinking.

He had the most captivating smile that I ever seen. I started blushing, then I nervously laughed. "I guess I can dance," I replied as I took his hand and let him lead me to the dance floor.

Grabbing my waist from behind, Montrell started grinding on me. I really wasn't into all that booty shaking shit, but at the same time, Montrell chose me to dance with, so I pulled out my best twerk moves, acting like I was the captain of the twerk team, and bounced my ass all over his dick.

As we were working the shit out of the dance floor, some bitch approached us and threw her arms around his neck.

"So I can't get a dance?" she asked as she started slow grinding on him.

"Hell yeah," he replied as he turned around, wrapped his arms around her waist, and started slow dancing with her, leaving me standing on the dance floor looking stupid.

I thought that was the end of anything popping off between Montrell and me, but I was wrong. As the night went on, Montrell would take a break from dancing and talking to other girls just to come over and sit and talk to me, and by the end of the night, we'd exchanged numbers. Montrell promised to call me, but he didn't. During school, he would ignore me, but that didn't last too long. A few weeks later, Montrell made good on his promise. He called me, and after we had sex that night, we became inseparable.

So it was then that I discovered that all I needed to have was a little patience. Yeah, I saw him with other girls even kissing and holding them as we would exchange classes. That didn't bother me, because when we spoke on the phone, he would talk so sweet to me and tell me about his dreams. My foster mom told me that love is patient, and then I realized she was right. My mom used to wait on my dad to come home, and he used to wait on my mom. Even through the fights, they wanted only each other, so love is patient, and I was patiently waiting for Montrell.

Carmen Lashay, T. Nicole, Ty Leese Javeh, Eden Mireya, Sparkle Lewis, Reign, & Armani

Love is Kind

When Montrell asked me if I wanted to hit the movies the following weekend, I couldn't be happier. The day I lost my parents was coming up, and I wanted nothing more than to go to the cemetery and see my mother. As I got ready for my date, one of my house monitors came in with a box from the bakery.

"Hey, Ms. Sherron. What's that for?"

"I know what today is, and I wanted to bring you a cupcake."

"A cupcake?" I walked over and opened the box, and there was a red velvet cupcake with cream cheese icing.

"Well, Lee Lee, when my mother died, I was a senior in high school, and we may have not lost our mothers the same way, but I still feel your pain, and every year, I take my mother's favorite cupcake to her grave site while I visit."

"Thank you. I usually just go and place flowers and leave."

"Well, this time, try to stay for a while and talk to her. I promise you will feel 100 percent better. Now finish getting ready. I heard about your date tonight."

She walked out the room, and I continued to get dressed. I never really got a chance to learn much from my mother when it came to boys, but what I did know, I would make sure to apply it to my life.

Once I was dressed, I said goodbye to Mika, my roommate and best friend. I took the bus to the cemetery, and I walked to my mother's headstone. Thank God that it was close to downtown; as bad as I wanted to spend time with my mom, I wanted to go out on my first date. I sat her flowers on her gravesite and sat down to have a chat.

"Mommy, I miss you, but you already know that," I said aloud and then began to look around to see if anyone were out here with me.

God, I felt so silly sitting here, talking to myself. I stood up and brushed my pants off and was quickly about to can what I thought was a stupid idea. I spoke to my mom quickly and wanted to get out of the cemetery because I was feeling dumb.

I looked at my watch, and I still had time before I had to meet Montrell at the movies, so I decided to walk instead of catching the bus. The ten-minute walk seemed to go by quickly. I made my way to the theater, and there was Montrell, standing outside, talking to some girl from our school. He slid her a bag with two pills inside, and she kissed him and walked off.

"Umm, excuse me? Why would you invite me here if you was going to be hugged up with her?" I placed my head down because I didn't want him to see me crying. He lifted my head with his finger and wiped away my tears.

"That girl don't mean anything to me. She was just buying something from me. You don't have anything to worry about, girl. Now stop crying, and let's go watch this movie. I hope you're not afraid of horror movies."

"Actually, I kind of am." I looked up at him and smiled. When he returned the smile, that was when I felt like he really cared about my feelings.

"Don't worry about it. I'll be here for you to grab onto."

As he took my hand, butterflies started in my stomach. I was more nervous than what I was before. He held my hand throughout the entire movie, and after the movie, he caught the bus with me all the way to my group home.

On the ride, I opened up about my mom and dad. He listened and wiped my tears away. I felt like we connected on a different level. The only person I told about my parents was my best friend Mika. We stayed up half the night talking about Montrell, and with the advice that she was giving me, I felt as if she was like the sister I never had.

After talking to Mika about Montrell and getting her thoughts about our interactions, that was when I realized how kind he was.

Love is Kind.

Carmen Lashay, T. Nicole, Ty Leese Javeh, Eden Mireya,
Sparkle Lewis, Reign, & Armani

Love Doesn't Envy

2 years later

I didn't want to do anything but go home to
Montrell and go to sleep, but I knew that wasn't going to
happen. As soon as I walked in the door, Montrell threw a
duffle bag at me, and I was back out the door to make a
drop. I called Mika on my way to the drop off point, and
as usual, she was at the shop, running her mouth.

"Mika, do you think we can just do a dinner for
your birthday?"

"Come on, Le. Yo' ass never wanna go out.
Montrell's bitch ass got you doing drops, and you do
them with no complaints. I ask your scary ass to go to the
club, and you act like you're too tired to go!" she
screamed in the phone.

"Mika, chill out. I will come, but you know
Montrell be tripping when we go out, tho'."

"Oh, I know. That's why you need to come out.
That man shouldn't control you!" She huffed and puffed
like I was getting on her nerves when all I was trying to
do was keep peace in my house.

"Mika, I will be there after I cook dinner and make my last run for Montrell. Girl, I been so tired lately. All I do is eat and try to sleep when I can."

"Wait a minute, Leticia. Don't tell me your silly, in-love ass is knocked up?"

"Mika, I have to go. I don't have time for yo' ass. I'll see you tonight."

After hanging up with Mika, I walked into the trap 11 house where I did my usual drop offs. As I walked in, I could smell nothing but Cush. I knew Montrell's brother was there because I saw his car out front. I hated running into him. Ever since I got with his brother, he kept telling me that his brother was no good for me. I didn't listen, and every chance he got, he made sure to remind me.

We said our hello's, and I made my way back home. On the way home, I decided to cancel on Mika. I hated when Montrell acted like he was mad at me. He could get physical, but I knew it was because he loved me.

As I pulled up to my house, I saw Mika was already there, and she was probably dressed like a damn slut. Taking in a deep breath, I got out my car, opened the door, thought I was seeing shit.

Mika had her hands in Montrell's pants, jerking him off. I slammed the door, causing her to jump. Montrell simply stood there, looking like he didn't give two fucks.

I ran up on Mika and started throwing blows to her face. I was getting the best of her until Montrell pulled me off. Out of breath and with tears in my eyes, all I could muster up and say was, "Why?"

"Leticia, miss me with that bullshit. You knew I liked Montrell way before you decided to make a move on him. Yo' ass always got whatever you wanted from the staff. The one thing I wanted, you took from me!"

"Bitch, you are supposed to be my sister! I shared everything with you!"

"Girl, shut yo' weak ass up. Montrell is supposed to be mine. You don't know what to do with a man like him. You're weak just like your mother was weak for your father!"

I looked back and forth between the two of them and couldn't believe this bullshit. All I could think about was my mother saying.

"If he's your man, you better fight for your man."

"Montrell, I want you to choose right now. Who you want to be with?" I placed my hands on my hips and looked at Mika. This bitch didn't know who she was playing with. I knew he would choose me, and when he did, Mika stormed away from my house.

"I don't ever want to see your face ever again, you no-good ass hoe!" I yelled to Mika as she made her way down the street, looking dumb in the face. She turned around, smiling ear to ear as if she'd won the lottery or something.

"If that's the case, you might not want to marry Monkia's father. See you later, baby father." She blew Montrell a kiss, and I damn near passed out.

…

Two days after all that shit went down, Montrell left, probably to be with that jealous ass bitch of a so-called friend. As I lay in my bed, still feeling heartbroken, I pondered on the thoughts of love. I didn't know why love felt this way. Love for me had always been painful, from my parents to my man, but I guess this was really love.

I heard Montrell come in, and I still lay in the bed. He opened the microwave and slammed it shut. I knew his ass didn't think I was going to cook for him after all the bullshit that recently came to the light. I didn't give a shit about him eating; he could go be with that low-down, dirty bitch. I bet she never told him how she tried to fuck me. Who was I kidding? He probably put her up to it so he could have both of us.

I closed my eyes, acting like I was sleep so I wouldn't have to deal with him. "Leticia, wake up *now*! I'm hungry, and this house stinks. Fuck have you been doing?" He sat down behind me and shook me.

"Montrell, please. I don't want to even look at you after what you did. You can leave my house now." I pulled the covers over my head.

"Lee Lee, I'm not going to tell you again. Now I gave you two days to get yourself together. I am hungry, so get the fuck up now." He raised his voice just like my father did with my mother.

I refused to be quiet like my mother would as my father said whatever he wanted to say to her. I had to be strong for myself.

I got out the bed and walked in my bathroom. As I sat on the toilet, Montrell lit a blunt. After using the bathroom, I started cleaning up, not because he told me to but because it was time to get myself together.

"Leticia, can you make that baked chicken you make?" he yelled from the bedroom.

"Montrell, if you want to eat, either you go buy food or have Mika cook for you!" I called back and busied myself cleaning.

I had to catch up on my homework because failing wasn't an option for me. As I was doing the dishes, I heard Montrell come in. He grabbed me by the back of my head and slammed my head into the cabinet. I grabbed my head as a lump started to form.

"Montrell, please stop! Why do you have to put your hands on me?" I asked between tears.

"Bitch, you don't ever know when to shut your fucking mouth! You're one lazy, weak ass bitch. You want to know why I'm fucking Mika?" He kept yelling in my face, and with every word, he sent a blow to my head or stomach.

"Please, Montrell! Please stop!" I cried out, but it seemed like it made him feel more powerful.

Carmen Lashay, T. Nicole, Ty Leese Javeh, Eden Mireya, Sparkle Lewis, Reign, & Armani

"Shut the fuck up!" He grabbed me by my hair, slamming my face into the dirty dish water. I closed my mouth to keep any water from getting into my mouth.

"I should kill yo' dumbass. You should know better than to talk back to me!" *Whamp!* "Next time I tell your dumb ass to cook me dinner, you better do it!"

I lay on the floor for five minutes, unable to move. As I lay on the floor, I heard my mother's voice.

"Get up, Lee! Come on, baby girl. You have to be strong."

As I pulled myself up from the floor, I felt like my head was going to explode. I started throwing up, and the taste of blood lingered in my mouth. I couldn't move as Montrell stood in the kitchen door looking at me like I disgusted him.

"Mika is strong, unlike you. She knows how to use her voice. She would never make runs and let me walk all over her." He scoffed as he stood there, smoking a blunt.

"Trell, I have to get to the hospital. Please, I feel like my stomach is on fire."

"Bitch, you think it's a game? I told your ass I was hungry, and your ass isn't going anywhere. Get the fuck up."

"I can't. please, get me to the hospital."

"Leticia, Leticia, your ass just don't learn." He kicked me in my back, and I fell face first beside the stove. He grabbed me and pulled me up to the stove, turning on the burner. I felt the heat coming toward my face. I put my hands up and burned my palms. He laughed as I screamed out. He dropped me to the floor and started kicking me in my head. The last thing I heard was, "Your ass is going to die tonight just like your weak ass mother."

I couldn't believe that he and Mika were so quick to use the things that I shared with them about my mom against me. Thoughts of my so-called friend flooded my head as I thought, *love doesn't envy*, as I tried to hold on until things went black.

Carmen Lashay, T. Nicole, Ty Leese Javeh, Eden Mireya, Sparkle Lewis, Reign, & Armani

Love Is Dead

We need to get her into surgery right now, or she won't make it.

I didn't know where I was, but I was hanging on to the life I had left in me.

As I closed my eyes, I could see my mother's face so clear. She looked just like I remembered. I reached out to her, and she held me tightly.

"Mommy, I miss you so much. Why didn't you hold on?" I asked as she brushed my hair like she used to do.

"Leticia, I wish I could have held on, but I couldn't. Your father was so abusive, and I turned a blind eye. What your father did to me wasn't love, and what Montrell is doing to you isn't love. Baby, love isn't painful. Love is joy and happiness."

The lights were bright, and it seemed as if my mom were fading fast. I heard and understood what she said about love, but I needed to know more.

"Mom, you loved Daddy. You took everything he dished out. Isn't that love?"

"I didn't show you the definition of love. What I thought was love ended in my death. It's not your time to go, my beautiful, sweet daughter. Hold on. Be strong. Love is like the stars that you see when you gaze up throughout the night. It's something so precious and true that it simply holds you tight. When the time is right, and your heart is healed, you'll open your mind and heart to the true love that will be revealed. Go back, my sweetheart. I'll see you again one day, but now is surely not your time. At least not today."

My mom began floating back as things started to go from bright to dark. Loud beeping caused me to jolt from what seemed to be a cold place. As my eyes popped open, doctors and surgeons were looking at me weird.

"All clear," the doctor announced, and the staff seemed to be at ease.

"What happened?" I spoke in a voice that didn't sound as if it were my own.

The nurses coached me to rest, and I had to know what was going on and why I was in the hospital.

"Just relax. You lost your baby, but we were able to save you. Please, don't speak. We have to get you settled," the nurse spoke with so much care.

Carmen Lashay, T. Nicole, Ty Leese Javeh, Eden Mireya, Sparkle Lewis, Reign, & Armani

I began to weep and mourn for the loss of my child, and knew from this day forward, love wouldn't make me blind.

Love is patient. It is kind. Love shouldn't envy, and love is now dead. What is this thing we call love, and why does it hurt? I guess that's a question for the masses because love might put me in dirt.

The True Definition of Love

Using the rail on the side of the bed, I pulled myself up into a sitting position. I slid one leg at a time to the side of the bed then proceeded to slowly stand up. Sharp pains shot through my body, causing me to double over from the agony. Even though my body was in tremendous discomfort, it was nothing compared to the pain that I was feeling in my heart. Losing my baby was one thing, but facing the reality that Montrell was the cause of all my pain hurt the most.

Taking a few deep breaths to brace myself to take the first steps, I closed my eyes and silently prayed that I made it over to the chair by the window. I was already tired of being cooped up in the hospital bed, and I wanted to at least feel as if I were taking in the fresh air from outside. I took the first step, and the pain in my abdomen seemed to have increased.

"Come on. You can do this. It's just a few more steps," I coached myself as I took another step then followed with another.

Slowly, I made it over to the chair and sat down. As I stared out of the window, I started noticing how everything appeared to be so small from up here. The cars reminded me of watching the cars on my father's race track that he used to have on display in the basement that he and his dad built together when he was a kid. I chuckled to myself as I thought about how his face used to light up every time we would watch the cars race around the track. It was the last thing he and my grandfather built together before my grandfather died.

"I wonder what you was like, Granddaddy," I mumbled, thinking about how I never met him, being that my grandfather died when my daddy was only a child himself.

My daddy loved me, this I knew, but as I sat in the window, I couldn't help but wonder if he truly knew what love was. The things that he did to my mother and the things that Montrell did to me were all done out of love, they said, but as I sat here, staring at the couples as they are walking by, I saw them holding hands, and the women smiling as if they never had to endure the type of pain that my mother and I endured all for this feeling we crave called … love.

A tear started to slowly drop from my eyes as my thoughts switched to the vivid dream I had of my mother when I was in surgery.

I didn't show you the definition of love. Her words played over and over in my head as I tried to figure out what her words meant. I know she loved me, and she showed me every day. When she woke me up, she always stroked my hair before kissing my forehead and saying good morning. Her touch was so gentle, and her voice was pleasant. She never raised her voice at me, nor did she ever put hands on me. She was always so kind, and she always smiled no matter how much pain she may have been in. That was a talent I picked up on. Whenever Montrell would beat me, I would wake up in so much pain, but I would ignore it and still greet him with a smile.

The door opened, and a familiar sounding voice greeted me with the same type of pleasant sound as my mother's voice.

"Ms. Sherron, hi," I spoke as I slowly got up to make my way over to the bed.

Although Ms. Sherron was smiling, I could see sadness in her eyes. She rushed by my side and helped me onto the bed. Then she pulled the chair so that she was seated at my bedside.

"How you feeling, baby?" she asked, taking my hand into hers.

I shrugged my shoulders as I shook my head. "Numb, like I'm dead inside," I spoke truthfully.

Ms. Sherron shook her head as tears formed in her eyes. "Leticia, I tried my best to keep my mouth closed and let you handle your own relationship, but it was no secret. I never liked Montrell. He was always bad news to me. I see now that I should have done more. Maybe I could have found a way to step in, then maybe we wouldn't be here today."

"Ms. Sherron, there was nothing you could do. I love Montrell, and I would've fought harder for our love had you stepped in. Even after all of this, I love him, and he loves me. I know that we have our problems, but we will work them out."

"No, baby. You can't go back to him. Laticia, this isn't love. A man is never supposed to put his hands on a woman, and a man that claims to love you would never.

You have to end this relationship now, Laticia, before it gets worse."

"Thanks for being concerned, Ms. Sherron, but Montrell loves me. It's just that he gets mad sometimes… I got to get better at doing what I'm told. That's all."

"Laticia, this is not on you. You did nothing wrong, believe me," she stated as she held my hand close to her heart and looked deeply into my eyes. "Laticia, I hate to do this to you, but I have to get this off my chest. Your mother… She didn't deserve what happened to her, and neither do you. If you stay with Montrell, it'll cost you your life. One way or the other, I'll lose the best thing that ever happened to me. Break this cycle now, dear. Your life is worth so much more." Tears spilled from Ms. Sherron's eyes as she spoke to me.

Ms. Sherron couldn't have children, so when I came into the group home, she immediately took to me and had been a mother figure to me ever since.

We talked for what seemed like hours, and it was finally registering to me. I didn't understand that the true definition of love started with me loving myself; and what I was looking for, I couldn't possibly find within a man.

Carmen Lashay, T. Nicole, Ty Leese Javeh, Eden Mireya, Sparkle Lewis, Reign, & Armani

From this day forward, I no longer had to choose love. I only needed to choose myself. Now that was my definition of love.

I closed my eyes and dreamed of better days, knowing that I had this new take of the word love.

Love is Strong

The definition of love is simple There are many kinds of *love*. There can be self-*love*, *love* toward a friend such as platonic *love*, *love* in romance, toward family, toward God, or toward an object or idea. ... Lust and *love* may be thought of as different. Normal friendship is a form of *love* that can be distracted by lust and misunderstanding.

Ms. Sherron explained the true definition of love, and as I prepared to leave from my hospital stay, I was walking in love by allowing myself to love myself.

I collected my things and headed toward the exit of the hospital. Slight pain reminded me of why I was there. I looked toward Heaven and smiled and simply said, "Thank you, Mom. I now know what love is."

As I stood outside of the hospital, to my surprise, Montrell was there. Feeling empowered to stand up for myself, I spoke.

"Montrell, whatever this was that we had is no more. From this day on, I choose me."

"Lee Lee, I don't have time for this shit. Get yo' ass in the car before I get mad."

"Trell, as a woman, I'm breaking the cycle that was somehow passed down to me, and I'm telling you that the type of love you give to me is unwanted. You are free to do whatever it is that you want, but I'm telling you now, if you don't want to end up where my father is, you'll take heed to my words and leave me alone."

"Who the fuck screwed wit' yo' head? Fuck wrong wit' you?" he spat, getting closer.

I backed up toward the entrance, and thankfully, security was right there and was able to step in on my behalf.

"Ma'am, are you alright?" the security guard questioned.

"No, he's trying to attack me," I spoke sternly, and the look on Montrell's face was priceless.

"Fuck you, bitch! This shit ain't over!"

"Oh, but it is, Montrell. Oh, but it is," I spoke with certainty, knowing that I was stronger and wiser, and as Ms. Sherron stated, I knew I had a place to go.

Montrell pulled away in a haste because security warned for a final time. Moments later, Ms. Sherron pulled up, embraced me, and simply said, "Let's go home."

I smiled, knowing that I was now standing as a strong woman, strong enough to face a battle and walk out a survivor.

Carmen Lashay, T. Nicole, Ty Leese Javeh, Eden Mireya,
Sparkle Lewis, Reign, & Armani

Epilogue

"Ms. Sherron, I don't think I could face him after all of these years," I said as we pulled up to the correctional facility, and I prepared to look at my father for the first time in over twelve years.

Ms. Sherron informed me that he'd been sending letters for years but decided that it might not have been the best thing for me, seeing that I was in the home when he took my mom's life.

"Lee Lee, you're strong, you're wiser, and if for nothing else, you deserve closure however you decide to obtain it. Think of this as part of your healing," she stated.

I'd been going to counseling and really digging deep to understand the deep-rooted issues that were within me.

I took in a deep, cleansing breath, checked the mirror, and walked into the visiting line.

After being checked in, searched, and escorted to the visitation room, I nervously waited for the man that I once called Daddy.

With my nerves at an all-time high, I sat bouncing my leg up and down while holding my head down, playing on my phone.

"Princess, is that you?" a voice that didn't sound like anything I remembered spoke from behind me.

I was afraid to look up or back, but slowly, I stood to my feet and turned to face my father.

"Daddy? I spoke as my words were caught in my throat.

Surprisingly, the years hadn't treated him bad. Aside from muscles and a few gray hairs, he looked everything like I'd remembered. He hesitated with trying to embrace me, and you could tell that he was having a battle from within.

Wrapping my arms around his neck, I spoke. "Daddy, it's alright. I forgive you."

Tears wet my face as I held onto him as if I never wanted to let him go. Breaking our embrace, we sat at the table, and he began speaking.

"Princess, for years, I've struggled with what to say to you and how to explain things to you regarding my actions with your mom's death. I know that the words 'I'm sorry' won't bring her back, and I deserve to live out the rest of my days in this cage," he spoke as his eyes welled with tears.

"Daddy, you don't have to explain," I stated as I started feeling bad about hearing the hurt seeping through his tone.

"No, I do. You deserve to hear this. Nothing I could say would justify my actions. As a father, I've failed you, and after being locked away, things really started to make sense. What message did I send to you? What lesson did I teach you? I was supposed to be your provider and protector, but I robbed you of so much more. Princess, it would be easy to make up excuse after excuse, but that won't solve anything. Know that with each passing day, I never stopped loving you or your mom. I regret the day I ever held my hand up to her to harm her. Princess, I don't want you to end up with a man like me. I want you to find someone better than me. I don't deserve your forgiveness, but I'm thankful that you said you forgive me."

He was crying, and many of the inmates started to glance our way. He didn't seem to mind as it appeared that he wanted to get things off his chest. We talked until visitation was over, and as I stood to prepare to leave, I hugged my daddy goodbye, and he said, "I love you, princess."

I looked into his eyes and simply asked, "Daddy, what is the definition of love?"

The End

34854735R00210

Made in the USA
Lexington, KY
28 March 2019